NOW LOOK

NOW LOOK

SYDNEY LEA

Down East Books

Camden, Maine

Down East Books

Published by Down East Books
An imprint of Globe Pequot
Trade division of The Rowman & Littlefield Publishing Group, Inc.
4501 Forbes Blvd., Ste. 200
Lanham, MD 20706
www.rowman.com
www.downeastbooks.com

Distributed by NATIONAL BOOK NETWORK

Library of Congress Cataloging-in-Publication Data

Names: Lea, Sydney, author.
Title: Now look / Sydney Lea.
Description: Lanham, MD : Down East Books, an imprint of Globe Pequot 2024.
Identifiers: LCCN 2023040706 (print) | LCCN 2023040707 (ebook) | ISBN
    9781684751945 (hardcover) | ISBN 9781684751952 (e-book)
Subjects: LCSH: Men—Fiction. | Alcoholism—Fiction. | Male
    friendship—Fiction. | Self-realization—Fiction. | LCGFT: Novels.
Classification: LCC PS3562.E16 N69 2024 (print) | LCC PS3562.E16 (ebook)
    | DDC 813/.54—dc23/eng/20231002
LC record available at https://lccn.loc.gov/2023040706
LC ebook record available at https://lccn.loc.gov/2023040707

PROLOGUE

The world may be changed. No one hopes so more than George Mayes. He tries to remind himself that every day he wakes up to is a new one. Corny? He scarcely cares. And it's not a snap for him to stay with the present anyhow; it never has been. A slew of yesterdays keep crowding his mind, perhaps more than ever just now. There's never been a guarantee—of anything.

He's still George, though, and Evan still Evan, please God.

George has no doubt there's plenty he needs to make up for from so many of those yesterdays, the ones that got him where he is now. He knows that he tends toward melodrama, too easily imagining whatever present he's in to be the permanent one, containing everything his life will ever contain. That's not so much different from living in the future, which sometimes seems a dire prospect, sometimes liberating, but which, of course, remains forever unpredictable.

July before this, in the unnerving visit George remembers, Evan was in his seventy-eighth year. He weighed little enough that George could slide him to the other side of the cab like a small child. So thin you could spit through him, the way Evan always claimed you could through the paddle Joe Mell made for him down at the Indian Point some sixty years back. Astounding, how many of this old drunk's idioms have crept into George's own interior language.

George wasn't alive when Joe fashioned that paddle, and yet, however vainly, he believes he can appreciate what went into it. He even briefly knew Joe Mell, if Joe could be known to a white man, or in fact to anyone, loner that he remained. The paddle's wrought of clear ash, and its shaft has decades of Evan's sweat in it. Like so much else, it implies a narrative George would love to recount, and will never be able to—not the half of all he's been told and all he's witnessed.

Pushing the seat back as far as it would go, George turned the engine over. The old man didn't wake up.

George was once a young man, and Evan Butcher no sot. George fights as hard as he can not to think of his friend that way, no matter what's gone on—the heartbreak, the pain, the news that has always seemed to get worse for the Butcher family.

It's been a long time since he and Evan first met, and he's gotten less and less innocent about the world since. So his naiveté about that heap beside him in the truck's cab was something willed. It still is. There are just certain things he can't let go of. He'll cry if he does—not for the first time.

George could make a quick and orderly catalog of quick and disorderly deaths. Like anyone, he can count up other losses too since his youth: a bit of wind, a bit of spring in the legs, a first wife, and trust in most people's decency. Good riddance also to some sordid stuff in his own character. And some less sordid than perverse. For almost thirty years, he's fought to govern his damnable sentimentality, which at times can prove nearly catastrophic.

But yes, there are some things he's stubborn about keeping, whether or not they do him any favors. He won't let his earliest vision of Evan vanish, not on his life. Can't anything he craves be real? Can't he hold onto something? He immediately scolds himself for self-pity, because in truth he's held onto a lot more than he ever deserved.

He felt heartache that last time he saw Evan, but it was mixed with rage. There the old boy sprawled, one knee on the floorboards, one hand reflexively grabbing the seat as it could. A little anxious, George leaned toward his passenger. Slower breathing than nature intended, for sure; it seemed to come from somewhere so deep that George couldn't bear to think about it. But at least it was breath.

Rattling toward the county road, the little truck bobbed in the ruts of the graveyard lane. Its headlights showed names on lichen-yellowed stones. Harley Ferguson. Billy McPeake. Louis Maclean. On and on. There were more dead folks here than live ones in the village now, most of the woods jobs gone south or overseas, the younger generation moved to pastures they hope to find greener.

It was said that Harley Ferguson could lift a full keg of nails off the ground. Billy McPeake, some claimed, lived all one summer on nothing but watermelon and vanilla. Louis Maclean was the best storyteller in a place full of storytellers. "A man of his time," Evan always called him.

But what's a man's time, a woman's? Where *were* the women? George half convinced himself there were only a scattered few among the buried men. No truth to that, of course, but George knew a lot of wives and sisters and cousins who did still live, while almost half of Evan's working chums were gone, one way or another, before George ever laid eyes on Woodstown.

There lay Lemont Brazier. LEE-mont, the old ones said. Oh, how they said. How they said and said and said. Yes, Louis had the reputation for stories, but none of the old-timers was a slouch with them. Not Evan, for certain.

Just before he reached the town road, George read *Bradley Llewellyn*. He knew Brad fell into a logjam on the Percy River in 1934. He knows about that awful accident—from Evan, of course, who at nineteen was on just his second river drive that April. The crew fished poor Brad out at Crooked Rips the day after he went under. Evan spoke of how they poured a carton of salt into his bedroll and wrapped him in it.

"Like corning venison," as he once put it, sad-eyed, "and salt were dear." Then the bateau bore that pitiable lump all the way to the drive's end at the sea. Thirty-nine days. "Cold spring that year," Evan added, "praise be."

George stopped at Llewellyn's stone that night. Though he knew what it was from too many prior night visits, he wanted to look again at the shape, a bit like an arrowhead, somehow fastened on top. Carved of wood, it crudely represented the bow of a canoe, the stern having rotted away long back. George can't remember when. But he thinks again: what's time, after all, when you can't keep the years sorted anyhow?

The cemetery sign now showed only the first syllable of *Woodstown*, the second fallen like the sternward half of Brad's canoe. So goddamn much gone down, George mused. Though he's ashamed of it, he can fall in love with a purple mood. That night, the sky was clear, and within hours the sun would come up to light the countryside, same as always from the start of forever. But poor little Georgie had the blues.

Out on the gravel, when George goosed the throttle, Evan's other knee slipped off the seat. His body twisted so that he was propped on his elbows now. He looked to be at prayer. Maybe that was it, George briefly fancied. Evan wanted to say a word or two to his chums in a hallowed place. But of course the man was simply passed out; he didn't have any noble goal. Never mind bloodshed. Never mind the paths chosen by the twin grandsons. Never mind any of that, George said to himself, as if he could just boss his mind around. Evan was only drinking because he drank. That's what drunks do.

George had to be gone next morning, and it was already after midnight. He'd only had the single week, four days of which his wife and girls were spending in a New Jersey seaside rental. He knows he's blessed as husband and father, but a single day on that saltwater, filthy with condoms, cardboard cartons, beer cans, orange peels, junkies' syringes . . . well, it was more than he cares to cope with ever again, even in beloved company.

Smudge-gray surf; crowds of oiled people whose idea of a vacation is lying in sand doing nothing. Everybody's kids cranky with sunburn and not enough sleep. That same sand in your bed. No thanks.

George, to his shame, is still one judgmental soul, which has never been good for anyone, least of all him. But despite himself, the beach town's pink and yellow ice cream shop rose to mind as he drove Evan back to his village, the most improbable place on earth for such reverie.

That little joint was dolled up to look like something from the early fifties of his own boyhood. Gulls squabbled there for scraps of cone or whatever. For some reason, that scavenging struck him as worse than their fussing over the ocean's detritus, which the birds did as well. The sweet odor of the store; the silly peaked hats on the pimply soda jerks; the jars full of chocolate sprills—jimmies, they were called when George was his daughters' age. Maybe they still are. He shrinks from the memory of everything there. But why should any of it matter?

When the girls weren't much more than toddlers, before the disasters, he and Julie took them on what proved to be their only seaside vacation. Everybody agreed afterward that Dad should just go bunk with the mice in his ratty old camp up north. They could take the full family vacation over the winter holidays.

George is not such a grownup, he sometimes fears. He hadn't behaved well at the ocean. On the other hand, he did keep the Maine place up, more or less. He needed to pass at least one short spell there each summer. Julie knew that then, and still approves, though she can't begin to fathom her husband's affection for such a place.

That last week in Woodstown had been a bad one, the worst since he corked his own bottle. He hauled Evan Butcher home from the cemetery six times in as many nights. George got pretty used to the short walk across the weedy old baseball field. He'd been watching his friend and mentor's decline for more than five years now. But rescuing him from the marble orchard every single evening was something new, dire.

He recalls how he turned on a flashlight to find his way through one of the gaps in the outfield fence, and then through the alders behind Timmy Beeson's barn, where good canoes are still built on his grandfather Pappy's molds. Not as good as Butcher canoes, maybe, but good, all right. They're mostly sold to out-of-towners now.

A woodcock might whistle up from an alder thicket and plunk back down. Bitterns—post-drivers, Evan called them—might thump in the wetland. George could have enjoyed his stroll. Otherwise. It was at least a tad better and certainly easier when Evan stayed in his shop to drink. The prior couple of years had changed that.

At the dogleg by the church, George braked, noticing the forward quarters of a moose. He could just make out her dull eye. She'd been hanging around town all summer, and he'd seen her in full daylight a couple of times that same week. She wasn't a very big cow, but if she decided to bolt across that skinny road, she'd be more moose than Evan's road-weary pickup could handle. She stayed put, though, her ears cocked at the truck clattering past.

Well before Evan decided to pass out there nights, George had been to the graveyard plenty of times over the years. Never a good idea. He scarcely knew why he did it. Those visits were like looking at old snapshots, for him a gut-busting experience, even when he doesn't know half the souls in the photographs. Something hurtful always stares back at him from those pictures. So what could it have been, this graveyard impulse in him—and in Evan?

Brad Llewellyn, drowned on a river drive before George drew breath, is still no more than a character in a story. So how can George mourn the man so? Our stories may keep us going, he thought, but they all end the same over time.

Where in hell had that gloomy notion come from? He knew he should just stamp out the woeful mood. He remembers shaking his head, trying to purge it. So many details came back, though, and do. And every charge of recall can spark another, and that one another, and that one the next.

He had to force himself to concentrate on the skinny road as he hauled Evan home, but that moose in the headlights made George remember sitting on beach rocks at Semnic Lake, watching Evan work a call fashioned from a coffee can and a shoelace.

"Keep looking right across at the dead stream," Evan whispered, sliding rough fingers along the lace. "Be a moose in it 'fore long."

Wetted, the string made a grunting noise as Evan worked it, and the can amplified the sound. George had never seen a moose, could scarcely imagine one, so what happened next was something out of phony, romantic, and plain bad north woods movies: a bull trotted onto the lakeshore as if on cue. George half believed it was some sham. Or else it was wizardry. The animal's velvet peels were grimy and bloody on the antlers, and the greenhead flies made a halo around them. You could see that even across the water.

How often George gawked in the early years at what seemed, sure enough, to be magician's work. Once, as they rested on the Semnic carry, George snapped a skinny underbough from a tree, handed it over, challenging Evan to identify it without looking.

"Breaks like a cedar," Evan said. Cedar it was.

"How could you tell?"

"I've felt of a stick or two."

Evan has taught George enough in the decades since then that the trick seems less amazing now, but back then it felt magical, all right.

Taking Evan back to his shop last July, George also recalled a spring day when young Ben Patcher came by Evan's place, black flies thronged around his head too. Maybe that was the connection, a memory of flies around some creature's head, for the love of God. Ben kept waving his oddly delicate hands to break up the swarm. He wanted to know what to do about a sow who'd gone off her feed.

The three of them left the dooryard. George can still picture the white puffs of dust they kicked up from the roadbed. They crossed the tannery bridge, that cloud of blackflies staying right with them, thickening when they reached the sty.

Evan glanced at the pig, then turned to Ben with an expression not quite amused, and not quite not. "She wants her tail cut off," he said. And before Ben could react, Evan pulled his dirk knife from its metal scabbard, on which his father must have etched 1915, year of his birth.

How George wanted to play savvy! He looked away, though, and would have closed his ears if he could. After a minute he peeked back. The sow hadn't made a sound, hadn't even bled much; she stood there briefly, staring down at the severed tail, pink as an angleworm in the dust. Then she gobbled it, quick-stepped over to her trough, and started working it end to end. George mused that her head moved like a type-writer carriage.

How would that head look when Ben held a pistol behind one ear and triggered it? George shivers. That's what surely happened to that sow come slaughter time. When a gun is fired at close range into a skull, are the brains literally blown out, or is that just an expression? It's not like a duck or grouse or woodcock on the wing in any case, not even like a head-shot deer at thirty yards. Not like running something sharp into your skull, either.

A big moon had stayed up, so George cut the lights as he nosed the truck into the Butchers' dooryard. Poor Mattie must have been upstairs in bed. She likely thought it was too late in the game to stay up worry-ing over a husband she couldn't understand anymore.

George carried Evan into his shop, appalled again that he'd gotten so tiny, the arms that had once felt like braided cable gone soft and crepelike. Evan kept an army cot and an old-fashioned blanket roll in the shop. George thought of Brad Llewellyn in his own salty bedroll as he kicked Evan's to the floor. No need for covers. There was sweat on his friend's face and his too.

Outside, the river lisped through the bank-brush forty yards east. A loon in one of the back ponds cackled nervously. A barred owl pumped its eight notes into the air, and another answered, a sound like pshaw at the end, drawn out, sliding down and opening up before it quit. Amid all this, George heard choked snoring behind him in Evan's shop.

George spoke out loud: "That man wants his booze cut off."

I

Mattie scowled through her bedroom window, following George Mayes as he walked out the dooryard to the tannery bridge. Then the river alders hid him. On the way to his camp, ready to head down-country, was he? Nowadays she and George didn't talk like they used to. But who'd tote her husband's sorry carcass home now?

It was coming on daylight in their back lot, covered with maple whips now, some with a touch of flame already. Lord, she used to love the time between tree-color and snowfall, only that little bit of red in the woods to start, but the winds coming back soon, stiff enough to lay foam-lines side by side on McLean Lake, and the salmon and brook trout moving to the shallows come early October. When she was a girl, she used to stand on the bridge and drop pebbles, just to watch them shoot out and then slide back where they'd been.

She felt a change brewing even now, no matter the weather stayed warm. Two ravens were fighting a blow to get upstream, gathering two yards and giving up one, flopping around like laundry. She could just make them out against the gray. The mountain ash berries in her dooryard weren't even ripe yet, but the waxwings were mobbing them already. Oh, the light off those birds!

"You don't have to live with that old man," she whispered after George.

Well, time was, she thought of Evan as a hero too, that short year they were courting, when weather meant a thing or two, like she was just thinking. Buck deer in rut, say, and the town all women in daytime. The best-looking young fellow in the village, Evan, no two ways about it. He'd get done in the woods, working or hunting, whichever, and he'd be back from camp on Saturday evenings, so's to go out somewhere only with her. A dance, maybe, or only a moonlight canoe ride uplake. And they had all day Sunday—nobody but the two of them until Tommy was born.

Evan turned himself out so nice in those days. She used to wonder how on earth could his shirt get that white, and who made it that way? You could see it even after dark. Nearly the same for his teeth—he had every one of them then, never mind he chewed that awful snoose like any 'jack.

And under the shirt . . . "It'd make a mare to eat her own bedding," she muttered. Then she blushed, even though she was all by herself.

It wasn't just how Evan looked, though. He was a man among men, drove the Percy every April, first one hired by the time he was only nineteen, best paid but Biscuit the cook, who was on the drive since Evan was a baby. That river business scared Mattie half to death before he quit, praise Jesus. They don't drive timber by water anymore.

Winters he cut railroad sleepers. Ties, the company called them. Camp boss would go man to man at night, taking tally. "Fourteen," one of the boys would say, and it stayed about like that for everybody up to Evan. Twenty, twenty-four, twenty-six. Even thirty-two once after he heard Sebby Pierson meant to beat him. Evan worked himself about off his feet and Sebby went right back to the pack because her husband cut the thirty-two, and each last one an A-sleeper which Boston and Maine would be glad to lay down.

Even in his prime he couldn't do such a thing now. Not enough good wood anymore. In those days, plenty of fine trees stood handy by, south of Gary Pond in the black swamp. That meant Evan was home nights. It was sure a lot better than during the drives in spring, when she learned what lonesome meant. And she couldn't sleep for the thought of him trotting around on those damned long-logs or stepping out on a jam with a charge of dynamite on a pole. How could a man claim to love such a business? But Evan claimed he did.

Those days making sleepers he never saw their house in daylight but for Sunday in winter. He went off every day with a lantern and that broadaxe and a dinner pail and bucksaw strung on him somehow and not come home till after dark. She got up with him and waited for him nights. Plenty to do anyhow, especially after Tommy came along, but that didn't make any difference. Even when she was tending the baby or stoking the furnace or splitting kindling, a lot of what she did was wait for Evan Butcher.

Now look.

Mattie felt all slept out, early as it was. Plenty of memories to bear down, mostly the one—or three, more like it. She always tried her best to put the kids out of her mind, but it wasn't ever all the way. And there her Evan was, out in the shop, so drunk he didn't know he was in this world.

She stepped into a set of his drawers. He was skinny now, and Mattie gone a little to girth, which she didn't care a particle about. Then an old shirt, also his, not white. She trotted downstairs. The way to keep going, her mother always told her, was—keep going. She knew what she was talking about too: shingled her own roof as an old woman, and it never leaked a glassful, even though she moved away the very next year.

Old? Was that what Mattie just thought? Sixty-five was what her Ma was when she did that job. Then she left Woodstown. She had a little pension from the army, because Mattie's father got himself killed in the first war. Mattie never knew him, but her husband's money was just enough for Ma to get herself out of town. Forevermore bull-headed.

It can't be healthy if it's good weather every day and never different. She told Ma that, but look what happened. A few years went by, and then it started: just a little bunch in one armpit at first.

Mattie always wanted to be like her mother, but to add on a quarter century or so. And now she was seventy-eight and, on her way, because her mother was only seventy-two when she passed. Seventy-eight. How'd that happen so quickly? Mattie meant to keep the same gumption Ma had, but she wanted to live to a round hundred. Why not?

Well, why, considering?

There was a time she pitied her poor mother, living those years without a man. But any way you sliced it, if he woke up sober enough to talk a full sentence, her own man would tell the world to this day that a person could play checkers on his wife's shirttails. She never stood still. Well, that's Mattie Butcher, she thought, and it'll keep on being her. Couldn't change if she cared to, and she doesn't.

She stood in the kitchen a while till she caught herself studying the electric tea kettle, that drooling bastard. There showed a crack in the spout, and you almost lost one cup for one you boiled. She meant to find herself a new pot, because Evan wouldn't get around to fixing things, the way he was. Wouldn't even drink coffee now. Too busy drinking from another cup.

Plug-in kettle. Gas stove. Oil furnace. Lord God. All kinds of things changed, some for the better.

They kept their wood stove. Nice to fire up now and again come fall, taking a little chill off, saving on the oil, but not for old times' sake. Old times was splitting off cedar chips on the kindling floor first thing when you got up if you forgot or were too played out to do it the night before. One of Evan's sportsmen told her it was called killing floor down south, which was a better name, especially if you had the morning sickness. Get the stove het, then lay in a few sticks of whatever hardwood there might be to hand. It took half an hour on a good morning before you'd feel half comfortable.

She hooked up the drooler and found a teabag. Then she grabbed her molasses. People could say there was nothing to it, but she always felt healthier for the blackstrap. Let them think whatever they wanted. She never put much else inside her in the morning these days.

Evan was out in the shed, which she'd burn up if she dared. Lying on that awful bedroll, or maybe just in his clothes on top of his cot. She hadn't been inside the shop a dozen times after they left it. It was what they had for a house clean through the second year they were married. That was plenty.

Nowadays she could barely put her eyes on the little building for the memory of cold, a foot of snow by Thanksgiving, Evan in the woods. There she was, bare-knuckled in the dooryard, putting in studs and joists and stringers, fitting those two little windows old man Patcher gave them for their wedding. By and by it was nailing the waney boards on the upright, all they could afford. She might look at the shack easier if Evan would just yank those ratty wanes and put on some clapboard, or even butted planks. That wasn't going to happen, so she chose another window to look out.

She wiggled her fingers to thaw the memory of one of those mornings. She thinks how she suddenly felt something down below once, and when she got indoors, come to find out the sweat of her backside froze her cheeks together. She had to dip her hands in a water pail to tend herself.

Good old days? Pretty likely.

It was nicer looking out the south side anyhow, over to Addy Benson's house, which Addy kept up nice even after Thump died, and then past her to the sidehill. It still showed signs of a burn, Lord, thirty-five years since. The popple took over after, white as birch in winter, then the lovely yellow leaves in spring, which moved like riffles in a brook when the wind fluttered them in summer. Money tree, some called a popple, not because it was worth much, but when those leaves came down in October, they looked like coins on the ground. That hill was most of it gone to cabbage pine by now, red maple suckers in the clear spots. A popple doesn't live long; a lot of them fell down and rotted a few years back.

That old shop could fall and rot too, and Mattie wouldn't care, no more than if she stepped on a piss-a-mire. It was a start for them once, but good riddance after they got the big place up. A lot of better years in the big house, which she and Evan still call it. A lot of very good years, truth be known. Woodstown lost its best river fishing by the late sixties, but it got a reputation by and by for bass in the lakes, and when they paved the roads to just ten miles from town, Evan could make a dollar off rich folks, taking them out to fish and looking after a couple of their summer places. The sports were the real money trees, seemed like. You had to just tolerate a few, mucky mucks, but there was a decent one or two. Even that foolish George Mayes, and she'd admit it. George meant well. Why couldn't he save Evan, though? Save her while he was at it. Save something, for the love of Christ!

Now who was the foolish one?

Guiding was a fine thing by her and Evan both. And every inch he stood off from a falling tree or a floating log was a good inch, far as it concerned her, and not just on account of danger. When he guided, they spent more time together, like married ones ought. That didn't last forever, though, did it? What in creation did? Some good in the old days after all. Look what's going on now. The teapot spat on the oilcloth. That kind didn't whistle a note, which was a nuisance. That's why she burned the hole in it, so she shouldn't complain. Her own fault.

Could have burned the whole house down. She yanked the plug and filled the cup with the cub bears looking down from a tree. The picture of the trunk wore off a long time back, so the bears seemed like they were flying. Angel bears.

There was a little gray wad of something under them, which Evan used to patch a seep. She plain forced him to do that, because she wasn't giving that cup up, not on her life. Tommy made it for her when he was eleven or such a matter, a lifetime ago. He worked it out of a little jar of clay she gave him. Evan's patch job weren't much account, but it seemed like he didn't care about that or anything else these days.

There'd be no more cups, and no more Tommys right from when the doctors had to cut him out of her. No more Tommys even if they didn't. No more babies at all. Not in this godforsaken house.

She rode all the way to Centerville to get that big cut made. It was in an A-model older than God, but it was the only rig in town that would make the trip. Evan kept crying behind her from the rumble seat, just like a baby himself till she almost went deaf on it, as if she didn't have enough to put up with. It was more than a full day and night of labor before she even got in that Ford.

Mr. Patcher owned it, and he kept right on rolling, never a word, hell-bent. Lord, but he was a fine old rascal! Good family, all the Patchers. Forty-odd miles of bad road with frost heaves and her bottom about blowing out. Then came the ether, which smelled like death itself even next day. They dropped that cloth down over her face, and quick as that she saw a bunch of lumberjacks rise up in the air, not one face she could recognize. Next thing, their clothes fell off, and they were nothing but skeletons under. Their bones were all blue. Her mother kept shouting about the mess from the far side of the river and claiming she was dead too.

That didn't make any sense. Ma wouldn't die for years, but she hardly knew her grandson. It was going to Florida killed her. Mattie'd swear it. Nobody used to do that around here, but different ones made that same mistake these days if they could afford it. They didn't last down there, either, always some son or daughter taking a bus and driving them back up home in the dear departed's car, which they traded quick as they could along with their own for a better.

Oh, that was some trip to get Tommy born, the first on her side or Evan's not delivered in their parents' house. But they just couldn't get him out at home. If Mattie ended up in hell, she thought that day, she'd be ready. She still thought so, even if what she had right here was not the bed of roses people sing of, neither.

That George Mayes. He was a grown man himself with his own past, but he didn't know from Toby's ass what it was for her to be with this old man he worshipped. She never held much against the boy—she still couldn't help calling him a boy—but no, he didn't understand, did he?

Oh, Evan drank all his life. Which of the men didn't? Only the ones with the sugar or whatever. The rest liked a sip, and then some in a few cases. Not too much you can do if that's what they're after. A woman looked out for herself, because there wasn't always going to be someone else to do it.

Mattie filled the bear cup again, spooned in some more molasses, then some Carnation. She watched the milk cloud up before she stirred. Then for some reason she got thinking about young Wilma Whitten, next house past Addy's. Wilma came in two winters back, not so long after that business with Tommy's kids. She was small as twenty seconds, but here she stood with a big shiner on her like a prize fighter.

Alan. Again.

"Mattie, I can't figure what to do," Wilma told her.

"Do?" Mattie asked, though she knew plain as day what was meant here.

"He'll come in cocked and smack me, or yank my hair and tip me right over in my chair at suppertime, and that-like."

"I'd put the boots to him."

Wilma stuck her hand over her mouth, like somebody covering up bad teeth.

"A man in that shape couldn't whip nobody!" Mattie told her. Yes, a woman had to tend to herself. "I'd wait till time was right and tip him over, by the Jesus." Wilma looked white as a ghost. She couldn't say a mumbling word. "Tip him over and give him the boots soon's he lights."

She didn't have much faith in Wilma. Next day but one, though, here's Alan going around town with shiners in both eyes, talking about running his skidder up on a stump in the burntland. Hadn't raised a hand to Wilma since. Mattie smiled. Oh, he still cursed and howled, but never the hand. No, it didn't mean all peaches and cream for Wilma, but she took a step to the front, all right!

Would Mattie give the same advice today, or was she only madder than a hornet with all that went on? Maybe she just wanted to punch the bejesus out of something, give God Himself a licking. But that was still good advice she handed Wilma. It was lucky for Alan he never married Mattie, not that she'd have him. Black eyes wouldn't be a patch on his troubles then.

You could say this much for Evan anyhow: he never even grabbed her, and that wasn't just because he knew she weren't one to take things exactly like a lady. He did know that, but bullying wasn't in a one of the Butchers, drunk or sober, no matter what that wife of Tommy's claimed.

It'd be strange to some, but no, the hardest part was how Evan quit telling stories three or four years gone, maybe more. She was still surprised to miss them so much, because she heard every last river tale in the world a hundred times.

It was only that he told some corkers! One about Eddie and Nora Sullivan was her favorite. Come April, the Sullivans set up what they called a store about halfway downriver. A lot of work to get stuff in there overland, but the river drivers always felt ready for something besides beans and cream of tartar biscuits by the time they reached there. The Sullivans sold corned venison or beef, and maybe some chocolate, tobacco, or that beeswax goop for blisters. Not much else, but they got a nice take. All IOUs, of course, but nobody was going anywhere. They'd call in their cash once the crew finished the drive, except every few years a poor one that didn't make it. Mattie could still shake, just remembering how she fretted.

And they'd keep that little place open right through deer hunters, for what little custom they got way out where it was. Evan told about how the storekeepers took in an orphan bear a trapper brought them one spring, not much bigger than a barn cat. Eddie wasn't too particular about it, but Nora was soft-hearted, like women are. At least that's what Evan said. So they raised this cub up till he got big enough to go back in the woods, which he did, just slipped his collar and run off just before fall. So they went back home in town.

"It's better, Mother," Eddie told Nora. "That bear's where he belongs." But she was sorry over it.

Well, the next April was uncommon warm, so they had their windows open. The missus slept out back in the big bed but Eddie stayed up front to mind the goods, not that you'd expect a thief that far in. By and by he woke up in the dark, though, conscious of a great weight upon him. That's exactly the way he said it, which was just like Eddie— a great hand for putting a flower in when he spoke. That bear climbed in a window and got in his bed, and you didn't know but he was ugly after almost a year living wild.

"Evan," Eddie told him, "that were one of life's darkest moments." But after half an hour, that bear climbed right out again, and they never saw him afterward.

It was a good yarn, all right, likely half-true anyhow. But it was really how Evan could spin it that tickled her. She'd bet money Sully could never tell it half so good, and him the one it happened to! Thing was, Evan had this gift to look like any animal he ever talked about. When he told about the little bull terrier he had as a kid, you almost saw the dog, all nerves and quiver. If he showed you an eagle looking down from a limb, he really showed it. A treed 'cat. A swimming buck. Eddie's bear. All plain as pictures. He wasn't exactly imitating these things; he just knew how to *be* them. Hard to explain.

No, he never struck her, didn't so much as shout at her, not even those times when she figured he almost had a right to. Mattie had a tongue like a raven on her when she was a young woman, she'd admit it now, and truth is, she'd rear back and lace him now and then!

It was like the drink took ahold overnight and made him an old man: one day he's what she lived with all that time, next he's not. He just got very quiet. In his seventies and plain out of things to say, which certainly weren't Evan Butcher. And he'd stay like that, hardly any talk at all for days. Or else he stayed gone. Asleep in that rotten shop or driving the twitch roads about five miles an hour, pining around the cemetery till he passed dead away. One night he'd freeze if he kept up that damned silliness or roll off a bank.

Another cup of tea would stick her in the bathroom half the morning, but Mattie poured it. As good on the toilet as anywhere, only putting in time. The idea made her sad, for that weren't Mattie, no more than she could truly believe Evan was Evan these days.

Once the liquor got its grip, if they did go visiting or launched the canoe or just went to see some nest or raspberry tangle or the sun over Percy Dam, where their stinking log drive used to start—if they did any of that, she might as well be by herself. It was like he had another girlfriend these past few years and he couldn't stop thinking about her. He'd go through all the motions but you weren't sure he saw a thing. That other lover sure didn't use him right, but she stayed on his mind.

Some lover! Just a damned jug.

Time goes by like a short night's sleep. Here it was 1933, and her in a new blue dress, all out of breath, telling her mother: "I'm over to marry Evan." She knew Ma didn't like that, because she thought he was a lot older, which he wasn't, because couldn't she remember him and her together in grammar school, and him just maybe a year ahead? Well, he was a working man by then. Maybe that's what confused Ma.

But her mother was a funny duck in her fashion anyhow. Why would she go down to a place full of snakes and alligators and who knows what else if she was like other folks? Didn't matter how she squawked anyways because Mattie was eighteen. She was already half out the door on the fly in that boughten outfit, clicking across the bridge in high-heeled shoes. And now here she was, sixty years after, and all that a memory, was all. Here she was, drinking electric tea out of a half-broke cup.

Old Ben Patcher was J.P., and married them right in his kitchen, surprised as the next one. He dragged in a man and a woman for witnesses, visiting cousins, he told them. No one ever saw them around here. Both older than the state of Maine, looked like. Then she and Evan lugged their duffels up to the dam, and off they went in the freight canoe he used for running beaver traps. The beam was fat as a tar road, and it was flat-bottom, and Mattie was in her blue outfit still, looking at handsome Evan on the stern seat, paddling to beat hell, her scarcely believing he was there and she was, and they actually went and did this.

They slept outdoors on the sand beach that night, and many another. When bugs were bad, they bedded down in Evan's canoe out on the lake. If it rained, they stayed under a woodshed at somebody's camp. Never spent a night inside a real place all summer long.

Wherever they were, Evan paddled to work in the morning. It was guiding mostly because of summer. He'd be back at evening, and she couldn't wait to see him. Oh, she kept busy enough all day, berrying or getting wood or finding a little sprig of something for decoration and keeping it in a can all day, waiting to set the posies in the gap of a gunwale, right up in the bow. Or she'd just sit there and see what swam or flew past. Not a care.

Evan always trailed a Black Ghost fly, so they ate some kind of fish for a lot of suppers. By the time the leaves changed, the loons were getting out of the lake, but Mattie had tamed down one old hen by feeding her fish scraps and guts. That bird was the last to fly to the coast. Feeding her and making of would fill up a little chunk of daytime too. No, never a worry but for maybe that foolish loon would forget ice was on the way.

A few hairs grew out on Mattie's chin that summer. She tried to pluck them with her fingers, but weren't a mirror anywhere, and she never could get all of them. She had her tweezers and looking glass these many years later, but she went back to letting the damned things grow out again. Evan never said a word about how she looked once he took to his new ways. Back then he spoke up, all right, but not mean, only teasing about the scraggle on her face. It sure didn't slow him up much.

She took to the bathroom, sat there and suddenly tasted something. Tears! They surprised the daylights out of her. She called herself batty, right out loud, and went back to the kitchen. By and by she peeked out the shop-side window in spite of herself and saw what was left of her Evan, hair all anyhow on his head, blinking like an owl.

Once Evan Butcher hewed thirty-two A-grade railroad sleepers in one day. His shirt was white as his teeth. He wrapped her up in his hard arms all night long, hairy chin and all, even in the belly of a canoe.

Now look.

II

It would be a long workday: a lot to take care of with summer running out. Mayes Transportation needed to be ready, as it always has been, thank God, even in the bad old times. George meets his obligations. That was one excuse for letting those bad times go on so long. He wondered what excuse Evan was using that morning. George hadn't even seen him after he hauled him home from the marble orchard for the last time a summer ago. He'd ducked him this year, just didn't want to be with the old wreck.

"There is trouble with the ditch-side tie-rod on number thirteen."

He remembers how his bright new mechanic Rob Beam put it, right here in this very yard, on this very spot, after George came home from his brief trip to camp in '75. He'd hired him just a day before he left for Woodstown, so this strange side of him—his striving for eloquence—hadn't shown itself before he went north.

Why does this snatch of talk wing its way into George's mind? Something about being where you're supposed to be, maybe. Rob was a good one for obligations too.

Was.

George remembers everything about the kid's little speech that day, but why choose that one among so many? He has the gift, if that's what it is, of recalling things people say, right down to specifics. He can read this morning's news and forget it by suppertime, but he'll bring back the most unimportant scraps of conversation even from early childhood. And there are a few words and things he'd like not to keep handy, that he wishes could crawl from between his temples and turn into trees or butterflies or whatever.

He thinks, God in heaven, George, do something with your time here!

"It is corrosion," Rob told him that morning. "It is potentially grave trouble, I believe."

The boy stood straight as a soldier as he delivered his opinion. George, though never a military man, was tempted to cry, "At ease!"

What a mix of feelings he has of Rob from a decade or so back, when the boy was his star employee. And it's still hard to keep developments straight in mind: the early time of his own sobriety, and then his puny bus business, and then the business getting so big almost overnight that he couldn't handle it alone—and of course Rob's departure, George had prepared it, wanting the best for him. But he never dreamed Rob's going would be a devastation.

He prods himself, as so often, to clear away the wreckage of his past. The process requires more than scratching his head and madly fidgeting, as if he had a thousand pieces of a puzzle and had to cram them into a pretty picture all at once. How did George ever manage to be shocked by his world's intractability? How can he be confused even today by how Rob left?

It is potentially grave. . . . None of his other mechanics would have used *it is* rather than *it's*. And *grave* or *potentially*? Who threw words like that around a garage? Not even George himself, and never mind his fancy education, what little he's ever used of it. Rob was the best of George's early crew precisely because of his own strange gravity, which could stray into unwitting self-parody. Rob might say *epitome* in three syllables, for instance, rhyming the last with home. Or mischievous in four syllables: *mis-CHIEV-i-ous.*

Once George came to the shop in an evil mood, and that scene is clear in mind too. He can even see the contrails in the dull sky above, how they moved him to try out some cockamamie metaphor—some nonsense about entanglement. Pretentious internal blather. Rob remarked that George was "looking sort of contumely." He read a pocket dictionary on his breaks, and most of what he studied sank in, but of course not everything.

George thanks God he always resisted the temptation to straighten Rob out. Who was he to play the superior anyhow? He knew where Rob came from: good parents, but rudimentarily literate; bare-bones high school education for their son; no instruction for him in automotive maintenance, either, beyond what he'd gathered—a fair amount, as it turned out—from his shade-tree mechanic uncle, aptly named Jim

Beam, long since dead, liver big as a dinner tray. Jim had been a well-known character in Glassburg.

George admired this kid from the start. Rob's work was flawless, and he was dependable to a fault. George sent him home half a dozen times when he showed up almost too sick to stand. His cannonball shoulders faded into his torso like a goat's, and he looked like a linebacker; yet his health was surprisingly erratic. On bad days, even the bristles in his brush-cut seemed to wilt. He'd outgrow the bad health in his later twenties. He outgrew a lot of things. Or did George just wake up to what was what? His workplace changed to beat hell, in any case.

George can feel his face flush. He checks the angry retrospection, because it's no good to get riled up, is it? His mood should suit a moment of hope, after all. Isn't that what today is all about, hope?

"Do what needs doing," George told Rob that day.

After their brief exchange that morning, George's spirits improved. He lost what his wife calls his curly eyebrows. They'd manage with the number one bus until the thirteen got up and running again. He'd semi-retired the poor old crate four years earlier, used her only for rare substitute duty nowadays. They probably wouldn't need her, though. He could send someone over to the NAPA in Norris, or go himself, to fetch a new rod for thirteen. It would be back online by early afternoon if he knew Rob Beam. No job too big or small.

George recalls cranking up his fan that day, but then going right back into the yard and climbing onto the old one bus. Her paint showed so dull it wasn't even yellow anymore but the color of the county's dirt lanes, unpaved until the early sixties, when he started his business. He feels mild shock as usual to think that almost thirty years have gone by since then. He has many a good memory, but not all by a damned sight. Clear away the wreckage, he reminds himself. Hope's the watchword.

For all her used-up appearance, the one seemed about the same as ever that morning, which was—when? '84, wasn't it? Thereabouts. So even then she was two decades old, and more. Rob had taken the jumpers out and started her engine, and she sounded same as ever, moaning exactly twice when you kicked the starter, then catching, even in

January. George believes she'd do the same right now. It'd be like starting over himself.

No, it wouldn't. Forget the magic. What's done is done. It wasn't January that morning but after Labor Day, George's shirt soaked through by seven in the morning.

Today he sits, cool, in the office his new wife made him redo as soon as they married, air-conditioning all through the shop. No, it's that just yesterday the papers were full of the end of the Cold War, and the day right before that, he and Rob stood in that yard and spoke of a broken tie-rod, and it was not much farther back that he and Evan ran across each other in clear water off Prune Island. How can it be 1994?

He can't help thinking of Evan, of course. What if he parked in the Woodstown cemetery and maybe even spent last night out there? There's a lot of precedent. By now the rock maple branches at the grave-yard must be about half orange. George prays Evan had his wool jacket on. A chill can hurt an old man.

No. Evan is alive, or better be. He's in the world, but Lord have mercy, there's no sure thing. It's another of George's refrains for the morning. May Evan keep his eyes out for the miracle. May he quit moping around at night among those headstones, ghastly in the moonlight above Woodstown.

George is a man for prayer, though it's largely wordless and entirely creedless. It more or less amounts to picturing the faces of people he cares most about. Evan may be a more important portrait in that gallery than some would consider sensible, but the old fellow has so affected his life that he's been praying for the old guy over decades, never so desperately as now.

Evan's worth it, but he's also outside George's power, or any human's. *Thy will be done*, George breathes. By now he's well beyond caring what the smart people might think any more than he cares about what the various orthodoxies propose.

After he sent Rob to Norris that morning, he went on sitting in his original bus. There was a fleet by the '80s—not a fleet like now, but a whole lot more than at the start. The one wasn't even the one then. She was The Bus. He lingered on the sprung seat and sweated, just as the kids would be doing that afternoon unless Rob could replace the thirteen's bad rod before two. The newer buses came with air conditioning, better than George had in his office. He's worked hard at staying with the times; he's proud of that.

But for all his work, listening to the veteran engine's rumble, hoping Rob would be back in time for the afternoon route, hoping the boy would stay with him forever, but hoping too that he wouldn't, that Rob would break bounds, find something better, be his own boss—no matter all George's years of work, he found himself thinking how strange life looked.

It's kept looking stranger ever since, even to him. Especially to him.

III

"God, man!" Boardie Bennett snapped at the Fence Club bar, "Do you know what you're getting into? I'd rather drive a bus!" The memory of that evening is specific for George, however much he forgets from similar ones. There were too many of those.

He'd never know if Bennett really believed his crap about a night club, and doesn't care now, of course. He has a narrative of his life in the '60s, which he suspects of being partly contrived, but he's gone on telling his tale, at least to himself. It starts at this hazy conversation with that tweedy classmate Boardie. Boardman Bennett III, to give him his prep school due.

Their bizarre exchange, unbeknownst to George, would turn out to be a seed, which became a flower, which dropped further seeds, which flowered too. Much of the process remains a blur. In any case, George Mayes now tends a sprawling garden of jonquil-colored school buses.

The night club, an utter fabrication, needless to say, seemed appealingly anarchic after graduation. He pictured his move as a headline, a habit of his in those chaotic years: *Yale French Major Buys Bus.* And indeed, he did buy a used one. To the Glassburg school board's severe consternation, Walter Hack, the driver who'd served Glassburg even in George's earliest school years, had abruptly died. George could scarcely have stepped into Mr. Hack's job except in such an emergency.

The development represented one of the coincidences so frequent in his life since that George occasionally wonders if they're coincidences at all, though his sense of Providence is woolly at best.

At all events, not long after Mr. Hack's unexpected death, George bought the bus from the poor man's widow and set about driving what few school kids there were in his neighborhood, all year long, often inexcusably drunk.

Then he got sober. Then there were more buses. Then more and more families moved in with their kids. Then he had kids of his own.

That's about it in a nutshell. Maybe what he did wasn't whimsy after all. His life has followed the kind of logic a dream follows, not true logic at all, but some progression that keeps making sense. By what right is he alive, especially in light of all his vodka-sick episodes? His affection for the flow of his ordinary existence is something he couldn't have dreamed back when he spent every free minute sitting on a bar stool.

His account, of course, is too seamless, but for whatever reason George, drunk or not, has always longed to make his life a coherent package. He sees that in himself, though not his motive. Story just matters, period. He can't come to grips with experience if he can't tell it.

In his college days, George hadn't rushed any fraternities. If he could get at their booze, why bother? The legal drinking age was twenty-one in New Haven. That was what spurred him, not a desire to be anyone's so-called brother. He'd visit whatever frat let him in; then he'd tell lies there. Plain as that.

Fence, the fraternity in which he spun his jazz club fantasy, was the epitome of Old Yale: J. Press, Brooks Brothers, and Chipp clothing everywhere, paisley ascots flashing in the half-light of the bar, tasseled loafers dully aglow. Oddly, the brothers' ankles tended to be bare, even in winter. In the inscrutable Yale slang of his time, the Fencies were "shoe," a sort of high-bred version of hip. So the place was one of George's dearest stalking grounds.

"Drive a bus, eh?" George vaguely remembers stalling for time, warming up his argument. Once he'd drunk enough, he argued with anyone who took the bait, deliberately tending to extremes. He was liberal and conservative, warmonger and pacifist, redneck, beaux arts fop, ascetic and hedonist. A positivist. A religious seer, sometimes radical Protestant, sometimes Catholic, sometimes even Buddhist. He'd been a Rousseauist, and of course he'd been a Sartrean, the voguish mode of his era, though like most of his contemporaries, he had little idea what that meant.

Dissidence was the point. It didn't matter what he dissented from. George now recognizes this actually meant he had no genuine convictions of his own for many years. All he had were tricks, one favorite in particular. Whenever he considered himself overmatched, he'd put his improbable French major to use, inventing some philosopher to quote in the original. Next he'd translate the quotation, very slowly, as if seeking the *mot* that was absolutely *juste*, or as if addressing a child. The technique could humble an opponent—or so he intended—by pointing up his innocence both of foreign languages and of important European thinkers, never mind that the thinkers were phantasms.

Boardie Bennett happened to be standing at the bar in obligatory attire. He affected a world-weary sigh before making any point, and he was addicted to certain words, *vapid* the real darling. Some other members, rather avant-garde by the frat's standards, had put Miles Davis's Birth of the Cool on the house record player. Boardie puffed his cheeks, blew out, and announced he despised jazz.

George could start wherever he liked. "Pretty vapid, eh?" he asked, feigning a sigh of his own, his imitation of Boardie Bennett surely perfect. Bennett scowled, but he nodded.

"Soon as I'm out of here, I'll find out how vapid," George went on, but Boardie made no reply. George scarcely knew where he was headed, but he rambled on: "I'm going to open my own little club in the Village."

Remembering all this today, George can't help smiling, but he winces too—at his old pretensions, his sordid wiliness. A lot of these adventures were meant to be funny, true enough, but often they feel otherwise in hindsight.

He took Bennett for a pushover, which almost disappointed him. It was almost as though George were playing a horn himself, his first invention generating another, and that another, and on and on until the story shaped itself. He was confident his opening figure would come back as he wound down. His solos always made a whole; he didn't have to think; that just got in the way. George considered himself a master of improvisation.

He dreamed up an address for Club Mayes: 107 Beulah. Had he ever been to Beulah Street? Did it exist? No matter. The permits were long since approved, the renovation of the building nearly done, the mortgage signed, everything as it should be. This was the opening lick.

George could go anywhere now, riff, vamp, and fill. Bennett tried to hold his expression of boredom, but his eyes showed uncertainty.

"You hear that record?" he asked. "Miles is the opening act. He'll be there before the mortar's dry."

Bennett sighed again. Twit.

"Monk in the fall," George added, pretending to sip from his glass, though the glass was empty, damn it. "Trane's on board, signed up for Christmas holidays. Cannonball. Wes Montgomery, Grant Green, Kenny Burrell, Joe Pass." George was partial to jazz guitar. He pretended to sip again. There couldn't be a club on earth that could line up luminaries of this kind in sequence, but Boardie wouldn't know.

"The whole thing's so . . ."

"Yeah, vapid." George almost pitied this poor sap. He thought of Bernard Shaw's claim that the British upper class subsisted on fewer than twelve words. The Bennetts of the world must command eight. "Haven't you got any other two-dollar locutions in the bank?" George demanded. The pity had vanished, immediately replaced by indignation, along with real pleasure. Locutions. That sounded so right. Everything was right. George was right. He was on a roll.

"Vapid will do just fine," Bennett said, heaving another sigh.

"Fuck you," George answered, depressed.

He's shocked to recall how irritated he became. A fierce proprietary interest in Club Mayes flooded him, along with fierce loyalty to the master musicians who'd perform there, not one of whom this herringboned nitwit could pick out of a lineup. George might have been talking about Martin van Buren's cabinet.

But why on earth couldn't he do better than fuck you? Bennett ignored him, probably hadn't even heard him above the general babble. George needed more liquor. That was it. He ordered his fifth stinger and gulped it, but the situation had changed subtly. He couldn't quite calculate how. His show wasn't getting any traction. Time for one of his Frenchmen. But he couldn't come up with a name, though he was confident, if it came to that, he could explain why some Paris intellectual might care about an American jazz facility.

Suddenly it seemed that all the brothers at the bar were talking at once. You could almost watch their words collide and churn, like those things on the backs of garbage trucks, whatever you called them. They made a communal bleat.

"Communal bleat," he said, not loud enough for anyone to notice, it seemed. All the better. Communal bleat: he liked it. He'd use it later. If he remembered.

George felt claustrophobic now, as if he'd just fallen beneath all that bodily mass of drinkers, unable to sort one thing from another up above. He shut his eyes and concentrated. He reminded himself that he was sitting on a barstool in Fence Club, engaged in unlikely debate.

"Armand des Rosiers," he whispered. It had an appealing lilt. So what was the opening sentence in des Rosiers's latest book, published by Gallimard, of course? What was its damned title? Never mind. George decided just to plunge in. Things always worked out on their own.

"Dès qu'on néglige la fondation africaine de la culture nord-américaine . . . ," he began. "As soon as . . . one neglects . . . the African basis . . . of North American culture . . ."

Not one of those fat bastards was listening. Not a shred of curiosity in the whole house. No fucking curiosity! No fucking culture themselves. No fucking nothing. Here George was talking about elite artists, for Christ's sake! And these ignorant bastards thought *they* were elite!

He repeated his French phrase, shouting it this time. Heads turned up and down the bar. Amazing, how each face was so . . . shiny. *Luisant?* He'd work it in. He thought of the gleaming saxophones—*les saxophones luisantes?*—on the cover of The Gerry Mulligan Songbook. Goddamn good album, not a piano on the whole thing, completely different kettle of fish. *Bouilloire de poissons.* No, not that. It wasn't a French locution.

This des Rosiers hung out at the Sorbonne, needless to say. "Ça va sans dire," George called out loud. No one responded. Was this a dream? He couldn't come up with his scholar's field. *L'ethnomusicologie?* That would work, but it had too many syllables. Well, at least it didn't have a lousy French *r*. That was a good thing right now: he whispered "des Rosiers" under his breath and the *r* was as awful as it had been in *africain*. He tried again. He couldn't buy one for a million dollars, his uvula all fucked up or something. Case of uvula in crisis. *Uvule en panne.*

But now he couldn't come up with any French name that wasn't loaded with *r*s. What an asshole he was. Asshole, plucked clean. "Plucked clean!" George shouted at full volume. What the hell was that supposed to mean? Bennett had his back turned anyhow.

"Engaged in vapid conversation?" George mumbled, his vision doubling. No response. George studied the heads of two deer on the plaster. Each grew another, and all four stared back at him with a kind of glazed pity in their eyes. "Well, the hell with Fence and the deer it rode in on," George said, but his words still couldn't break into the crowd's noise. "Or moose. Or elk. Or whatever."

Whipped and he knew it. Plucked. *Plumé.* The stingers were gone, and his money. Time to beat it. He slid off the stool, stumbled against Boardie, spilling a dash of the dingbat's la-dee single malt.

"Hope you sober up by the time your, uh, nightclub opens," Boardie said, another sigh, of course, coming along for the ride. But the guy was pissed off, all right. There were a few wet spots on his pants, their creases so sharp you could shave with one.

George thought for a long moment: "Miles will be playing to a more sophisticated crowd than this one," he said, carefully navigating his way through sophisticated. He waved his arm at the row of pink faces luisanting along the bar. Pig mugs. His comment had dripped contempt, but no one got it. Well, he was goddamned if he'd ever come back to this pig-hole anyhow. Ignorant pigs. *Cochons.* Everybody knew that one. He didn't bother to say it. Yes, he was plucked clean.

He wanted to add something more, but each time he got ready, his voice ran back a long, bright tunnel in his head. He could watch it shrink. It looked like a tiny hunchback in a herringbone overcoat. Uh huh: tiny hunchback in there. Tunnel was luisant, and you could hear the growl of a bari sax played low inside.

Gerry! Somewhere.

Boardie Bennett's face was so close as he held George up that he remembers seeing its pores. "Stick with the bus, kid," Bennett said, kicking open the frat's oaken door.

"Start your own joint, shit-for-brains," George mumbled. "Club Vapid, why not?" But Bennett was gone.

It had been snowing for some time. Amazing. A little bee-sting thing was pricking his temple. "I'm outside," George announced. The look of the world crept up on him, astonishing. Outside. Snow. The storm seemed so wondrous it might have kicked up in the middle of May. How many hours had he spent in Fence?

"Snowing," George muttered. "Snow." He wanted to say something else, but he couldn't. Snow. *La neige.*

He slogged a few feet before he noticed the emerald MG roadster. He gawked at it, as if beholding some famous painting for the first time and finding something distasteful in it. He'd wait for whatever was making its way forward in his brain. Spiffy little car. Spiffy little beige top with spiffy snowy fluff on it. Very shoe. Little yacht club decal on the back window, très shoe. Oh, spiffy and shoe, vapid Boardie-boy's vapid shit-for-brains MG B. Fucking A.

George grabbed the windshield wipers and pulled himself onto the hood, impressed by his good balance. He turned in his tracks, feeling agile as a ballerina. Down with his pants, out with a turd on the cloth roof, driver's side, alleluia. Then he stood up again, even steadier, and floated down to the snow like an angel. Steam rose from the car-top toward Fence's fake gas lamp. George grinned ear to ear, alone in the wide universe. *La merde, c'est la gloire*, he said. It would have sounded absurd, and rightly, if anyone had heard it.

But at least his *r*s were back.

He kicked through the deep snow to York Street, then turned left toward Saybrook, his dorm. He kept up the moronic chant: *la merde, c'est la gloire.* He wanted something more original or bright, but he couldn't fetch it, alors. So he kept singing, snow waking from his shins.

He still questions his memory of that walk. Did he really stop in the middle of York Street and say out loud, "I didn't wipe"? How could it have been that, at the very moment he spoke, a window opened on the third floor, and someone tossed a roll of toilet paper that landed exactly at George's feet?

Yes, all that did happen. He remembers crossing one eye for focus and peering up at the open window. Nobody there, but he shouted anyhow: "Merci!"

The *r* was perfect now.

IV

One morning in June of 1961, immediately before graduation, George Mayes whispered the word *north*. He couldn't have said why. It was totally random. Dormitory life was about to end, and he had no particular place to go in Glassburg. He'd have to rent an apartment, no paycheck lay in sight from anywhere, and his savings, while keeping the wolf from the door, were scarcely capacious. But hell, practical concerns could wait. Meanwhile, he'd stay outdoors someplace in the sticks until weather pushed him back.

George knew next to nothing about that weather or about real woods, his boyhood landscape pastoral, not wild. He had no way to know his sojourn in the back country would sew a crazy, crucial patch onto a patchwork life.

Within a week from commencement, he'd bought a battered Grumman canoe and a carry rack from Myers Army-Navy out on Whalley Avenue. He strapped everything he could on top of his Volkswagen bug, headed northward for hours on end, choosing random turns at the intersections, following whichever road seemed to point toward a remoter country.

He bivouacked on a lake whose very name he wouldn't even know for a time. The black flies plagued him at the start, but he remembers his strange pleasure in speaking to almost no one for a couple of weeks, except when he drove for supplies to a store in a minuscule place called Woodstown, whose proprietor wasn't much for words himself. Those trips were infrequent, because he was cautious of his funds, at least for part of that summer.

So big-talking George kept quiet. Tenderfoot George tried to become a woodsman, an imperfect accomplishment at best. But he got along well enough on a mix of crackers, canned fruits and vegetables, and jerky, with panfish the occasional delicacy. The lake was clear as tap water, individual rocks and even sand grains visible as much as fifty feet down. He could drink from it at will.

His keenest recall, though, is clanking through a shallow channel between two islands in his Grumman, three or four perch in a bucket under the transom. He came on a man in his late forties, the first and last person George would encounter out there. The fellow wore a green crusher hat, a blue bandana, and, even in the heat, a pair of gray woolen trousers held up by suspenders so sun-bleached no one could have said what color they'd been when new.

Evan Butcher would have looked drab elsewhere, but in that setting he looked like a figure you'd meet in a dream. George sees that scene as clearly in 1994 as in '61: Evan in the stern of his canoe, a loon swimming close enough to take a mud chub from his hand.

Commanding. That was the word for this stranger, one that would fit him for a good, long time.

As George paddled up, the loon sculled away, the fish crossways in its bill. "You two know each other?" he joked.

"I guess probably," the man answered, appearing to scowl. His voice rang differently from any George would ever know, as it does even now, at least in mind. If only Evan will speak today. George will phone him. It's not the same as talking with him face to face, but if things go well, it will surely do.

Evan's three-word reply had been quiet, and yet it bore some quality that seemed near mystical. George suddenly imagined him as the Ancient of Days, who spoke with the voice of many waters. He recalled that phrase from an English course he'd barely paid attention to, The Bible as Literature. It was one of the few things he could summon from that class, or, really, from any outside the Yale French department—from which he didn't retain much either.

Evan's canoe was classic wood and canvas, every hair in place. "Nice boat you got there," George remarked.

"Canoe," the man corrected. "I wouldn't cross a millpond in your outfit."

George flushed. The Grumman could be noisy enough to drive a man crazy, true, and she rode so high that a puff of wind could spin her like a top, but he wouldn't have known what else to choose.

"Best I could afford, I'm afraid," he said.

"I'd ought to show you how to make a better," said Evan, a smile in the voice now, sudden, welcome.

"I'd like that," George answered, surprising himself by how deeply he meant it.

From that moment, things simply happened. Every few days during George's sojourn, Evan came back to the lake, whose name turned out to be Semnic, no doubt some corruption of an Abenaki word. In time to come, his new friend would in fact teach George how to build his own canoe. He never got handy enough to fashion one he felt really proud of, but what he did turn out has lasted him all these years. Who'd have imagined it?

Evan taught him how to paddle his canoe properly, without shifting sides every few strokes. Trees too. Animal tracks. He tried to teach him how they made the cream of tartar biscuits the river drivers ate. How to fillet a salmon. How to cast the fly to fool that salmon. How to tie it. A slew of names for certain backwoods bird so tame you could feed it by hand like his pet loon: Gorbie, Gray Jay, Canada Jay, Whiskey Jack, Camp-robber, and, given his wispy Yale education, his favorite, *J'écris*.

For years George dreamed of moving to Woodstown. Another time, another George. Yet, infrequent as their meetings would become, from that day in that June, Evan changed his life, partly by making him more aware of the physical world, yes, but that's too simple—or maybe not simple enough. Evan's nature and Nature's nature seemed so closely linked they couldn't be separated from each other. George would never reach such a state, of course. To start at twenty-two was already too late. Still, that fusion became an ideal against which he measured his own aspirations. He's now a bus man in what's become a suburb, so what he means by the ideal is hard to explain, if the story is not to be mere poetry or fiction. Or plain lie.

Evan's life has been a story, an intriguing one, at least until lately, its setting crowded with particulars so eloquent they never needed elaboration. George feels a momentary chill inside. Yes, it will have to be the phone. He can post the letter any time, after all.

V

Glassburg, Pennsylvania is a sprawl of office parks and strip malls and the rest of modern ugliness, but even here George wants his life, like his old friend Evan's, to have a proper beginning, middle, and end, unmanipulated by him. He's somehow certain that Evan has understood this about him. After all, the man's a storyteller himself—a truth that for the moment unsettles George.

Evan's own end looms, but it isn't shaping up to make his life coherent after all. George's adoption of that ideal may owe itself to its being the opposite of incoherent, the state in which he stumbled for years. George hopes Evan may remember that in the good times, he lived a noble and shapely life, and that he and George were conspirators, no matter how radically different their livelihoods.

Nor how different their environs. Development has progressively devoured what once was the natural world near Glassburg. Development! George sometimes spits the word. Didn't God do a good enough job? And yet he knows development has helped him prosper. He never moved to Woodstown, of course. There used to be life-threatening, soul-deadening reasons for that, ones that kept him from starting his own better story for too many years.

His north country dwelling turned out to be no more than a tiny cabin that had lain unused for years and teetered at the brink of ruin. It sat on land leased from St. Regis Paper. There's no water, no view, but George loves it, and regrets his long absences. He bought his little spread in '67 for four hundred dollars, and it remains his heart's home in some respects.

He'll hold onto everything associated with the camp. It was his, it is his, it will be his. *Erat eius, eius est, erit eius.* George has finally accepted that he'll never quite purge such snatches of a so-called classical education. They can spill from his mouth like orts. He's not so ashamed of them as he used to be. Yale was what it was. George is only what he is. *Ipse est enim.*

The camp needed a fair amount of work, but rough enough that, with Evan's coaching, he handled a lot of it on his own, jacking up the corners and resquaring the granite footings, stripping the tarpaper roof and putting on a galvanized, installing a woodstove Evan located down at the Indian township.

Evan built him a table and four chairs, two for the table and two Adirondacks for the dooryard. He made a single cabinet to keep the mice from George's meager supplies. On his own, George slapped up a lean-to woodshed and a privy. The camp provided shelter and warmth when they were needed, and that was enough. When he did move up, he reasoned, he'd see to other comforts, maybe even find a better spot.

But Julie and the girls are spooked by the very idea of Woodstown, its remoteness, the camp's lack of running water and electricity, the attacks of insects. There's the matter, too, of making a living. What could George ever do in those parts?

One day he woke up older than Evan was when they met. He had a young family for a man his age, a mortgage, and a decent income over six hundred miles to the south. If all through the '60s George considered his school bus business temporary, it's now clearly what he does. It took him an age to marry a second time, and his life's quality immediately soared. Nothing—not even her squeamishness about his favorite place—will allow him to fault his wife.

For almost a decade and a half before her, he'd lived a bachelor's life of controlled, sober depression. Controlled was better than drunk and disorderly, but it was still depression, which George didn't even recognize until she lifted it. He's a lucky man simply to have survived. He stepped over a lot of corpses to get where he is in the middle '90s. Anything else—and there's a lot—represents unmerited good fortune.

"What's yours is yours, George," Julie said from the start, not a possessive nerve in her system. He's been free to indulge his nostalgic northern pilgrimages ever since, and could likely have made them longer, but a combination of conscience and missing his family has kept them what they are.

Well before Julie came along, in the early years after New Haven, he was pretty much sloshed full-time, with the exception of that month in his tent on Semnic Lake. Evan wasn't much of a drinker in those days, the county was dry, and it seemed too much bother to travel for liquor. As soon as he got home from that Maine interlude, of course, George would travel miles and miles for booze when he had to.

He was drunk even on his wedding day, of which he has cloudy recollections. Staggering up the aisle. Dropping the ring. Scrabbling for it on his knees. A red-faced pastor keeping him from tipping sideways and snarling under his breath, "You're a disgrace." His bride Melody's poor family studying their hymnals or looking up at the vault of the Lutheran chapel. George hadn't invited anyone. He had no friends close enough for that. He had no true friends at all, in fact.

He can bring back the color of Melody's hair, brown flecked by red in the sunny months. He recalls her squinting her eyes when she laughed, something she did less and less as time went by. Besides such meaningless detail, he can't summon much. He knows people called her cute. He must have found her something like that himself. But what color were the eyes? What did she like to eat? Did she have hobbies? The moment he conjures a mental picture, it blurs.

Words are more vivid in memory—angry ones, as when George knocked into furniture or garbled his speech, all the while denying his condition, at least early on. On the first night of their honeymoon, he actually pissed from the edge of his bed in sleep. What a start. "I hate you!" Melody screamed as George clumsily dabbed with a towel.

She'd say the same thing countless times after. She had a right, God knows. I hate you: who'd told him that since his days on the playground? Maybe more people than he can bring to mind. For too long he just didn't care.

A blind man could have seen what was wrong with his marriage, with his life in general, with him. George couldn't. It didn't matter how often he woke up in their diminutive living room at three in the morning, their black and white television crackling like a fish fry. He'd stay conscious just long enough to crowd his legs onto the loveseat where he'd slumped, a Smirnoff fifth on the floor. How many times did he flinch at the whine in his ears and his throbbing eyebrows come miserable dawn? Another day. Same old other day.

Loveseat. That was a good one.

It's surely possible that what George tells himself of the marriage is just more drivel, and yet it may actually hold at least a germ of truth. He and Melody had fallen into conversation at the Rexall lunch counter in Norris, and that led to breakfast. George learned she was an only child, one, he inferred, both confined and pampered by her Pennsylvania Dutch parents. Melody was a receptionist at the vet clinic. He started the relationship because she wouldn't be the Radcliffe, Vassar, or Smith bride that most Yalies courted in those times. George called her more real. But who has he ever been to define reality, especially then?

George figured a wife might put some order into his life, which, despite his braggadocio, he must have sensed was needed, even if subconsciously. No wiser, perhaps Melody imagined that they'd somehow meet halfway. A wild man might juice up her quiet existence.

He juiced it up, all right, in every sense of the term. Poor girl. In his younger years, he'd never have dreamed himself capable of his crazy fabrications or of the cheating he started within months of their wedding. Could she really believe, say, that the female voice on the phone, which she'd chanced to pick up mid-conversation, was not some local barfly but a parts rep from the west coast? More astonishing, how did George persuade himself that his lies weren't really lies, his infidelities not really infidelities?

A crash in the garage snaps him out of his blue reverie. He pokes his head through the little window into the shop. "What's the rhubarb?" he asks, a little grumpily.

"No, rhubarb, George," says John Henry, one of his mechanics. "I just cut the pipe off this old wreck." He douses the flame and holds the torch up. The number ten bus, not so damned old at that, looms on the monstrous lift installed five years back.

George puts on a smile, though he still catches himself thinking Rob Beam wouldn't make this sort of racket. One of the poor twins once said Rob had a soft paw, right on the money, and unusually eloquent for whichever twin that was.

George rebukes himself for more daydreaming. He has work to do, like returning a call from the superintendent of schools, not a bad fellow, if only he'd get over the matching white shoes and belt motif. He rebukes himself again. Why should anyone's clothes matter to him?

More clatter. Well, George made his own racket in his day. Flung silverware. Broken dishes. Shattered furniture. One morning, he even smashed his wife's radio with a wooden pestle, for God's sake! How could her taste in music—Mantovani, the Conniff Singers, Percy Faith—have chafed him that badly? At least he's a lot better at keeping his irritations to himself now.

Poor Melody. Poor kid. They'd both been kids, in fact, with no way to foresee that bright young marrieds could quickly be companionless, that nobody'd keep tolerating the husband's conduct out of mere politeness. Guests began to fidget and sigh whenever George invented another text to bolster some half-baked opinion, translating his imaginary French source with the diligence of a schoolmarm. And soon there were no guests. Maybe some of his antics had been funny in college. Probably not. In any case, what adult wanted to hang around with some lush who'd break into a foreign tongue at the first sign of dispute?

In their early months together, George even pulled that stunt on his bewildered wife. He'd begin some spiel with *Écoutes, ma chère* or whatever, and she'd stare in bewilderment. Later along, she'd simply stomp out of the room, bawling her refrain, I hate you! George once even told her he should have married someone from Vassar after all. Skunk, all right.

Soon Melody's social life, so far as George could tell, came down to lunches or matinée movies or shopping outings with girlfriends. At first, he wondered whether there was more, but one day he realized he didn't care. Did she have a boyfriend? Let her. Was she pregnant? Did it matter? He had one demand: "Just leave me the hell alone!"

As for his own social life, he quickly became, or resumed being, a serial predator on all kinds of women, but he dropped even that by '64. He didn't want complication, conversation, distraction. All he wanted was what he called freedom, which meant getting as drunk as he chose, no matter that after the first gulp, the freedom evaporated. Liquor called the shots.

Social life meant one bar or another, where opinions and passions roared to life, then guttered at closing time. It meant flushed people shouting, laughing, challenging, weeping, apologizing. Their faces were more shape than feature when morning arrived, along with the inevitable despair, fogged memory, dread—which only more drink could remedy. Having repeated them so often, he does recall a few of his barroom tales, one in particular. It still makes him shudder.

Those years after college might so easily have blessed him, turned him into another man. The full catastrophe of the Vietnam War, in which his roommate Farley would be among the first Americans to die, lay a way off, and even farther off the cocaine blight of the '80s, which killed Farley's son. What was the boy's name? George has forgotten. Along with a lot of others, he'd thought JFK would lead everyone into a golden age, that he'd stay young forever, like them.

People persuade themselves of nonsense, he knows; it's a human weakness. He does it himself, even sober, hard as he tries to deal with life on life's terms. He still has absurdly wishful thoughts. Old habits die hard.

There was surely nothing blessed about George's life in the '60's, though he kept thinking there must be, which now seems a marvel, as if a devil had used some black art against him. "They don't call it demon rum for nothing," George says aloud from his office chair.

"Boss?" Herbie says through the little office window.

"Just talking to myself, Herb."

Even now, George feels his stomach tighten and his cheekbones burn if he imagines how low he got: that awful bachelor's duplex in Glassburg; the ketchup smears on the mound of dishes in his sink; the urine in his mattress; the vomit on his bathroom floor's throw rug; the cigarette holes everywhere, and holes too in the sheetrock of each room from punches he threw at walls in his solitary, inexplicable fury.

George started drinking before he drove his bus, but that wasn't what awakened him to the hold booze had. He kept tolerating his own behavior in those days, no matter his recklessness with kids' lives. But if he were to open a bottle of mouthwash now, the smell might make him retch, or maybe weep, or both, reminding him how he'd swig it at the wheel, partly to cover the scent of the vodka he'd already swigged, but mainly for its own alcohol. He fooled everyone, or at least the twenty-odd kids who rode with him mornings and afternoons, along with their parents, who seemed to regard him as mildly eccentric but somehow lovable.

Lovable!

No, he didn't suddenly peer into his rearview one day in 1967, notice a bunch of scrubbed faces, and wonder what kind of scum could drive drunk on public roads, threatening the worlds still lying unmarked in front of those innocents. The turn came instead one Sunday morning, when he bumbled into his kitchen, and in the corner saw a rat eating dog food left over from a month before, when he'd tended some vacationing family's basset hound. Jesus Christ. The dog's name was Luna.

For one of countless times, he tried to tell himself he wasn't a drunk, not really. He was just a guy with a hangover, because how could he just be some common, knee-walking wino? Not George Mayes, Yale '61. But nothing would do now; the jig was up. He was a man with a rat feeding on the floor of his apartment, an addict too depleted to do anything but let the rat be.

He spoke aloud: "I'll quit!" It would be that easy. "This time I mean it!" So he pledged for one of countless times. Then he watched in astonishment, as if he were looking at an unsettling movie. Someone else's hand opened a cabinet door; someone else's hand grasped the vodka bottle; someone else's hand tipped it up. Whose mouth sucked those remnant inches in one swallow? On the wrist below the alien hand, a watch read seven o'clock. George heard birds outside.

That was his last drunk—at least so far, he has learned to caution himself. When the vodka wore off, he lay on the sticky linoleum and wept for hours, wrenchingly. It felt like an athletic ordeal: how many more snap ups of grief and shame could his body endure? Yes, for the first time in his life, George understood why they called alcohol a spirit. It had clearly possessed him.

He wouldn't sit at the wheel of a bus again after that morning. He hired a driver, using all but the very last of his modest inheritance. Then he sold his Volkswagen and his metal canoe, along with various articles of unmaimed furniture, including his metal bed frame. He got a loan from Glassburg Savings, bought another bus, hired another driver. He slept on his floor and hitchhiked to work for half a year. Two summers later, he bought another bus on credit, hired another driver, and so on, until his buses were carrying more people than ever lived at

Woodstown, his heart's home, which he still faithfully visited for most of July.

The years bounced by. George's north country stays began to shorten in the '70's, and got shorter still in the '80's. But they always refreshed him and still do, just as his returns to soggy mid-Atlantic August have always brought him down for a spell. Not today, though, because everything is looking up. Isn't it?

He kept making it through the school years, and to his astonishment, turning more and more into a businessman. Once, no matter how foggy his mind, he knew the name of every kid on every route, knew if there were brothers or sisters, knew what each father and mother did for a living. Then suddenly he was operating a slew of vehicles. He didn't see the kids anymore, but even if he had, they'd be numbers. George had thirteen buses and drivers, with two retired drivers for back-up; he had a panel van for kids with disabilities; he paid two full-time mechanics.

Once there were even more mechanics.

Mayes Transportation now carries students to public, private, and parochial schools alike. It serves children of immigrants, of native Pennsylvania Dutch farmers, of professionals who have flocked to the new office campuses. He has heard from the high school drivers that it also serves boys and girls nearly as wrecked by alcohol or by something else as George was, not in his own school years, but not much just after, and for years.

By the '80's, George couldn't keep his own books anymore. He'd never had a minute's training in accounting. He'd barely scraped through the simple math classes he took as a schoolboy. He shudders to recall those stuffy rooms where other boys and girls somehow made sense of the runes on the chalkboard. They'd even argue about equations and formulas. What on earth did those classmates see when they talked like that?

There's still another crash from the shop. George lurches up from his chair, then settles back. You don't find help like Rob Beam every day. Herbie and John Henry are a cut above the norm; they just don't have the soft paw. Lord knows what may have become of Rob, no matter his talent. Him and that woman of his. Good riddance. At least John Henry and Herbie are straight-ahead guys.

He's been lucky. He might have gone belly-up any time, drunk or sober. The tax man might have grabbed him. He'd gotten by for almost twenty years with once-a-month temporary help on his paperwork, and some crooked temp might have noticed his helplessness with figures and done some skimming. Maybe one or two did.

Along came Julie. She wasn't the most experienced of the men and women he interviewed in '81; she may not even have been the smartest. He simply chose her on a hunch. She was only twenty-nine, thirteen years younger than George, but she won him by her self-assurance. She seemed to have a calm about her that he lacked himself, at least when it came to numbers. She probably had a cluster of things his soul cottoned to, even if he didn't know it. Call that a corny notion. George doesn't believe it any the less.

VI

George often suspects that what sees as his life's symmetries are products of his overheated imagination. The imposition of order, even if it's false—that's surely a natural impulse in one given to disjointed night thoughts. His doubts about such shapeliness can move him to self-pity: shouldn't he be rewarded for abstinence? No. not if he thinks it through. He quit a habit that was killing him. No one applauds diabetics for leaving the sugar bowl alone.

He's lucky his night thoughts have never made him drink, but they're no easy ride. He hopes they'll stay at bay just now. Fitting Tommy Butcher and Tommy's twins into his damned symmetrical pattern is no walk in the park. George sometimes fears he harbors a monstrous nihilism under his outward calm.

He drowned so many of a normal young man's disenchantments and pleasures in booze that learning to cope with the actual remains a struggle. He can vividly replay too many onsets of nebulous fear. The hunched back, the neck muscles in a lemon-sized knot, the left arm scarcely mobile. Such episodes have felt like preludes to death. He began to experience such attacks from the moment he gave up drinking and life turned into—life.

Those attacks have always caught him off guard. He can be going along more or less heedlessly, like anyone else with above-average luck, and then the wheels fall off. In those bleak hours, he's found himself thinking less of his life as saved than of his doom as forestalled.

He particularly remembers one ordinary night, Julie beside him in the king bed, beautiful in the jade glow of the bedside clock. He tried to lie still but tossed until she stirred. She'd be grouchy if he woke her. She wasn't callous; there are few who can understood dry drunks. Such episodes make no sense, but they happen.

George sneaked from the bedroom and reeled around the house like—well, like a drunk caught short of liquor. There's your pattern,

George. He pictured a jungle and himself as a tiny insect within it. Then he stumbled to the kitchen for coffee, knowing he wouldn't sleep again. By the time he carried his cup back to the family room, his jungle hallucinations had vanished. There were horror and despair enough in plain reality.

He noticed the television gadgets that Mary and Kate used for their video games. Their sound effects, even in mind, seemed hair-raising. Out the window, the shopping mall's aura glimmered in the distance. Its lights dim after nine o'clock, but they're never extinguished. That night he noticed a raccoon patrolling his trash cans, and the animal looked like an ogre. Just at daybreak, a grackle crabbed over the lawn; in his state, even a songbird could terrify.

George had grown up just two miles to the east, but where was the continuity? The dump where he and Pat and Nine shot rats was filled in now, a nuns' blocky, gray retirement home on its site. The town long ago razed the water tower where he painted his initials in '59. A traffic circle, showing route numbers and "Yield" signs like metal flowers, surrounds the little green where the tower loomed.

His bachelor uncle's Irish housemaid, Mary Conley, had in all manner of ways been his mother. He and Julie named their older daughter for her. But by that night, Mary'd been dead for years. That uncle's gentleman farm had become a municipal office park, its yellow stucco house chopped up and converted to town use as well, the shed rows and the gloriously scented milking parlor bulldozed.

Even as his outbreaks of anxiety raged, George knew he shouldn't be nostalgic if that meant forgetting how his neighborhood's metamorphosis provided him a livelihood. But reason was of little help in the bad old hours. Still is.

How can George speak of symmetries? He often thinks of Evan's only child Tommy, and how they met five years after that first magical month in Woodstown. To think of him is to think of others like Iggy Mook at George's garage, of other souls blighted by the same war. Tommy in and out of jail. Tommy's boys. All that followed. Violence raiding the world. Often, after the night terrors passed, he'd sneer at himself: yes, where are your patterns, George?

When he first encountered Tommy Butcher, it was shortly before he'd be gone again. From fall of '66 to the last of '68, he ran heavy equipment in Vietnam, constructing landing strips, where planes and helicopters dumped the wounded into what passed for hospitals. George would never hear Tommy speak about all this; in fact, he rarely spoke coherently at all once he finished his hitch.

Few of the Nam vets George knew shared war stories, except perhaps with each other, so George conceived his own pictures. Accurate? Dead wrong? How would he know? He played the roar of engines in mind, the screams from gurneys, the bellowed commands of medics and doctors. But what has he ever really known? That conflict may have been a tragic blunder, but having ducked it, he feels a guilt he can never quite appease.

In August of '66, just before deployment, Tommy spent two weeks' leave in Woodstown. Before he did boot camp, he'd been working for some years at a stud mill in New Hampshire and had recently married a woman there. The only name George ever heard her called was Poot, whatever that stood for. He remembers his unconscionable thoughts whenever he ran into her. In those days, he got a buzz on early, and his few inhibitions tended to be gone by noon.

"If you wasn't married," he once told Poot outside Billy's store, "I'd chase you all around this Christly village." He winces now to recall his boldness, and just as bad, his affectation of north country speech.

Poot seemed amused, maybe even something else. "If I wasn't married," she said, "maybe you wouldn't have to chase."

How quickly he could be titillated! She had a saucy way about her, the kind that had driven George to flirtations, inevitably futile, with a score of overworked New Haven waitresses and salesgirls. He quickly made calculations: Tommy'd be long gone when George came back to town next summer. He knew Poot could almost hear him figuring, but she never dropped her eyes.

It was George who looked away, as if studying the sign on the store, but he longed to breathe the scent of that dirty-blond hair, to feel the hardness of the hips that strained at Poot's jeans. George didn't know she was pregnant.

If he couldn't have this woman at least once, he told himself, he'd never get over it. How was he capable of such inanity? Lewdness was just his way for some time, even after he married Melody. To hell with a wife, with Poot's husband, even with good old Evan, the husband's father. He also wanted a pull at a beer or two from the six-pack Poot clutched against her. The cans wet her shirt. George liked that.

Nothing ever came of his designs, and after all the ill-starred history of Tommy's family, George thanks God for one thing at least that doesn't plague his conscience.

George and Evan had planned a trip to Semnic that July. They'd call it a celebration, a sort of five-year anniversary of their meeting. Though he didn't acknowledge it, even to himself, George's real intention for the campout would be getting drunk, the same as for any adventure. Not watching for wildlife anymore. Not marveling at the gorgeous calm of an unspoiled lake. Not even savoring treasured companionship.

It irked him to learn that Evan had asked Tommy, a virtual stranger to George, on the outing. The man was bound to change the atmosphere, but George couldn't very well tell Evan to rescind an invitation to his own blood. He even imagined sending the Butchers off without him. Poot would stay behind with Mattie, after all, and she always turned in early. On the other hand, Mattie was a keen one. Still is.

Disappointed that morning, George drank, though he'd have drunk no matter. He'd have done it if Tommy stayed home. The cat dies, have some booze. Same if it lives.

"We'll treat you to a ride," Evan said as they dragged his canoe to water, quickly picking up his spit-through paddle and handing another to Tommy, nodding toward the hull. George reluctantly stepped aboard while the Butchers, knee-deep in water, steadied the canoe. George lay back against the middle thwart, facing away from Evan. He didn't want to see Evan's expression and he didn't want Evan to see his. Sulking, he studied Tommy's back. They had a twenty-minute trip from Evers Lake to the Semnic carry. George hated to think Evan had seen through him.

The sky showed clear, the sun full, the air already redolent of fall, if distantly. George trailed a hand in the water, the regular dips and thrusts of the other men's strokes narcotizing him. He kept nodding, but at the cackle of a loon or a fish-hawk's shriek, he'd jerk upright. Why in hell was he so miserable so much of the time?

"Christ almighty, set still!"

George had shaken awake again. Twisting to look back at Evan, he nearly upset the canoe. The two others braced their paddles cross-beam and leaned the other way.

"What the hell's the matter with you?" Evan barked.

"I don't know," said George. "I'm sorry."

"Bet I know," Tommy muttered.

George gripped the gunwales hard on both sides. He might be the guilty party, but he didn't mean to put up with some redneck mill hand's mockery.

They reached the west shore of Evers and slid onto the sand beach. The carry to Semnic was short but hard, the trail fire-blackened from a burn in the '50's, tangled with berry cane and hardwood sucker. Not enough people used the portage to keep the brush down.

George's anger fueled him, even seemed to sober him. He yanked the three men's Adirondack baskets out of the hull, put his own on his back, and made to heft the canoe onto his shoulders, all in a series of abrupt motions. He had something to prove.

"What's the hurry?" This time, Evan's voice held the usual good humor—at least George hoped so.

Evan sat on a boulder. "We'll relax a minute," he said. George saw he wanted to smooth things over.

"Rest a while?" George asked, shrugging off his pack. "Easy for you to recommend, you old bastard. You got the only seat in the house."

"Oh, they's plenty of seats," Tommy said, dropping to the beach.

George wished he could purge the booze-fumes that cut through the scents of warm sand and the jack firs that leaned their way in a soft breeze. He sat on the beach too.

"How old is this burn?" he asked. He was pretty sure he knew the answer, but he wanted to keep Evan talking, and to keep his son quiet.

"Let me see . . . ," Evan began.

Tommy cut him off. "I was eighteen, Pop. We worked the other end."

Tommy answered a question he hadn't been asked, and George instantly resented the bond of son to father.

"Eighteen?" Evan said, arching his brows. "Then it must've been . . ." He paused to consider. "Must've been ten years ago, then."

George did his own quick computation: if Tommy turned eighteen in '56, then he was born in '38, a year before him. That caused an unpleasant inner commotion, which he couldn't make any sense of.

"Yessir, by the Jesus," Evan went on. "Started up in the middle of June and burnt most of the summer."

"Longer'n it had to." Tommy chuckled.

"Could be."

George was lost. He hated it.

"Now don't you get talkin' out of school, son!" The tone was mock serious. George half hated Evan's amusement too.

A long silence followed, but for the wavelets' rote on the gravel and the scolding of red squirrels. George took it until he couldn't. "What're you two talking about?"

"Well . . ."

"Somebody must've kept that burn goin'," Tommy interrupted.

Things might get ugly, George thought.

Evan paused to fetch a pouch from his trousers. Then he filled his pipe, tamping the tobacco with theatrical slowness, striking his match on a beach stone, holding the flame for several seconds above the bowl. He did enjoy a story.

"Billy Miles was the fire warden," he drawled, sucking the stem, "and he had charge of the crew. He sent Tom and me out here. We knew the country better than most of 'em; made a lot of tracks around Semnic when he was comin' up."

"I guess we did!" Tommy interjected. Couldn't he just shut up? "Couldn't use this carry," Evan went on. It was afire from here to the end." He pronounced each word slowly, as if George might not understand otherwise. Or did George dream that?

"We had that fire tamed down pretty good by September. But a lot of times the big ones'll burn underground till snow. Billy needed a watch."

"And you was available." Tommy chuckled.

"Nothin' much to do till deer hunters."

"Fire watch wasn't big money," Tommy added, "but it was money."

"Money, you said it," Evan replied, "and me so poor right then I'd have to puke if it cost a nickel to crap."

"Trouble was—" Tommy started.

"Trouble was, I believe that fire really was out."

"Believe it was," Tommy echoed.

"Billy'd take me off watch 'less it caught."

"Just a little coal oil and a match, was all," Tommy muttered.

"What?" George asked. "You didn't keep it burning?"

"Just so's you'd notice," Evan said. "Or Billy would. I knew his habits. He had trade at the store till us fellas went to work, then things got slack till noontime. So he'd mostly show up around 9 or 10."

"You was fightin' fire, time he come around," Tommy explained.

"Oh, she kept goin' till the snow flew."

It was a good enough story, and George laughed, but he wanted Tommy somewhere else.

The three of them finally stood. Evan groaned and complained his bones were used up. George strode quickly to the canoe, hefted it, settled the middle thwart on his shoulders.

"Hell, I'll carry it," Tommy said. There was a pout in his voice, which pleased George, though he knew the first leg of the carry—all upgrade and brush-strewn—would take a lot out of him.

"You'll get a turn, Tom," Evan said. "Lord knows I ain't going to lift her a particle."

George took off at a quick pace. He'd have to slow it imperceptibly if he could. The Butchers filed behind, Tommy with two pack baskets, Evan with the paddles, the cookware, and some metal plates and cups in his. They each had a fork in the packs and knives on their belts.

George was grateful for the breeze; it kept the insects down and fanned his sweat. He took care at a certain narrow pass, recalling how one June he'd lost hold of his canoe there as he waved at the black flies. He patched a tear in the canvas with spruce gum and a strip of shirttail, a trick, like so many, he'd learned from Evan.

At height of land, Tommy offered to spell him. "I'm doing all right," George assured him.

"Come on over to Nam if you're a hero." George twisted his head under the thwart. He could just make out Tommy's wry smile. He knelt and rolled the canoe onto the blackened trail, then snatched a basket from Tommy's grip and reached for the one on his back. Lunging away, Tommy unstrapped it himself. George remembers the flying sensation as he shed the canoe's weight. These days he remembers the same sensation after backpacking his daughters. He can sigh over that if he chooses.

Even after he put on his pack and set out, holding Tommy's and Evan's by their leathers, his body seemed to rise on air—a good feeling, and the exertion had cleared his head. He walked on like a new man, taking pleasure in Tommy's awkward progress through the berry patches and loose coals. He hoped he'd drop his goddamned load, the way he'd done himself that time.

It was only minutes by water from portage's end to the Semnic beach on the west shore. Evan and Tom would sleep in the lean-to there. In his sojourn just out of college, he'd never come on that shelter. It turned out the two Butcher men had slapped it together the year after the burn. George hadn't known that. The knowledge didn't please him.

George pulled a square tarp from his basket and strung a length of rope between two gray birches. He flopped the tarp over the line. It would be enough to ward off the dew or even a light drizzle. If the mosquitoes thickened after dark, he'd put on a bug veil. The Butchers, like most native sons, didn't worry much about insects. He dragged his bag inside, unrolled it, and despite his pledges to himself, swigged from the fifth of scotch in his bedroll. Why scotch? It represented one more delusion—that he'd drink less if he drank unaccustomed stuff.

There was another fifth in the pack basket, also wrapped in clothing so as not to clank on the trail. He'd save that one for himself. He scooted out on his backside, jug in hand. Sun flashed off the glass and got in George's eyes. He blinked. "Anyone for a little cheer?"

"I'd drink a tap," said Evan, without much enthusiasm.

"May's well be drunk as the way we are now," Tommy added. George didn't know exactly what to make of that old chestnut. He didn't like it, though.

Evan fiddled inside his pack basket and pulled out three smutty tin cups. He tossed one to his son and the other to George, who walked carefully to where Evan sat, poured him an inch, no more.

"That whiskey's twelve years old, Evan," George bragged.

Evan downed the drink in one quick swallow. "Small for his age," he muttered.

George chuckled and topped him up.

"How about you, Thomas?" George asked, all fake heartiness.

"About the same, thank you, sir," Tommy chirped, his fake politeness a transparent insult in response. George pretended not to notice; he poured an inch into Tommy's cup, turned his back, filled his own.

The deer had long since stripped the evergreens' under-boughs behind the lean-to. Evan had to walk fifty yards or so into the woods to break some off. He came back and snapped three softwood sticks across his knee. Then he pulled his knife from its odd tin sheath, skimming the blade along the outside edge of the plank he sat on, making shavings. Each plank was a waney-board, as they'd say at a mill, the last cut made by the saw, the rounded portion of the log, showing up on one side. Evan, and maybe Tommy, must somehow have toted them out by canoe, carry and all.

Over the years, Evan had shaved a few inches from the outermost wane. It was after one, late for lunch, so he balled up the latest strips like paper. He settled them into the beach-stone hearth and lit them, building his fire as he went: first the skinnier cedar, then the thicker. Tommy went down to the beach and returned with an armload of driftwood. Within minutes, they'd made a high blaze. It wouldn't last, but this kind of cooking didn't take long.

Evan peeled the cheesecloth from his bacon and put six slabs into his pan. He twisted his knife-blade in the lid of an extra-large bean can, enough to pour through. Settling the can in the ring, he sat back and resharpened the knife on his whetstone. Taking a sip of his whiskey, he breathed a drawn-out "Aaaah."

For George, it was like watching all this without being part of it. Evan leaned forward now and then to turn the beans with a bandana or to flip the bacon, but his gestures looked like ones from a half-remembered dream.

Evan and Tommy exchanged words now and then, but each time George began to sort them out, they would fade. At one point, he saw the men turn toward the lake. More words. Tommy got up and shaded his eyes. George followed his gaze and saw an eagle in mid-air, bullying an osprey for the fish in its talons. To keep looking felt like too great an effort, though, so he didn't. He wasn't hungry, and he wasn't happy.

George passed the rest of his afternoon in what he'd later call a nap, then woke into uncertainty. The sun looked surprisingly low. Was it morning or evening? Where was he? His neck and shoulders ached from the carry, and from being propped against the lean-to's sill.

His bacon and beans had cooled on a tin plate, the congealed fat slightly nauseating. He squashed a mosquito on his arm. Red as a cherry, it had clearly been there a long while. And where were Tommy and Evan? Remorse mixed with anxiety. Had they stranded him for bad behavior?

By the time the others came back, a pink sky was fading in the west. Tommy carried a half-dozen white perch, gill-slung on an alder sprig. Evan had brought a spinning rod. He'd saved a wad of bacon fat to catch the first fish, then parts of its own body to catch the next five. George knew the trick, which didn't always work, though it had this time.

"Rested up, are we?" Tommy asked. There was no mistaking the sarcasm.

"I should have eaten something," George said weakly. "That sipping whiskey got me woozy."

Tommy grunted. His father just gazed at the lake. George did too, the surface turned to pewter. A raven, letting out a metallic yawp, flapped by, enormous in the twilight, then vanished against a ridge.

The perch were delicious, and so were the spuds Evan fried for a second course. As usual, their goodness had partly to do with where they were. The full moon rose abruptly over the burn, flooding Prune Island until it was almost bright as by noon. Not far from shore, the men could see rings on the lake's surface.

"Hatch of bugs," said Evan. "Fella ought to have a fly rod so's he'd eat trout 'stead of perch."

"Perch was all right by me," George answered. "Anybody want another tap?"

"I'd drink a little whiskey," Evan said.

"Pass," said his son, unfriendly.

"More for us, then," George remarked, feigning good humor again. He poured a full cup for Evan and one for himself. "Drink hearty," he said. "There's another jug in my mansion there." He hadn't meant to say that.

George and Evan sat on opposite sides of the dwindling fire, Evan still in the lean-to, and George on a rock. Tommy squatted on a blow-down some ten feet off, facing the water.

George broke their silence: "Remember that fall you called up the moose over there?" He pointed at the deadwater.

Evan nodded.

"I thought you were magic," George went on.

"I guess by the heavens I was," Evan joked.

"You was both probably full, is what you was," Tommy said over his shoulder.

"Could've been," Evan answered. If there was any inflection in the words, George couldn't make it out, but Tommy's comment struck him as another omen of a mean turn coming. To this day, George is too quickly irritated by criticism, especially when he knows it's just. Not that he'd been drunk back in '66 when Evan called up the moose, but he was now.

He walked past Tommy down to the seawall heaped onto the beach by ice. With no clear notion what he was doing, back to the water, he lifted a sizeable rock with two hands, jerked with his legs, and cast the weight back over his head toward the lake. It flew five feet or so before splashing in the shallows. George turned to see the ripples spread in the moony brightness. The top quarter of the rock stood over the surface.

"What the hell was that for?" Tommy growled.

"Just to see if I could." The rock probably weighed forty pounds.

"Whoever gets his canoe skun up will be glad you was able," Tommy said.

George merely scooched down and grabbed another rock, slightly heavier.

"Like I said, you want to be a hero, why don't you come to war?"

"He's only jealous, Evan," George said brightly, pretending to make light of the whole game. But he dropped the second rock in the sand. His tongue felt thick, and his stomach muscles stung from the first heave.

Evan just sat where he'd been. George could see his body and even his clothing in the moonlight, but a shadow obscured his face. George vowed to quit whatever he was doing: why involve the old man in his pettiness?

"What in hell would make me jealous of *you*?" Tommy asked after a pause.

"Watching me do something you couldn't." So much for the vow. Why couldn't he let things be?

"Shit!" Tommy spat.

"I'm looking," said George.

Tommy swaggered over and put his hands on the rock George had dropped. It lay so close to the lake that his heels were in the water. As he lifted, he lost footing, wet moccasin leather slipping on wet stone. He hefted his rock aside so it wouldn't fall on his feet.

George snickered. "Good one!"

What followed came so fast that probably none of the men could quite believe it, including Tommy. He charged.

George felt a flurry of body punches, but they weren't square. He fought to clear his head. He looked over at Evan, still as the seawall. Tommy took advantage and hit him. It wasn't a punch, really, more like a flat-handed swat, but it caught George on the nose. His head seemed to swell like a balloon.

He staggered. He could feel more than see Tommy coming on again. But he was lucky enough to get a hold on both shirtsleeves, stopping the punches for a moment. The two men grunted and wrestled. Tommy's laboring life had made him the stronger man. George was about to take a whipping, but rather than scaring him, that only rekindled his anger. With all his power, he yanked Tommy toward him and thrust his head upward.

The head-butt caught Tommy off-center, on an eyebrow. Blood gleamed in the moonlight. Kind of pretty, George mused, idiotically. He waited for another charge, which didn't come right away. Tommy hustled to the lean-to and grabbed the axe.

George bolted for the water, dove in, and flailed for distance. He looked back: Tommy was hauling on Evan's canoe, and George felt an instant of relief. He couldn't do any harm from there—he'd have to drop the weapon to hold the paddle, or the other way around.

But then George would have to come ashore in time.

"Son."

George heard the word as if nothing else in in the world was audible, no near clamor of loons, no scrape of the canoe's hull on gravel, no huff of his own breathing.

Son. A muted sound, no urgency in it. Even from out in the lake, George could see Evan's body, the drab suspenders, the crusher hat, the woolen pants, but his face still lay in shadow.

Tommy unhanded the canoe and stood. He walked to the lean-to and laid the axe beside his father.

You've swam enough," Evan called. George dog-paddled in and doddered jelly-legged uphill.

"Shake hands," Evan directed, taking two or three steps forward. They obeyed. Between the moon and the dull glow of firelight, George could at last see the older man's face. The eyes shone.

VII

*P*lethora.

Rob read the word aloud, but softly. Then the definition: an unhealthy repletion or excess.

Repletion? He found a clean patch on his lube suit, wiped the burger grease off his index finger, and flipped ahead in his Shorter Oxford English Dictionary, open on the tailgate.

Repletion: the action of eating or drinking to excess.

How'd that figure? For no good reason, hundreds of miles from Glassburg, he recalls one morning when George told him the company had a plethora of problems. From what he heard, once upon a time George was very much a plethora man himself in the drinking way. But that was a long time ago, from what he heard too. So what did the boss mean? George never stood for drunks. Take a belt on the job and you're down the road. Strike one-two-three unless you start going to those meetings with him. Some did, different times.

Rob remembers that day's sandwich too. Great Scot, it tasted good! He'd taught himself to say that somewhere. Great Scot. He wiped his finger again and returned to the page, dropping through plethory—just an old-fashioned version of the other—through things no one would ever use: plethron, plethysmograph, pleurenchyma. Then he landed on pleurisy.

It rang a bell. "Pleurisy," he breathed. It sounded like something a cat might say, too quiet almost to make out. A lot of *s* in that one, a lot of hiss, seemed like. A lot of . . . sibilance.

Rob remembers reading the full definition, which ended with "pain in the chest or side." Oh yes, that was it. What they thought his Uncle Matt had, but it turned out a lot more serious. Poor Matt beat his older brother Jim into the grave. No one could believe it, Matt living so clean and Jim—well, Jim liked his tea, as his parents said.

It wasn't long till Jim followed Matt, though. Old Jim Beam, put in his grave by Jim Beam plethora. Rob liked that. The word, not the death. He always read his big dictionary on lunch break. Some of George's crew used to rib him about it, but Rob didn't care. They'd be working for somebody else till they went Jim and Matt's route. Him? He was headed out of that rut. Maybe not right then, but he'd get out by and by, or he'd die trying. He'd had his own eight- or ten-year plan. Things might take that long, but he'd save every penny he could. He vowed he'd be gone by 1990 at the latest. He beat that deadline, all right.

"Plethora." He repeated, still too quietly for anyone to hear if there'd been someone around. He savored the way his tongue stuck out as he pronounced the *th*, the outbreath on the *o*.

Poor Uncle Jim. He never had any kids of his own. Probably just as well for the kids, but Rob couldn't say a bad word about him, Jim being the one who got him started as a mechanic. Rob remembered how he'd sit on a sawhorse under the big beech tree with the chain hoist over a limb, and somebody's motor hanging off it like a side of beef in Uncle Matt's butcher shop. Parts lying all over the lawn. It was a wonder the old rascal ever got them back in the right places, or even the right engine, but he always did. He could have been all the mechanic anyone ever wanted. Maybe he was.

Jim had dreams too: he wanted to build a real shop after Rob got out of school and they'd go into business together. Rob would get married and raise kids and they'd lug his tools out and drop them on the same lawn and lose them, but it would be a lot of fun, and he and Rob would make a pile of moolah. He always said *moolah*.

His uncle talked about his plans every time Rob came by. He'd sit his nephew down in a beat folding chair and he'd always take that horse. He'd have a tall can of his daytime drink, Peel's beer, in one hand, a rag in the other, and a Camel hanging off his lip. It amazed Rob how long the ash would get on the Camel, even with Jim jabbering about where he'd put the lube bays, or the alignment rig, or whatever.

Jim wore an orange ski cap all year round, rolled back so it sat on the back of his head like those beanies the Jewish folks wear on Saturdays down in the city, hardly bigger than a silver dollar. People stared at him, and you knew they were wondering how that cap could stay on. It was the one clean thing he owned. His drawers sagged halfway to his knees, and all his shirts were a nightmare. Even in his casket, his hands were black as coal. But great Scot, he was one handsome old boy! What would he have looked like if he took any care of himself?

How did Aunt Thelma stick it out, God love her? That was a mystery too. So was the shop. What would it really have looked like? Rob never exactly believed in Jim's daydream, but he did try to picture a place like that. George Mayes was a good enough boss, but yes, there's more to life than just working for somebody.

Rob checked his watch. 12:25. Time for one more. He flipped through the book and laid his thumb on a word by chance. *Terrain*. Rats. He knew that one. He wrapped the dictionary in a pillowcase and put the bundle into his oversized toolbox. Safe and sound. Weatherproof.

Rob Beam could make his uncle's dream a reality. Even back then, he vowed he was master of his own terrain, or he would be soon.

VIII

After he married Julie in late '83, George virtually erased what memory was left of his first wife, but not by act of will. It simply felt that he and Julie had been together forever, and the births of two daughters—Mary in '84, Kate in '86—buttressed the feeling. There was doubtless something wrong with all that, but it's how things developed.

With the demands of business and family, he fantasized less about moving north, and whenever he thought of that, he felt a dull sadness.

"Off in your gloomy place," Julie sometimes observed.

"Just thinking about school stuff," he'd lie. He knew he couldn't fool her—and that she'd pretend he had.

Living in Woodstown had always been a fantasy, even when the idea glowed most brightly. As for now, his life feels closer to whole than almost anyone's he knows—disasters everywhere, and not just the wars, the political mayhem, the poverty, plagues, assassinations. He thinks of all the personal misfortunes, split-ups and wrecks, of how often people's ruinous pasts suddenly explode into the present. Blood, rubbish, and pain all over. So much in tatters. There but for the grace of God, he thinks, reminding himself not to bet the whole shebang, not even a small part, on the whole shebang.

But the part he has in mind today isn't small, is it?

After Kate's birth he only got to his camp for that week and change every summer, but he still stops at least once a day year-round to wonder how things are going there. He was sickened by his last visit with Evan. How much bounce could the old boy have left? What in hell has he been thinking these past few years?

Well, what was George thinking, back a couple of decades? You wouldn't call it thinking. And now here he is, kids and wife and home and buses, safe as a man like him can ever hope to be, while Evan's up north, anything but safe. There's time for that to change, though. There has to be.

Has Evan ever been safe? As a young man, he worked jobs so dangerous that losing companions, especially in the April log drive, could almost seem routine; but at least he knew how to be careful back then. Carelessness with alcohol lasts right up to the crucial decision . . . if it doesn't finish you off before you get there.

But this just can't be the end for George's friend. It can't be.

"There's always a trap set for you in the woods or on the water," he'd once warned George. In his better days, he hadn't expected traps in other places. Every time Evan felled a big tree, he was face-to-face with peril; and of course, when the river men ran the booms to the coast, he was tempting the Lord, as he said. Death always paddled alongside. It's been trying to bring Evan on another trip for more than five years.

George has listened to tales of the drives so often that, against all reason, he can imagine he's been on one. He feels the spray on his skin, smells the tannin of logs skinned by rocks, hears oars knocking against their locks in the bateaux. Some daredevil scrambles out on a logjam to free it up with a charge of dynamite, masses of timber shooting up like rockets, a scent of nitro. George used to love his floods of imagination.

These days trucks carry logs to the mills. Everything's history, and George an inept historian. He almost wishes he'd never gone to Woodstown at all. What can he do with all this stuff? What can he save? What can he say? His old urge to narrate is a bully, but he can't play anybody's savior, and his words can't even explain why Evan and his domain need saving.

George once believed the experts' claim that keeping the logs out of the rivers would make the water clean again. He chalked Evan's objections up to understandable wistfulness. Now it looks as though the old man had a point. Roads crisscross the woods, crowded with trucks. Vacationers use them too; hunters; anglers; poachers. They reach each last lake.

Even if he found time now for the retreats of his early Woodstown days, when he and his friend would ramble back, as Evan liked to say, so deep it'd scare them to death, George couldn't find many real wild places now without a good deal of road travel. The nearby waters are full of power launches, much of the woods chopped almost bare, their products so easily carted out by road. Why can't he let it all be? Things have changed. But he can't avoid it—sometimes his heart is just unruly.

As machines have prevailed, the loggers' hands-on skills are vanishing. Trucking's risky in its own way, especially in winter, but not like the drives, and nowhere near as colorful. Colorful matters to George, perhaps too much, but he can't help that, and he can't stop lamenting how the drivers' stories have grown quaint. Younger people scarcely believe them now, and they don't want somebody's picturesque lore to start with. They like their entertainment on the screens whose blue glow fills windows in every house and trailer, even in tiny Woodstown.

George looks at the back of an envelope, where he's scrawled a list of business matters—he still hasn't phoned the superintendent—and homey ones too, like picking up Kate's skates at County Line Sports. Reminiscence can be a sickness, just like the bottle. It may not kill you, but then again, it may. Dwell too long on tatters and you'll end up tattered.

Even by the late '60s, of course, George began to witness changes more radical than the switch from water to highway for forest products. Sleepy Glassburg, now a town of malls and offices, watched its young men go by the dozen to Vietnam, while more privileged ones carried on at their campuses, or, like George, devised ways to stay out of harm's way.

As the Vietnam fiasco escalated, George's part of Pennsylvania was full of boys between cultures, the farm life gone and nothing yet to take its place. A lot of them figured they might as well enlist. The draft board made little effort to recruit George; it was '67 before he even got called for a physical, and then a letter from Dr. Dutson effectively ended his dealings with the military. Somehow George still has the letter in the old man's spidery, barely legible longhand. Doc Dutson's been dead for years, but George clearly remembers his puckered face and wispy hair.

Was Doc Dut a good man? "He was like the rest of us," George says aloud.

"What say, boss?" It's Herbie, passing George's office door.

"Only muttering to myself, Herb."

The doctor was a Quaker, whose moral smugness could sometimes be off-putting. George remembers the embroidered dove that hung on a wall in his waiting room, made by orphans or amputees or refugees; he can't recall. It was crude enough that George rolled his eyes each time he saw it. Drunk or not, he could be relied on for judgment, generally ironic.

He thinks of other strange details from Dut's practice: two big vials in what he called the surgery, for instance, full of some blue liquid. George vaguely remembers seeing such bottles in the pharmacy window when his parents were alive.

The old doctor's Parkinson's disease made him shake and mumble. Once, as a child, George stepped on a nail, and he can still picture Dutson dipping into that blue fluid with what looked like a turkey baster, then shuffling back to the table to rinse the puncture. As he walked, the old man quaked, all right (the pun would be inevitable for anyone), leaving an indigo trail behind him.

George suddenly wonders where that ancient wooden table has gotten to, with its brass gynecological stirrups, its lathe-worked legs like ones on a Victorian billiards table. Is it in a museum, perhaps? He hopes so. It makes him sad to think of all that quaint gear simply gone. Same old George.

He'd gone to Doc Dut a week before the Army physical. "Let's chart your history of asthma," the doctor immediately suggested, though the affliction had not been serious even in boyhood and George had entirely outgrown it by the time he went to college.

George should have left matters at that, and gratefully, but he couldn't help asking how the good doctor felt about saving a physically able person from the draft, knowing that some other soul would take his place. Dut looked peeved by the question. His reply was elaborate, or at least long-winded. Most of the words were so muffled George couldn't make them out, and he can't remember any now. He'd been full of vodka, of course.

He reeked of vodka too when he got to his draft physical, which infuriated one of the military physicians. The man cursed out Dutson's letter and Yale in the same breath.

"I wish to Christ you kids had gone to a Jesuit school like I did, where they've taught the same way for four hundred years."

Drunk as he was, George asked, "Learned to bleed your patients there, did you?"

He'd never seen a person literally hopping mad. The doctor was short but his hands were huge; he looked ready to throw one at George's jaw, but a colleague, likely thinking more of George's drunkenness than of the phantom asthma, signed the 4-F recommendation.

Yes, in time he'd experience remorse over ducking the Vietnam disaster. It wasn't that he'd shared none of Dutson's ethical convictions, but back then he mostly just wanted to live. His was nothing nobler than the self-absorption of an addict, which would govern him until a certain morning in a squalid duplex.

By the time a land mine killed his senior-year roommate near the demilitarized zone, George's thinking about the conflict had become less crass; for months he felt a fuddled sadness, subtle as mild headache, for Farley. Still, he drowned it in the usual way.

Farley's death should scarcely have affected George at all, except abstractly, the two of them having been no closer than he got with any of his college acquaintances. George can't even remember how they came to share their room. He can evoke Farley's soft speech, his occasional mild stutter, his open, midwestern countenance. The boy disdained any coarseness, and George provided plenty. He remembers his roommate's reaction to the turd on Boardie Bennett's MG. "That's just depraved, you know?" He stood up from his chair when he heard about it, and George expected more trouble than he got.

Yet even that rare show of temper remains less vivid than abstract. Did Farley threaten physical violence? If so, how did George react? Farley was a strong man, center on the football squad, heavyweight wrestler; he could have torn him to bits.

Farley was scarcely intriguing, but he certainly was serious. Or maybe he was intriguing, and George just blind to that. The poor guy wouldn't have been the first or last he misjudged. He had two aims in his short life, which seemed at odds to George. He intended to marry his Indiana sweetheart, who'd never seen the Yale campus. George could only judge her by a photograph, which showed her standing against a photographer's fabricated sky, garish as the girl was ordinary. And, having earned a commission in the Marine Corps, Farley longed to see action somewhere as soon as possible. He got both wishes.

In George's most distinct memory of his roommate, he's standing erect on a terrace at Saybrook College to accept his commission. The rest of the ceremony had struck George as pointless: the tearful parents, the Latin phrases, the silly mortarboard hats and robes, the plaudits

—both inflated and banal—showered on scholar and athlete. More inflated twaddle about future leaders. But as he watched his roommate strike that military posture, shake hands with some officer, then thrust his scrap of paper heavenward with a whoop, George's cynicism turned to gloom. The quadrangle's mock-Gothic buildings weighed on his spirit. Saybrook's trees had come into pastel early-summer leaf, and the sky showed cloudless, yet a darkness seemed to drop on the courtyard. George had to blink to be sure it wasn't real.

He never saw Farley again. They exchanged a few noncommittal postcards, then fell out of touch. George would get only the rudiments of his classmate's later life from the stiff form letter his father sent to his son's Yale acquaintances: he'd married a week after Commencement; nine months later, a son named Gerald arrived; after three years at various bases, the last in Germany, he became one of the first American soldiers—called advisers then—to fall in a country that few Americans could have found on a map.

The sadness of the death grips George now far more than it did back then, yet he reserves most of his sorrow and guilt for the fallen or permanently maimed kids from moribund farms and the desolate inner city, the ones who fell without ever having cherished Farley's dreams of glory—or George's own savvy about how to stay home. They were drafted, they went, they died.

George recalls one of his mechanics, a cheerful Dutchie named Zebedee Fuchsluger. Leaving for duty, the kid had smiled and put his fate in God's hands, though he contrived that gesture, George reckoned, to reassure his parents. George had closed the shop early so there'd be a proper send-off for Zeb at the bus station. The boy's father wore a double-breasted suit in which he might well have been married, his mother a dated floral house dress. They were clearly not much given to their son's joviality, which made their smiles all the more poignant, so hard were they trying to appear at ease, holding hands in the squat terminal, much older drivers and grease monkeys here, a noncombatant boss there. The stoical effort failed, and they both wept for Zeb, who'd be killed within the year.

George also saw the war's effects on the several Vietnam survivors he hired after their service. They'd come and go. Some seemed to return unfazed; others just couldn't readjust. In '71, a certain Carmen Doddi worked a month for the company and then, even though American fortunes were going from bad to worse, he re-enlisted. Does he still walk the earth? George once had a dream of him sitting on Dr. Dutson's table. The big, embroidered dove came to life and swooped down to cover Carmen's body. When it swooped back to the wall, he was gone.

George shakes his head, taps his list with a pencil. One of his men, either Herbie or John Henry, is shouting out in the yard. George should go see what's up. Instead, he thinks of a boy named Ruth, inevitably called Babe, who joined Vietnam Veterans Against the War shortly after signing on with Mayes. Babe took some scolding from the others, but, bent on his agenda, he ignored them.

Ever more persuaded of the war's injustice himself, George let Babe use the company copier and phone for his own purposes. But once Babe began to devote more time to his moral enterprises than to the garage, he let the kid go. He felt some mix of embarrassment and remorse to do it, and Babe's calm only made matters worse. "That's cool," he said when George fired him, grabbing his jacket off a hook and stepping outside, carefully latching the office door behind him.

George wondered if some vengeful scheme might lie under that composure; the far-off look in the young man's eyes had perturbed him. Now he thinks Babe's devotion to his mission made the interruption of his working life look trivial.

There was so much turnover at the shop in the '60s and early '70s that George sometimes strains to recall the names of these characters after almost thirty years, but others can swim back unbidden. Iggy Mook is a name you'd remember anyhow, even if you hadn't given it to the police. Iggy'd become spectacularly heavy after his days as a Navy Seal, when, for reasons George couldn't quite understand, he saw nothing of the ocean. He traveled with a Special Forces unit, whose specialty was penetrating NVA lines.

Iggy moved agilely, even delicately around the shop, not at all like a man burdened by weight. He rarely spoke, and he zealously protected his tools, which were the only ones he used, not the company's. When a job called for some implement, he didn't have, he'd ask if he could go buy it. At quitting time, whether he'd used them or not, he methodically cleaned every tool in gasoline, blew it dry, and laid it back in his immense box.

Some of the others were amused by such obsessiveness, and some were annoyed. One lunch break, a burly mechanic named Dick Huffman hid Iggy's tray of socket wrenches in the van for the students with disabilities. Iggy discovered the prank. How could he have known Dick was behind it? He just did.

George heard screams. Rushing onto the floor, he put a hand on Iggy to calm him, and was struck so abruptly he felt next to nothing. Yet as he fell, he noticed how Iggy's jowls still quivered from throwing the punch. Then all went dark. To this day it fascinates George that he remained conscious while tumbling and unconscious just after. In any case, that quaking face is stamped on his memory. Truth is, he can see the whole garage in that instant: the lifts, the girlie posters, the hissing air compressor, the rack of spare tires, the clean yellow of a new bus, the stunned expressions on everyone's face but Iggy's. By the time George came to, his attacker had vanished, but not before beating the hell out of Dick.

"He used everything," someone said, "hands, elbows, feet—even his fuckin' head." Dick lay against the wall, a lug wrench by his hand. He'd never gotten to use it in defense. Blood seeped from his ears.

Dick would be hospitalized for weeks with broken facial bones and a ruptured spleen. Iggy had gone back to his rented room and yanked light fixtures from ceilings, shattered the toilet, reduced glassware to chips, beat table legs into splinters. Finally, he'd scratched the word *eagle* on the bathroom mirror. No one knew what to make of that. He was never seen in Glassburg again.

Once more, George notices his list. He has to bear down just to remember what it is. How could it possibly have led him to Evan Butcher, to violence in his garage, to reflections on a tragic war—if indeed it's the list that did all that?

Does George want a story? Well, he's got one, and he may be in the middle of the latest chapter, where he's always hoped to be. He conjures the old platitude: Be careful what you wish for.

IX

"It's like right now," Julie's words surprise her as she wakes up. What she recalls is from a decade ago. She hoped it would stay like now for as long as she lived.

When she woke up back then, it was in a maternity ward. Her first daughter needed nursing. She thought that life just seemed a miracle. No, thinking probably wasn't the word. Dark-haired baby, right there on her chest, lively, ringlets quivering like grass in the wind as she sucked. The dark would fall out in time, and the blonde come, though Julie didn't know that.

She knew what dreamed up was nuts, but for right then all of the people she cared about, especially this baby girl, would live forever. Death was only some stranger she would never have anything to do with. Life might be strange, but it was—kindly.

1984: Mary's birth year, which will always be her idea of what a good world should look like. All she could think of from the time she met George kept getting kindlier, too, if there was such a word.

She didn't walk into that dirty little office of George's and suddenly boom! Hello, Dreamboat. She just needed a job, and even if she got this one, she never figured it'd be for any longer than it had to be. Which means you can't tell a thing.

Julie recalls burping Mary that night, patting her tiny back. She wishes she didn't know now what she would know, and not so very long after that night. But she tries to put it all out of mind, not for the first time. It's hard. All the bad things could have happened this morning too, like someone pulled pictures out of a wallet. There was before and there was after. She would give anything to stay with before. Not that life's all hell-on-wheels since, not at all, but it sure isn't kindly every day, the way she dreamed in that hospital bed.

Julie's first impression on the morning she met him was that George was doing all right for himself, far as she could see, which wasn't that far, because she wouldn't have known one end of a bus from the other. All she knew was, there were quite a few of those buses, and a good-sized crew taking care of them. The way the men dealt with George made him seem like a pretty good boss. Unlike some, she could tell you. She went into that place with her eyes wide open. She'd been around the block a time or two by '83.

Julie made a point of looking nice for the interview. She couldn't have known George's office wasn't exactly the Hilton. What a rat's nest, in fact. A couple of unframed papers from the state department of transportation tacked crooked on a wall, and a desk that probably came from a school, considering George's business. There were two metal chairs, one for him and one for her, which would throw your back out if you sat in it too long.

And cardboard boxes! Three deep against another wall, and each one with a number and a letter: C-3 , 4-K , 7-A, whatever. George tried to explain his system after he hired her, but he couldn't, really. He must have lived a charmed life. A wonder the tax people never came calling.

She looked out a window at a couple of gas tanks and a salvage yard—that's what Julie heard George call it later—with a wooden fence around it. Another little window into the garage was more like a hole, no glass. The company name had gone to pieces on the biggest window. All that was left was *MA* at the beginning and *N* underneath. When people drive by now, they see MAYES TRANSPORTATION, and painted, not decals. That was one of the small things she took care of right after she brought in decent furniture. File cabinets, wooden chairs with seat pads, a nice desk with drawers in it for a change. Even a water cooler.

George whined about the expense. He said he didn't need to impress anyone. He had all the business he'd ever want, and it wasn't like there'd be a whole set of new schools built any time soon.

But Julie told him, "You're a pro, George. Why not look like a pro?"

They were on that first name basis from the kickoff. Not a lovey-dovey thing, or if it was, she didn't know it at first. George just put her at ease, no airs about him. You could've called him clumsy, which was fine by Julie. She knew how some men act suave, or sweet as puppies when they're hiring you, and then it's good night nurse. Or they keep up the sweet stuff because they think they'll be taking advantage in the other way. And some think they can act like tyrants and still get to the other, and you're too dumb or timid to cause any fuss.

She learned a lot from her time with high and mighty Mr. Geoffrey Zink at Norris Business Machines. But he learned something too. She'd rather take in laundry than put up with any man's hogwash after that circus. She could report to Zink's wife and the whole county what Geoff was like when he wasn't puddling up over a Lions Club donation to a blind person or giving some Chamber of Commerce spiel to the papers. She thought about punching his card for him, though she'd prefer it if he just drove his damned Lincoln off a bridge. It didn't take her long to quit NBM.

Julie figured George was probably no saint, and he isn't. Who is? But she liked whatever she saw. It was almost cute, how he got flustered when she asked him about his books.

"Books?" he said, red as paint.

Turned out his so-called records were those boxes or on the backs of envelopes and old scratch pads that some insurance salesman or parts company gave him, all tossed together and stuck in a three-ring binder with a rubber band around it, more stuff he probably picked up at one of his schools.

Even the binder had one ring that wouldn't snap. On the outside there was a picture of a cartoon Indian, Straight Arrow. Julie remembered him from the cards her brothers had saved from the days when they came in shredded wheat boxes. They had tips about wild animal tracks and making fires and such. They were gray with green ink and had a smell she still remembers. She thought it was pretty awful herself, though she didn't know whether the odor was because of their age or if they had always had it, and she sure didn't know why her brothers wanted to keep them for years.

When she asked George how he managed to keep things straight with a system like that, he blushed again, right into his hair. "I'm not sure things are straight around here." He admitted it. He told her he kept each month's cancelled checks and receipts together, then hired a temp to come in and make sense of it all. Julie wouldn't be surprised if one or two cut some checks for themselves. Kelly Girls, he told her, and not very often the same one twice in a row.

There was a woman who did keep coming back, though. Just to see if there was any work, she said, even after Julie set her own desk up right across from George's. Now she could read this Darlene like a book, not worth trusting here to there. She wanted more than money too. She came tippy toeing on her skinny high heels, wearing a skirt that would shame a hippie, even when minis were biggest, ten years ago or so. To Julie, she looked like a raccoon with all the eye shadow. Her hair was hard and almost white as chalk. She kept chirping Georgie this and Georgie that, which no one called him. Darlene didn't pay Julie any attention, and the softie wouldn't kick her out of his office to walk the streets like she was meant to. Julie took care of that one day. Whew! This lady had a mouth on her like nothing you ever heard, a regular tramp.

George was honest too. He told her he'd interviewed some other people, including a couple of men who had accounting experience too, but he hadn't made up his mind. So at least he wasn't spinning some fairy tale. Julie even liked that he had such a sorry-looking office, no matter she changed it later. They'd have been more comfortable talking in one of his school buses; at least their air conditioners worked, and the seats were softer. But his little rathole was good enough for him. He was humble enough, then. When Julie found out later he went to college in the Ivy League, la-dee-da, it about knocked her over!

His so-called books were a mess, but she figured double entry for a simple outfit like this wouldn't be too hard. As long as George was being honest, she'd be that way too. She asked about pay, vacation time, the whole nine yards. He answered every question. Julie didn't find much to complain about, so she came right out and told him she wanted the job badly, which surprised her and seemed to surprise him as well. She grabbed a piece of smudgy paper from his desk and wrote down her phone number before she left, bold as could be.

That same afternoon, George Mayes called her up and said, "You're hired." It made Julie wonder for a moment if he'd really been so honest after all when he told her about her competition.

"What about those others?"

"I want to hire you."

"Why?"

"Hunch."

Julie could see him blushing right through the phone.

Now people will think what they want, because she and George got married just about a year from that day. Some probably guess they had sparks flying from the get-go, and maybe they did, but no, she didn't know it herself. Maybe he liked her sense of humor, and true enough, she and George have gotten through some scrapes and even heavy arguments because they always end up laughing at each other. There's a little magnet plaque on their fridge that says, HOW IMPORTANT IS IT?

Julie knows this much. She didn't play any platinum-head-Kelly-Girl-oh-Georgie number. What he saw, he got. And he was just as natural too. He offered her a cup of coffee that morning, which he made by dipping one of those coils in water and pouring some instant mix right from the jar into the cup, no measuring about the deal. The cup was nasty, black as coal, and Julie could almost swear he turned it over at the basin to dump a dead spider or fly. Then he just rinsed it out. That cup probably never really got what you'd call washed. Julie isn't fussy, but she'd have left that awful mess alone if there wasn't just something about the guy. She drank it.

Julie noticed his hands too, square, and short-fingered for a man as tall as he is. But they're strong enough when he needs them to be. They still make her a little lovesick.

Sitting there with a standing fan making more noise than cool, she realized she liked George's face too. It had some kind of sadness in it. She didn't know why until later, if she really did even then. Maybe he always had the sadness without understanding it all the way himself. That made her think there was kindness in him. After some people go through stuff they understand what sad feels like, so they can be good to people who feel the same. The look is even a little sadder nowadays, no secret why.

Julie remembers looking down at Mary after she fell off the second breast. There was a little bubble on her lips. She thought about ringing the nurse, but things just seemed right this way. She fell asleep too, baby and all.

X

Evan got up, unsteady. He stared at a window of the big house. Mattie never stood there on the south side. Or was that her after all? Seemed like he saw something. Hard to tell with sun on the glass and all dark inside the house. Mattie's bad for dark in a room. Christ, his head hurt!

"I suppose she'll let me get away with it," he muttered. His knees were bad too. He got himself knocked around in the woods of his time, but his legs was worse lately, no two ways about it. Not that Mattie'd buy that for an excuse. But how much could an old man take? Or old woman? How'd Mattie keep on taking things same as always?

He just had a dream of himself with a stamping axe, driving the company figure into the butts of pulp logs hung up among the islands on that little feeder stream. He forgot its name, forgot everything these days. It comes into the Percy at the first rips below the dam. Company wanted to save those sticks for a better head of water one day. Dry April, the one in his dream. The stamp was three *x*'s and something looked like an eyebrow on top.

He could walk right out on a boom back then, no peavey, no pole, no nothing. Walk out and stamp wood by hand. Or if your wood got hung up, he could put the dynamite to it. Sometimes you needed just the cap to get it moving. You could feel that lumber through your boots, tight as a spring and aquiver. It drove Mattie half-crazy when he told her how that got up in your feet.

Evan took two or three steps and caught his toe on a clod no bigger than a mouse. Stumbled almost to fall, then said right out loud: "You could stand on a log in the water and now you can't hardly stand up on a township . . ."

Let Mattie tell him the meaning of that. Let anyone. Nothing against her at all, forevermore a good old gal. Better than he deserved.

I'll see to things, he swore. This ain't me, please the Lord. This ain't Evan Butcher. Not sure what you'd call it, but it ain't anybody he knows.

But who the hell then? Oh, his mind's all balled up again.

XI

The start of school in '67 felt as hot and humid as Mississippi. George can still feel how his bus trapped the heat. The weather got so liquid he had to run the defroster even with the kids on board just to be able to see, and he drove with the doors wide open. That was against all the regulations, but the cops looked the other way.

They didn't know all they were looking away from. There were too many mornings when George was vodka'd up even before he started. Sometimes he had to close an eye to change the doubled white line back to single. He kept a bulb of garlic in his shirt pocket, and it got pretty ripe, especially in the heat, by the time he pulled in at the grade school. But let a cruiser's lights flash, he figured, and he'd bite into the garlic like an apple. Oh, how clever.

The one-time lights did flash, the trooper went right past after somebody else, or something, but George had already bitten off a chew. The taste and stink were still there in the afternoon, and to cover them, he stopped by Farrell's Pharmacy and bought some sort of blue mouthwash. There was a pull-off on route 307, a mile from school. He swung in and sat on the bus's steps, swished the blue stuff in his mouth, and spat it out.

"What the hell's in that?" George asked out loud. It tasted worse than the garlic. But when he read the contents, damned if alcohol wasn't at the top of the list! A couple inches remained. He tipped the little bottle up and gulped.

"Why not?" he breathed.

The mouthwash burned his throat and blossomed in his gut. Not half bad. Better than the taste, anyhow. George grinned. Who'd ever suspect this one? Back at the wheel, he checked his mirrors and rumbled ahead. He barely made it through the route. That blue drink had given him a jolt, true enough, but after he dropped of the last child, his bowels made it to his apartment's bathroom in the nick of time. One more good idea gone bad.

And yet the blue gargle had given a little boost to his buzz, and the thought of his canniness—why, it felt like those old French charades. He began to experiment with other unlikely things. His gut paid now and then, but in time he came on Listerine. It went with him every morning for the year.

He'd stop at a pharmacy or a grocery store to buy it, then pull off at that same place and chug before he picked up his riders. George's eyes would tear, and sometimes his stomach heaved, but he had his fix. He'd buy the Listerine early in the morning, because if he got it the night before he wouldn't save it. He knew that much about his addiction, even if he didn't call it that yet.

The challenge lay in choosing stores. He didn't want to go into Farrell's every day. He was a local boy, after all. The ancient Farrells had been friends of his dead parents, so he prayed for a different young clerk from this time to the next. He made a point of buying other trifles too: a magazine, a bag of chips, a key ring, what have you.

One day Mrs. Farrell asked: "Do you have gum problems, George? Because there are better treatments."

"Oh, Dr. Zahn is on top of it," he replied, though he hadn't seen the aged family dentist since college. He'd hear rumors the old boy wasn't fit for his job anymore, though that scruple wasn't what kept George away.

He kept getting up earlier and earlier, hard as that was with the hangovers. Sometimes he'd drive eight miles to Green's Landing, where a little grocery conveniently opened at 6:30. Other days he'd drive farther, all the way to Kuehntown and the county's only real supermarket. That was best if he had time to get there and back. The place had enough customers and employees even in those days that George was just another client. He could meet the checkout girls' eyes.

How, in spite of sickness, could he sometimes actually have enjoyed that Kuehntown trip? Route 74 was pretty straight along the Glass River, and George liked to look for waterfowl in the flats: mallards, teal, an occasional raft of geese. The flocks put him in mind of some old times with Evan Butcher. He'd lean on his horn, just to watch the birds flush. So much energy in a duck! Must be nice, he'd think.

Haze rose over the farmer's fields, and the low sun shone silver through it, pretty. He was squandering gasoline by not driving his Volkswagen, but he preferred riding high.

Anyone who knew him well—though was there anyone?—could have told him he was squandering time too. George figured he had plenty of that, though. He reserved the hours between morning and afternoon routes for sleep in his apartment, persuaded he was lucky just to be there, separated from Melody, no woman putting him under a microscope anymore. He could crack a beer or swig something harder whenever he damned well pleased, and, except for the driving hours, he followed his own schedule, to call it that.

In fact, the days between 1966 and late 1967 were a marvel of idleness. All he needed to plan was to drink. He slept away his middays mostly because being awake meant getting drunker. Even he knew there must be a limit to what he could take in and still drive, no matter he kept pushing that limit.

Getting up early for mouthwash and guzzling it had him good and tired by 9:30. A hard yank of vodka at home, and he'd pass out in minutes, his radio on. He kept it tuned to a station featuring Motown artists. Smokey Robinson, Martha Reeves, David Ruffin—all sang him to sleep dozens of times. He might croak *My mama told me you better shop around* or *Summer's here and the time is right* or *I got sunshine on a cloudy day* or some other lick before plummeting into stupor.

Then one day he broke his radio in a fit over some group he despised. He must have mistuned his dial. He can't even remember which band enraged him. Some phony English group, probably. The Dave Clark Five? Gerry and the Pacemakers? Who knows? Whoever they were, George smashed the little radio against a wall. For months, the plastic shards nestled among the dust bunnies on the floor. The wound in the sheetrock stayed there for as long as George did. He never got around to buying a replacement radio until he sobered up.

Lord, those rages! Just as well he lived like a hermit when he wasn't at work; he didn't even venture into bars that final year, just brought his poison home. So his tantrums didn't do much harm to anyone else. Not that he didn't want to: George had a couple of quiet resentments, one especially. But how could he be faulted for that?

Evan had put a stop to the fight at Semnic Lake over a year before. When he and Tommy shook hands, George actually said, "Let me know if you ever need help of some kind." It was an odd thing to say, as if the words came from somebody else, because he kept seething even after poor Tommy went to war. No hard feelings? Plenty.

George meant to look up Tommy's wife come the next summer. That'd be a sweet sort of revenge. He'd been scheming right there on the beach, even as he was apologizing. But Poot took off before he got back to Woodstown. After Mattie told him that, all he could do was play out his little fantasies. He pictured Poot's tight jeans there in front of Billy's store, when he craved her and her beer both. Those daydreams were so witlessly and tritely pornographic that they astonish him looking back.

When his bladder filled in the night, George often stared into the mirror over his grimy toilet. To think of his old self-loathing still makes him cringe, the way he called himself a maggot or snake or whatever. And yet nothing kept him from throwing back more vodka. He'd never get back to sleep without it, after all.

Much of the time he lay wide-eyed anyhow, until at length Tommy Butcher seemed to appear on the ceiling. George frightened himself then, because soon he'd sneak up there too. He could somehow watch himself do it. Tommy's muscles had felt like bricks, but this time George held the axe.

Soon his arches would cramp, his visions of bloody retribution curling his toes tight as barrel hoops. He'd try his best to talk himself out of fury, but he was a hard man for anyone to talk out of anything. Would he really take an axe to another man? No. God, no. Pure imagination. That didn't hurt anyone, did it?

George would be out of the apartment before 6:30, headed for his pharmacy or grocery hooch. Even weekends saw him up early. He couldn't lie in, his wakefulness a curse. How he wished he could sleep off the booze, the night phantoms, the ruinous thoughts of Poot, of Tom. But he never put himself in a position to do that, no matter how often he pledged to.

Saturdays, he treated himself to breakfast at the Rexall counter in Glassburg, though hunger didn't take him there, and neither did Listerine. That was one store that he wanted to be sacrosanct.

The paraphernalia on the familiar short counter, or, as George preferred, the Formica-topped tables soothed him somehow. The napkin and toothpick dispensers, the fat ketchup jars, the honey pitchers made to look like hives. That lunchroom was as close to a homey scene as he could find. He even felt affection for the big orange-and-blue sign outside.

He enjoyed watching Leo too, the soft-voiced cook, a dumpy man but with arms like a prizefighter's, covered with Navy tattoos: schooners, mermaids, an anchor. They looked like they belonged on another body. Leo was a marvel of efficiency. No matter how many orders he took, he filled them with remarkable speed, moving deftly from one set of burners to another, never seeming to hurry, never botching any.

Most of all, George treasured Rose, the Irishwoman who waited on the scattering of tables. She had been a friend of his late Uncle Emory's housemaid Mary Conley, who, for discomfiting reasons, had been his surrogate mother in George's younger years. Rose and she were both Belfast-born Catholics and parishioners at the same Glassburg church. The lilt of her voice and certain phrases—"that's it all," "it's half nine," others—fetched Mary back, and depending on how much George had drunk by breakfast time, the memory could bring him close to tears.

Rose saw it all. "There now, ducks," she'd say, laying a plump hand on his arm. "I know, I know."

"I'll never forget her."

"God bless."

There were times when George did watch actual tears tumble onto his plate as he bent above it. He hid them from all but Rose. Those episodes seemed a purge. They'd have embarrassed him if other people than the sweet waitress saw, but they made George feel responsive in ways he generally didn't back then.

Delusion? Melodrama? Very likely. He'd have fought anyone who called him on it, but he wondered even then if there was anything about him that wasn't an act. He sometimes calls that part of his life the Years of Performing Arts now. But his love for Mary was no performance. It can't have been.

"Not a mass goes by I don't say a word for her," Rose told him every Saturday. George was no man for church, yet her words brought him odd comfort.

George's father had run a small, fairly successful hardware store not far from that Rexall, where he remembers now and then sitting at the counter with his dad and sometimes his mother as well. Once George went to grade school, she passed a lot of her day with her husband, clerking at the store if business was brisk, just keeping him company if not. From all George has ever heard, they were happily married, right up until 1948, when George was nine. His father was three years back from the Pacific, enjoying America's economic boom in his small way.

Then both parents were murdered.

As a teenager, George came upon a stash of newspapers in his uncle's basement. Uncle turned out to have been a bit of a hoarder, not only of the daily papers but also of coffee cans for some bizarre reason. Skimming a few years' worth of those papers, George clearly saw that the crime against his parents lingered in the headlines for a month and more, ones like *Police Baffled by Glassburg Attack*. George's mother and father had been discovered in the store's cellar, their heads savagely battered. That was that. The killer was never found.

Evidently there had rarely been anything at all like it in the county. In his desultory reading, George did come upon violent crimes, perhaps one every two or three years, but they almost always proved to be ones of passion. Just home from the service himself, a carpenter named Max Berndt got word of his wife's wartime affair and stabbed her lover, but he recovered and moved away. A plumber named Nunzio fought with another member outside La Loggia Ruggiero Bonghi, their Sons of Italy social club in Norris. It was just a drunken brawl over a woman, but Nunzio landed an unlucky punch and caved in his friend's temple. The poor man spent two weeks in a coma before he died, and his assailant two years in prison for manslaughter.

His parents' deaths and their aftermath are blurry to George. He knew almost no details as a child, and only pieced the story together from those newspaper articles and flimsy local anecdote when he got older.

That horror has to be part of his own story, but it somehow escaped him then. He's puzzled, in fact, by his years of near indifference to it, and remorseful too. On the other hand, no one ever helped him know how to react. Things just happened. Then more happened. To this day, he's not sure who sold his father's building to whom. He assumes the proceeds went to his great uncle and guardian, and its remnants, after covering his Yale fees, were part of the paltry sum George inherited at the old man's death.

He went to live with that uncle of his mother's, who was his only competent relative. George's grandmother was very much alive, but at a shockingly young age had lost her mind. Back then everyone called it hardening of the arteries. She lived in a Lutheran rest home near Green's Landing. George saw her perhaps a half-dozen times as a little boy. In retrospect, his lack of broader family connections in those years puzzles him.

It was the grandmother's much older brother Emory Unger, an enterprising fellow who'd made considerable money as a paint merchant, who took George in, almost without seeming to notice. Emory was tall, glisteningly bald, and still all business in his late sixties. George would come downstairs in the morning and join him in the austere dining room that looked down on his pond, but he'd stay just long enough for a quick greeting.

"Are you prepared for school?" Uncle Emory would always ask, eyeing him over rimless spectacles.

"Yes, sir," George replied, truthfully for the most part.

Then Emory turned back to the newspaper, eating with one hand, as if unconsciously. This was George's signal to leave the room, and he did so more than willingly. There was something daunting about his great uncle, though George still can't define it, and the kitchen was a haven from whatever it was.

Those were the years that turned the housemaid Mary Conley into the most important presence in George's life, on a par with Evan Butcher. By the time he got out of bed, she would already have been to her five o'clock mass. Any later service would get her back to Mr. Unger's too late to make his breakfast, and he was an indifferent employer. He never had much of a word, kind or even otherwise, for his housemaid, but she knew the slightest deviation from his routine would irk the old man.

Breakfast had to be served at 6:30, Monday through Sunday. The paper had to be at the right-hand side of his placemat. The breakfast was always two poached eggs with dry toast, darkened almost to black. To this day, the odor of burning bread brings Emory's stern face to George's mind. Two glasses of water, one with ice, one without. What was that about?

On his uncle's left sat a small silver bowl full of what Emory called soda mints. He'd swallow a single pill after every meal. George didn't know what they were for, but it never crossed his mind to ask. Things were what they were. You didn't ask Uncle about any. And when George put questions to Mary about his guardian's habits, she always nervously deflected them for some reason. She likely didn't know herself.

Mary prepared chicken for her boss on Monday, beef on Tuesdays, lamb on Wednesdays. Then the same fare in the same order, Thursday, Friday and Saturday. On Sunday evenings, he took a light meal—a single dry waffle and a cup of Postum—and went up to his bedroom at seven. So far as George could tell, his great uncle had no friends. He never entertained, never even left his house day or night except to do his inscrutable business or to survey his considerable property.

Emory took no interest in running his house. This was all up to Mary, who was therefore free to make sure George had whatever he wanted. In the mornings he could choose sausages or bacon or his favorite, the Pennsylvania Dutch dish called scrapple, which Mary dusted with flour and fried. He liked to pour corn syrup on it.

But the best meal came late on Sunday afternoon. He can't remember now who dreamed up his bizarre favorite sandwich, peanut butter and tomato. Mary served it on a special Sunday plate, which showed images of a cowboy riding a spotted horse. She'd eat from a loaf of Irish soda bread herself, spread with butter and coarse marmalade. The two sat at the kitchen table for over an hour, listening to the radio serials: *Nick Carter, The Great Gildersleeve, Sky King, Sergeant Preston, Henry Aldrich, The Fat Man, Gangbusters, The Green Hornet*. George recalls those hours as among the most purely blissful he's ever known. The programs. The root beer in a mug Mary had frosted. The sandwiches, especially in summer when the tomatoes came straight from the kitchen garden she tended, warm and full of juice. George once told his wife, "If heaven isn't like that, I'll boycott the place."

Mary died just after George's junior year at Yale, six months after Uncle Emory, ten years after his parents. Grandma Unger must have lived on in her nursing home, raving. To his shame, George never even knew when she died. Who ever went to her funeral?

George experienced only a vague heaviness of spirit at his great uncle's passing, along with the usual awe, which lingered even as the man lay in a closed casket. George's reaction, to the degree he can call it up, resembled the one to his parents' slaying, though now he was a grown man.

He often wonders why his mother and father remained so obscure to him for such a long time. Mary, on the other hand, was never a blank. Her memory would go on stabbing even his drunken heart. He still aches to see her alive, though she'd be impossibly old. He wishes his children could have known her. Thirty-some years back, he swore he'd never get over missing her, and—however faulty his thinking otherwise then—he was right about that.

Rose seemed to understand and approve. It's why, with all his might, George put off his true Saturday benders until after he'd visited her at the Rexall.

But there'd come a time when even that modest gesture of restraint disappeared.

XII

It's been a chore to live with a drunken son of a son of a son. But Mattie's a good one for chores, always was, never bothered her even a mite. 'Course chore wouldn't describe this mess.

God don't send you but what you can bear with His help. That's the sort of talk Wilma and different ones give her, same as those years ago. And she remembers thinking, well, it sure better be God, because I don't mind any of you amateur preachers dropping by to give me a hand, not all that often, anyhow, and me fifty-three years old that very October and Evan working all day!

Fifty-three. That seems young enough now, but back in '68 it felt like Methuselah to Mattie. Maybe someone gave her yesterday's loaf of bread or whatever, then stood there acting like they just donated their eye to science. So, whenever she heard all that cheerful talk, two words came to her mind, and not "Happy Birthday," even if she's not one for coarse language.

Who on God's earth would've figured so much of that time raising Tommy's twins would look okay to her, compared, these twenty-odd years later? At least Evan was on the go day-in-day-out back then, not laying dead to everything over to his shop, or else out to the cemetery. Old days weren't so bad next to that. 'Course she didn't know this trouble was coming downriver then, not out of Evan anyhow. Out of Poot, yes, but you expected that. Who'd have two kids and then it's right on down the road quick as a thief?

It was what Mattie could do to stay civil with Wilma when she started in with her pick-you-up talk, and it still is, even if down in her heart she knows it weren't Wilma, for the love of Pete, who put Mattie in that old mess years ago, and in this one too. On the other hand, her troubles weren't her own fault, either. Yet and still, who got stuck with the child-raising?

The boys' father was off in East Bejesus dodging gunfire, and the twins' hellcat mother who-knew-where, and here was Mattie, bogged down with kids that looked so much alike you could hardly tell one from the other. And it weren't "Let's go see Gammy today." It was living with Gammy, no holiday about it, as if her and Evan didn't deserve a little rest after all their work to get by, and after raising Tommy . . . who she kept praying wasn't blown to bits in some jungle, never mind he was always a hellcat in his own way too, God love him.

Tommy'd be coming home sometime. At least she and Evan hoped so every straight day. But you wouldn't leave little twins for him to look after, especially the way he sounded in his letters. Nutty as a chip-lifter. No, you wouldn't leave kids with him if they belonged to your worst enemy, which you might say they did once upon a time.

She never did like that Poot. You couldn't take to a woman with her look, or even with a name like that. It just sounded like trash. Poot, by the Jesus! She flirted with every last pair of britches in town, even when she was big as a sow bear with her boys in her. She even flirted with George, which he gave right back at her or any other little sweetie he saw. Not now, he don't. But one time, well . . . you mightn't think Mattie notices much, but you don't put much past her. Call that bragging if you choose.

Poot's probably still her daughter-in-law, because she just took off, bedroll and all, never even a note to Evan and Mattie, so you know she didn't settle anything. She and Tom were still married, far as law was concerned. Tommy wouldn't hear about all that anyhow. Mattie couldn't blame him. He was just running heavy equipment over there, not shooting, but even that might make him a target, because what she heard, those people attacked anyone, anytime, anyplace.

No wonder he went half loony. She and Evan thought of keeping the Poot business from him, but it didn't seem right. Nowadays she wishes they had, but then Poot would have answered the letters that came. Quite a few too. Tommy never could get the hang of school at all; he quit after tenth grade, and not many teachers was sorry to see him depart. He hated it if he had to write anything, because he could just about do it, so of course he was never a hand to send letters before. But now, after he gave up writing to his so-called wife, it seemed like he sent these wild ones to her and Evan about every day. Sounded like Old

Mother Hubbard backward for all the sense they made, only you knew it was nothing but confusion and a sick heart over his useless woman.

She and Evan wanted to write letters too—to someone, somehow, somewhere—to see if they couldn't get Tom shipped back, even if it meant the hill in Bangor with the rest of the touched folks. At least he'd be alive. But who'd you write to? It'd be like dropping a leaf down their well. Mattie threw out those letters of his, all but the one or two that still looked halfway sensible, because she can't stand to think what her own boy was going through to rave like that.

Poot! Gone, thank God and Greyhound. Or it would've been thanks, if only there wasn't this little matter of being on the tired side of fifty and having to bring up her kids. Mattie could tell them apart, really. She just had to remember, "Donnie's got the mole under his ear." Otherwise, two peas in a pod, except one slept while the other fed from the bottle, then the other woke up just when that feeding got done. It was a good way for her to learn the real meaning of played out.

Evan was up with the crows to go guiding or chopping, so he took to Tommy's old room for sleep. Mattie almost forgot what that felt like herself. What shut-eye she did get was in the middle of the morning, because the babies had their one and only long nap together at about nine. Weren't for that, she'd've been under a stone by fall. Evan could visit with her when he rode out there now. It was awful, though, thinking that sleep made the best part of a day.

She'll bet that Poot is in a bar somewhere, wearing a patch of a skirt like the models on TV, even if she's fifty or such herself by now. Going home with whoever has a car. Never a word from her since she left, but the cat don't change her whiskers, by the Jesus. A bar is where she'll be going, sure as the sun will shine.

Which it looks set to do, all right, and her awake and worried half the night, same as back when all she ever managed was just going to the kitchen after formula for the woke-up one, hardly time even to get the stove het, and back to her room to push the rubber tit down the next mouth.

Back then, she'd see her door swing a little. Grandpa blowing a kiss.

Well, some things were good and they wouldn't change. That was what she figured those mornings.

Good things didn't change. Now ain't that rich?

XIII

It was only I saw red!

I blew into that burg from some other fifty-cent one, can't remember the name of it. Just caught the first thing smoking out of there, same's I did coming, same's I ever did anywheres, seems like. It's all been a while, thank God in a way. One town wasn't too much different from the next them days, unless you found you a decent jungle and kind persons which'd let you hang around some. I liked that kind of moving around the country, but it's only memories.

Railyard bulls run me out of the place in Maryland, and I'm thumbing and riding and next thing it's Altoona, and then this town of Norton, I believe it was called, or something like it—not big enough to get lost in but big enough you got you a day or two before you're the sore thumb. And then you're on your way out of there because there's no future in what ain't even really a city. People get to know you pretty quick, and odds are they ain't going to like you particularly. Doesn't matter you mean no harm.

So, I figure: I'm a pretty big guy, I open up my knife in whatever store looks easy, I clean out the register and I'm two hundred miles away before you blink. Not a lot of cops in a place like that. Easy, as I told you. I thought so anyhow. No harm intended.

What else you going to do? Place like that, you can't hit the stem. Put your hand out and some good citizen calls up Paddy to cuff it. I swear I never made a habit out of robbing before, not any type whatsoever. But here's this quiet-looking couple in their hardware shop and not a customer to kingdom come, so I walk inside quick and say, Let's have the cash. Hardly even think before I do. I make them turn the sign in their door to Closed and go way back in the corner away from any nosy people.

It's cherry-picking, because they give me their money, what there is of it, fast as you'd say Jack Robinson, and it's only keeping them out of harm's way a little while so I can lam that gets me figuring, hell, it's a hardware store, so it has rope, and rope ties people up, and that's all I meant to do to that fella and lady. Your best plans can go in the shit-can before you're halfway done.

The basement's where the rope is, the lady tells me. The man don't say a word. Looks like he's in his own little-bitty world. I almost want to tell him: Listen, I'm no killer; this is all only a bluff, but yet and still don't be calling it. I should've gone ahead and said something like it too, turns out, but how the hell you going to do that?

Down we go. Now I tell you what, you'd think the walls down there was made of mold. It smells and I say so, not that it matters one bit. Don't know why I even tell them, but you can see mister's not happy, like this wasn't a stickup but some housekeeping test and he flunked.

These poor people probably never even heard of a stickup but in a movie. They don't have no way to deal with it except think about anything in the world but what's going on here, which I guess he was doing. He gets to breathing like a horse, practically, awful mad. So yeah, I want to tell him, this is getting robbed here, not some health department inspection! He's a blue-ribbon booby.

Anyways, there's rope down there, but it's on a spool. I need to haul some of it so I can get it wrapped around them good enough to light out. But I am holding my knife, so I say for one of them to do it but no funny stuff. I'm trying to figure how I'll tie them up and still keep the knife right in my hand.

And that's when the devil shows up. The missus is pulling off the rope. Then something tells me, watch out. I yank my head back and that hammer only catches the tippy-tip of my nose. No blood, just a sting, like. If he catches me on the side of the head I'm either dead or laying there with my lights out and the cops can take their time.

I don't even know where the hammer came from, but I smack the little fart one with my elbow. Like I say, I saw red, partly because he tried such a dumb-ass trick but also because if somebody bops your nose it will cause anger. Anyhow, he goes down and I grab that hammer and—swear to God, no one wishes this didn't happen like me—I lay a bunch of licks on him.

And the woman, she just sits in a heap on the stairs and now it's her which looks like she's in a trance. Maybe she's passed out. I can't even tell. Yet and still her eyes're open, so she probably saw what I done and I'm still mad as a bull and I don't think twice. If I whack her the same, then she don't talk to anyone. I guess you murder one person, that's all a judge needs, so two don't make a lot of difference. Then I just cave her in too. Funny. She saw me coming at her but she didn't even scream or squinch.

When I went in that store I didn't mean to lift a finger. But naturally this whole business changed those people's lives. Finished them. Maybe they had kids, and I feel poor about that to this minute. But my life got changed too, I'll tell you what. I'm an old man now but still got the same job I had pretty quick after that all happened. I ended about okay as I have any right to, but you can't help thinking about if things were different.

I changed the sign to CLOSED FAMILY REASONS and stuck it back on their door. Then I sneaked up out of a cellar bulkhead behind the shop and through some woods and caught a ride with a farmer. He told me sit in the truck bed, and it was fine by me. No questions to answer. What I took wasn't enough to kill someone or go to jail for. Two sawbucks, a five-spot, and three measly ones. But I'm in deep shit, can't get no deeper.

Some other guy drops me in Allentown, I buy a ticket on the 'Hound to Detroit, and I ride a box to another place. I stay a day, maybe hit the stem an hour. Not much luck, but enough to get myself fed some way. Then I catch another train, another place. It goes like that, and for a lot of weeks even after I got here I'm thinking about sheriffs coming and troopers and dogs and everything else you heard about, but nothing ever happens.

I got a conscience, though. I been living with doing the worst you could dream for forty years and more. Believe me or don't believe me, it makes me to suffer, and I wish everything was some other way than this, and I'd see what life would be like if none of it went on.

Way back I told the Abbot, but I only said a crime was done and my heart is uneasy. Not the details. He don't pry, says I'm forgiven, says we're all sinners. This was in confession, even though I'm not Catholic. I bet he knows that, but still he wants me to say hail Marys and other stuff I never even heard of. He's a good guy, I truly believe. He's not supposed to know it's me, or anyone, because that's what the rule is.

Then again, who in hell else would it be? He leaves me alone about all that, though.

This is Nebraska, but for me it could be Mars or somewheres. The brothers don't say hardly a thing morning to night. Seems like their hired man and cook just up and died one day all that time ago, and no one saw it coming and I saw an ad in a bank window. So I cook for the brothers. They never complain, even if I know the food ain't that wonderful myself. I don't get much money, but some, and I have a roof and I have something to eat and old clothes that came out of a chest they keep.

I help with the gardens and the hives too. I kind of enjoy the bees. They are very interesting, you know that? People are good as I ever deserved, that's for sure. And where would I spend money anyhow? I quit smoking all those years ago. They don't let you smoke. Never did. Quit and you're hired, Abbot told me. Funny. I swear I smell a cigar on him sometimes, but it's not my business. So no smokes to buy. Soap in the shower, paper in the toilet, laundry. I can get along with just things like that.

My hooched-up father and my poor mother—saints protect her—must've died a hundred years ago. Pretty sure they weren't looking for me. Only the cops were, and they must have did a poor job, or they gave up quick, because here I am a free man, sort of. I could get out now and nothing would happen, I bet, but I'm okay here. You couldn't dream up a life like this back when I was a kid no more than you could fly right up to a star. My life is all different because one day I saw red, like I say. Nobody can ever tell what's around the bend. There's a lot of funny things happen.

No one knows who I am. Where, neither. Only the brothers, and brothers don't talk about their own. Or about much of anything.

XIV

A golden age, or ages. Ten and eight. George knows it can't go on forever, but even though Mary and Kate are old enough to be capable of surprisingly adult conversation, he believes they still admire him, at least most of the time. Who knows? They may keep on with that. Plenty of other sweet surprises have come his way.

Stuffed animals in their beds still, and the hankering for stories, even the ones they've outgrown—*Goodnight Moon, Where the Wild Things Are*, whatever. Sunday pancakes cooked in goofy cartoon shapes, or as close as he or Julie can come. But they have questions now too, questions about God, say. Not "Does God have teeth?" as Kate asked when she was four. Instead, things like "How could He let Tabasco run away?" George lamely suggests that life can be mysterious.

Tabasco was a mixed-breed dog, mostly spaniel of some sort, they adopted from the pound when the girls were little more than toddlers. George and Julie kept the true account of her death from them. Louie Catlin, the local cop, knocked at George's office door one afternoon, the dog's collar in hand.

"You don't want to see the body," Louie said. The car had been going fifty, but that was the speed limit. This was no one's fault except Tabasco's. Sadly, this was the only time the poor mutt had ever wandered away from home.

Yes, a change will come for Mary and Kate and their parents. The only unchanging thing in life is change. George knows he's sentimental or downright stupid, wanting things to be forever what they were once. Some would ascribe this to the early shock of his own parents' deaths, but that never really struck a chord, at least not until very lately. He ought to be glad there's such a thing as change anyhow. His drinking days were no Shangri-La.

There may be change afoot up north too. No way to be dead sure about that, he reminds himself for the hundredth time, but if there is, it's change only a fool could reject.

He suspects his real nostalgia is for those too brief years with Mary Conley at Uncle Emory's farm. Not that he craves exact replication, detail by detail; it's an abstracter sense of well-being, something that could never be destroyed, the peanut butter-and-tomato-sandwich, the root beer-and-radio feeling. It all does come back now and then, to be sure, though in disguise. It's as futile for George to describe his feelings now as it would have been when he was a boy, but all of it's there somewhere, no matter the explosions in the lives of people he's loved or at the very least thought hard about.

Innocence wouldn't be the word for what he wishes on his children. If his own childhood is the measure, there's no such thing anyhow. He thinks of certain collusions with his friend Patrick Shannon, from the neighbor farm's family, and of Nine, as everyone called him, the ninth of eleven O'Meara kids. How did Nine's parents manage? They ran their own little farm, but they both worked at Weymouth Asbestos in Norris too, his mom on certain afternoons and his dad on the 3:00 p.m. to 11:00 shift five days a week.

They were at those downtown jobs, in the barn, out in the fields, tending to their two younger children, or dead asleep. So Nine had a lot of unsupervised time on his hands, and he was usually the one to get their mischief going: painting huge red initials on the village water tower; pelting trucks with mock oranges; stealing Uncle Emory's station wagon late at night and cruising his pasture lanes under the stars.

Those three pulled other, nastier tricks too. One in particular makes George shiver, knowing that his own Mary and Kate are not all that much younger than the three boys were then.

"We need to load some rocks into this bag," Nine announced one late afternoon.

"What for?" said Pat and George in chorus.

"Load 'em up and I'll show you."

Pat and George followed orders, and Nine set the paper sack in the middle of Lewis Lane right before dark. They watched from the woods as a long, skinny guy, top down in his aqua Buick, took the bag head-on, blasting his oil pan and careening into the O'Mearas' corn field. The boys were hiding behind a brush pile. George can still smell its dew-dampness and hear rodents rustling through it. They clutched each other as the man bellowed furious curses into the night.

Back then, they were scared to death the driver might find them. Today, George thinks instead how the man might have struck the bag with a wheel and flipped, or wrapped himself around a tree instead of bogging down among the cornstalks.

And what about smoking in their hayloft forts at Uncle Emory's? The barn could have gone up like a Roman candle. What about jumping astride the old boy's horse at midnight, three strong, no rein or saddle, just hell bent, bruises the worst they ever suffered. No broken bones. No punctured lungs. No gray matter smeared on a fence row.

When Nine's father Mickey dropped dead, closing the tailgate of his pickup on a veal calf, the O'Mearas just moved away. Where? George never knew. He wonders what happened to his red-headed friend with the gapped teeth. He remembers his way with animals, his enviable baseball card collection, his sure aim with a rifle, but he had no idea where he and all those brothers and sisters went, not where they may be now.

George's heart aches for Nine sometimes. He can put himself right back in the O'Mearas' dirt drive, standing wordless as their Plymouth, four kids inside, mattresses tethered to its roof, trailing a tractor cart full of household effects, bucks out the lane, the widow O'Meara at the wheel. The oldest brother and oldest sister drive off first, Mickey Jr., who's barely gotten his driver's license, follows in the pickup truck with three more siblings. George and Pat watch it all, dazed but too proud to cry.

As for Pat, George heard he got shot up in Nam, but came out of it all right. Apparently, he has a company fifty miles distant. He and his crew tend potted plants in the office parks that have spread into old farm territory all over the region. He should look Pat up. He really should. How does anyone just let an early friendship dissolve? George is simply afraid they won't have enough in common now. He's a bit of a coward, if the truth be known.

But who on earth would share much with a man like George Mayes, an Ivy League brat who first drove a school bus and then owned a fleet? And George is not the only oddity. The neighborhood's ugly, flat-topped buildings stand in pastures where he and those friends played ball games, marines, and cowboys and Indians, in woods where they hunted crows with a fabulous owl decoy. The schools seem built to look like jails, George thinks. People in suits and dresses work in the other buildings. None of it makes any sense.

No wonder he's more or less a loner except for wife and family. His young adulthood was no fairy tale, Lord knows, but his boyhood now seems like one, and there's nobody to share it with anymore. Back then, all he knew of swag and commerce came from one small movie theatre. Jabbering Lou Costello. Gaunt hero Gary Cooper. And the Hollywood gunslingers long since forgotten—Hoot Gibson, Bob Steele, Johnny Mack Brown, the rest—all in Boot Hill now. Beauties like Ava Gardner and Jane Russell.

George recalls the dark trickle of sweat running down Ava's spine and under her belt as she climbed some stairs in Bhowani Junction. She wore a drab military uniform, but the damp stain brought on a stirring the boys understood only imperfectly. He smiles at their ludicrous banter while they walked home.

"What would you do if Ava Gardner showed up here right now?" Nine challenged, as if the famous star might have found herself walking from Glassburg to Norris and strayed onto Uncle Emory's farm.

"Tell you what I'd do . . . ," George began.

"You'd be scared shit, is what," said Pat.

"Would not!"

"Would too!"

Age-old playground back-and-forth.

That was a kind of innocence, when you get right down to it. But was innocence an unequivocal good? Is it? What about Santa Claus, say? Last Christmas, Julie found Kate in tears. When Julie asked her why, she answered, "Billy Mason said there's no such thing as Santa!" Was the swap of that myth for so-called reality truly a benefit? You shouldn't lie to your kids, no. But life's complicated, George lamely concluded yet again, useless as the claim clearly was.

His recollections can't all be sentimental fabrication, though. Hiking back from O'Mearas, for instance, he always passed the so-called colored graveyard, puzzled to see the broken glass on moldering rock walls, bottles hanging from tree limbs, horsehair garlands cinched around certain stones. One of the markers read, *Slew by a sinner.*

George understood nothing about that place, which was surely the chief reason it unsettled him. But back at Emory's, he could compose himself, because, no matter the hour, Mary would always be waiting with a cup of tea, laced with sugar and cloudy with milk from the separator, which had wheezed in the pantry that morning. Those things were ever certain. If anyone provided the continuity he seems still to crave, it was Mary.

Once, when he was eleven or so, George had a dreadful case of diarrhea, so violent that he began to imagine something worse. When he saw blood in the toilet bowl, it was as though a great, gloomy pipe organ were playing deep inside his body, something more ominous than he'd ever known. He woke up Mary, who came down, wrapped in a pink robe, hair in curlers, her toothless mouth dark as the night outside. He could see her struggle for good cheer, God bless her.

"I'm bleeding!" George croaked, though now he felt better just for her presence. Mary determined, however, that the blood he imagined was no more than skin from his favorite sandwich's tomatoes. George remembers his sudden relief. Not far from young manhood then, he was still willing to rouse an old woman and have her inspect the waste from his bowels, the worst consequence some petty embarrassment.

He never told Patrick or Nine about this, of course. You didn't go around talking to your buddies about something like fear, still less of love. Yet even here in the bosom of his family's affections, the memory of that bizarre episode tells George a lot about love's nature.

He hopes the girls feel such absolute trust. Julie's the likelier parent to offer it, and he can foolishly feel a touch of jealousy about that. Not that he hasn't made his contributions. If it weren't too hot or cold, when the kids were smaller, he'd put one or the other into a carrier fashioned from a Woodstown pack basket. George cut holes in the weave for legs, swathing them with chamois. The packs you bought for children back then were both flimsy and costly.

How often must George have hiked Mary or Kate up and down Finland Ridge? He misses those trips, something belonging exclusively to him and his girls. He prayed they would recall the outings when they were grown, and fondly. In rhythm with his steps, he'd sing a nonsense tune that Evan used to sing, without, it seemed, even knowing he sang at all.

> I bought a mule,
> He's such a fool
> He never paid no heed.
> I struck a match
> To the end of his tail
> And then he showed some speed.
> Oh, go 'long, mule,
> Don't you roll them eyes.
> You can change a fool
> But a goldang mule
> Am a mule until he dies.

Often the daughters sang along, but at least as often they fell asleep. George could linger at the top, looking down on the valley and its few remaining farm-plots, surrounded by the sprawl but still neat as checker squares. Like graceful skaters, vultures wheeled languidly overhead in the drafts off hill and river. They could hypnotize.

To be sober was the good thing, without which others wouldn't exist. If he ever got careless, he could go back in a heartbeat to a place whose horrors remain vivid, as he means to keep them. You can change a fool but a goldang drunk am a drunk until he dies. He seemed surer than ever to remember that with the breath of a daughter on his neck.

Those moments when he carried his girls were so profound he had to conjure something or someone to thank. Whatever it was still is, and it contains even more meaning than that stony outcrop on Finland Ridge. It's a place. It's air. It's music. It's the old, reassuring voice—in fact, it's all these together. It's as real to him as Glassburg, because he's been there more than once, even if the first visit was the crucial one, the one that has kept the others coming.

The girls have outgrown their rides, but whether or not he can get to Finland Ridge, George will always recall that modest height and all its associations, just as he hopes his daughters will, for reasons of their own. And whether or not this indefinable spirituality warms his blood in one moment, he can summon times when it did, when he simply knew he'd live and that that was a holy condition.

That he never completely lost hope in his furious years owes itself at least in considerable part to a half-literate Irish spinster who smelled of rosewater and powder after her mass, who wore squeaky fat-heeled shoes and a plain white uniform, whose starchy blouse abraded his cheeks when they embraced. She had special, serrated knives for tomatoes in a special George drawer, as she called it. Dear Mary. Heaven-sent, no doubt in his mind. That's not mere hokum. Mary's care for detail, for particulars, still signifies love. You could trust her, and for that, life itself could feel trustworthy.

XV

Dear mom and dad   novembier 11 68

Its a hard thing I bet having Donald and David but yet they could not be with no better in times thats this terrible. From the pics you sent me their sure twin's all right and no dout about THAT. And terrible time's cant be over quick enough to suit me and will be quite soon I believe. Then I will see the boys for myself. Good huh. Here its much colder than many people would ever think after dark and I dont care if I NEVER see another drop of rain. Time will come tho when its sunny all over and here I am not just talking about Nam because the hour is at hand as the prophets tell us. I hope you and me and the boys live to see this thats all and I feel in my hart we will. So there I said it. Im sad thinking about Poot leaving before she even got to know D and D. But in the good time shell be back because shes not a evil person. Evil person's has ran things many years and still is doing this but will not forever. Speaking of running Im still running the D10 cat which me and other mechanics keep very good because you cant afford it not to run beleve me. Charly will try and blow up the landing strips which they sometimes can do. This is when me and the cat realy go to work. I have had it in a dream that Ill be alright and will live on so my boy's and me can go fishing. So my thoughts are at piece. Poot has not wrote you I bet because shes feeling sheepish of what she done but will see the light. Mean while we must wait for the change Im talking about. Its hard I know. I know your doing every thing that can be done for my little fellers. I thank you for this because I know you are good perent's because you raised me haha. But thanks and I mean it!! If I hear another one of them loud birds that comes around only at night and then dont shut up till its light again I will personly bulldoze there nest ha ha ha. Not really but really their a bother.

Your son Tom

XVI

K ate still had the child's knack of speaking in italics. "You always fall *asleep* at the movies," she said that evening.

Why did this feel like an attack? His daughter was poking fun, and George knew it. Still, he thought the comment implied his failures as a father. He saw how silly that was, but his reason could quit him, sober or not, in a wink. He has never quite shed his fear that he may be unworthy, which sends him far too quickly into a self-defensive crouch. This memory is from two winters ago, for the love of God! Move on, he thinks.

His friend Al, sober forty years, once told him something so simple he can't forget it. "If you want respect, do respectable things." He has tried that to the best of his ability for thirty years. Al is gone now, but George imagines him standing right in front of him, his red beard swept sideways, as if by a gale. "Do what you always did," he sometimes added. "Get what you always got."

George had just suggested a film to his daughters. Lapsed into sullenness, he instantly forgot which one. Why does the memory of such penny ante stuff two years back preoccupy him on a day that may be auspicious?

George remembers Julie saying, "Oh, don't pout."

George rolled his eyes, sighed loudly.

"He does sleep in movies, doesn't he, Katie?"

"Don't call me that."

"Call you what?"

"Kate-EE."

"Why not?"

"Because we have Jule-EE and Mare-EE, and I don't want to be another EE."

"Don't forget Dadd-EE," Mary teased.

"You're stupid and gross," Kate replied.

103

Was all his family as crazy as he was, and if they were, even though none had ever seen him take a drink, was that his fault? "I don't always sleep," he challenged.

"Only about ninety percent of the time," said Mary.

"Ninety-five," Kate corrected.

"Well, if I do, it's because they usually aren't worth staying awake for."

Why on earth should he have offered his cranky cultural commentary to mere children, especially his own? Lunatic. He's a skeptic about most movies, it's true, but why such an asinine need to voice his disapproval to whomever might listen? The old egotism. Hard to kick.

He understands sometimes that his yen to be listened to is a vestige from his days as a barroom fabulist. And yet a lot of movies, especially the ones that strive for depth, do strike him as all but laughably committed to their own significances, as subtle as cudgels. The more he hears one talked up as brilliant, or above all innovative, the more likely he'll find it banal.

For some time Hollywood has considered Oliver Stone an intellectual. That about says it all, as far as George is concerned. Suddenly, we were watching films, not movies, or we saw blockbusters like *Star Wars*, in which technological effect passed for imagination.

George's attitude goes back to the '60s, when people started calling themselves visual, as opposed to verbal, which as far as he could tell meant they didn't enjoy reading or were too lazy for it. Like so many things in his world, it all made him yearn for his boyhood, when he and his pals could go to the Orpheum in Glassburg, with its velvet ropes, its great Warner Brothers cartoons, even Lowell Thomas's boring news briefs. Jujubes for adequate ammunition, Milk Duds for superior.

George, Pat, and Nine particularly prized the horror flicks. When the dreadful things—*The Thing from Another World*, *Them*, *The Creature from the Black Lagoon*—first showed up, they'd bolt from the first row. Whenever the threatening theme music played again, they did the same, squatting behind a partition. When it stopped, they rushed back to their seats. Almost every kid in the place did same. No one seemed to mind.

But how could George have gotten so worked up over newer movies that late afternoon? Did his children's ribbing really launch him into such self-important opining, even if it was unvoiced? What is it kids say? Get a life. Well, he has one, but curbing his impulse to judgment will be an ongoing challenge.

"We ought to take the sleds out," Julie suddenly said that night, looking to change the mood.

"Hey, I like that," George answered. The girls dutifully groaned, but they were quickly off the couch. The snow had fallen all day, and now the stars were out. There was a big moon too, and by its light George could see to the bottom of their hill and the frozen stream. Some night bird lifted from the ice and plunged into black pinewoods, all in a flash, its beauty the livelier for brevity.

He did like the notion of sledding, skipping the movies altogether. The wind would feel right on nose and cheeks. He all but jogged to the hallway closet.

"Dad, you are so weird!" said Kate.

"Weird is right," said her sister.

"Weird?" George asked.

"You're like a little kid sometimes," Kate replied.

Being childish has too often occasioned those sulks over slights real or imagined, like the one he'd just shrugged off, but it has also meant that, even in his middle fifties, he can be playful.

As the girls struggled into their winter outfits, he remembered driving Uncle Emory's battered Jeep through snowy pastures, Nine and Patrick on a toboggan, a rope hitched to its crude bumper. It's a wonder he never turned the Jeep over, fishtailing, cracking the whip. His friends splayed their legs to one side, then the other, to keep from flipping.

George remembers an owl, motionless as a palace guard, perched low one afternoon in an elm at a field's edge. Each time the boys finished a circuit, he checked to see if the bird had flushed. It never did, though the engine roused cottontails from their burrows under the snow to zigzag all over the meadow. The owl seemed not to care. Strange. In fact, the whole white world looked strange—exotic somehow, but also promising.

Nine drove so poorly that everything changed when he took the wheel. Once he actually snapped the tow rope bucking to speed. Patrick did a little better, but George felt content that he, rather than Nine, could be best at something for a change. He preferred driving more than he did riding the sled anyhow.

Nyaaaaaaaaa! Pat and Nine would squall as the Jeep slewed through a turn, a sound combining delight and terror. The trees' ice by the pasture was bright with sun, glorious. The weather was bitter, but George felt nothing but well-being.

And then there was the hot chocolate, dense as a melted candy bar, which Mary somehow had waiting for them, no matter when they came in, ice balls in their hair, snot frozen on face and mittens, fingertips ridged with cold. That drink would have been worth going to war for.

Now his daughters, finished with getting into parkas and boots, rushed out to find the sleds. Julie came downstairs in a red union suit. She opened the mudroom closet to find her quilted bib overalls, but George stopped her briefly, admiring her long figure. "You're still my girl," he whispered, looking her up and down and feeling some heat.

"And you are a certified madman," Julie answered, though her smile was fetching enough. They kissed. Not quite passionately, and not quite not.

The family took run after run, George with Mary piled on his back, Julie with Kate. In the rare silences, an owl, this later day's owl, called from the bog to the south, another answering from a near ridge. Despite the chill, George felt a different tickle of heat in his blood.

The time of backpacking and sliding with the girls is over. George could swear he hears a string quartet full of weepy tremolo when he thinks about such a matter, but he can usually snap out of such dejection without too much delay. The moment's what counts, and in the one he recalls, parents and daughters raced, capsized, threw snow at one another, squealed and shouted, not exactly like him and Patrick and Nine but close enough, in fact better.

Standing at the top of the hill, George kissed Julie once more, if chastely, on the cheek. She smelled like the fresh air itself. That outdoorsy scent made him fall in love again every time, but there was a lot else to do that, day by day, over and over.

Once the moon climbed completely clear of the ridge to the east, George slipped away. All he could find in the kitchen was a can of prepared cocoa mix. That didn't matter. The girls had never sampled Mary's hot chocolate. Once again he recognized that in all those drunken years he'd longed for moments like that evening's. He just hadn't known it.

XVII

Poot looks good for forty-nine. Tweezers for a couple chin-hairs. She gave up being blonde last year but even dark she can turn a head or two, some of them a lot younger than her. Baltimore's nobody's seventh heaven, not her part anyhow, but she wouldn't go back to Tommy up in the sticks if you smacked her with one.

And she finally got rid of Hughie too. Huge-ie was more like it, once he had her roped and didn't do a damn thing but pump gas, drink about a million gallons of beer and put the Eye-tie sandwiches to him. Huge-ie, all right. He didn't like it any when she called him that. Too bad. He had no pride, didn't care about you didn't even see his belt buckle.

She just couldn't look at him, let alone . . . you know. Once Hughie Junior was up and gone, in and out of that desert war without a scratch but signed up for the long haul, looked like, which was okay by Poot, because the army'd keep his nose a lot cleaner than his s.o.b. father ever kept his—once little Hugh was gone, it was bye-bye, Daddy. She ran out the door almost before their son's transport left town. She can't believe she put up with what she did almost twenty years.

This isn't living like a queen, no. But working the register at Wendy's and having this ratty little apartment seems like she died and went to heaven, compared. Papa Hughie wasn't just a tub of guts. He was one mean bastard too. Not mean mean like Tommy. Huge-ie wouldn't beat you up then laugh if he heard one whimper. She took that from Tommy maybe three times. Then she wasn't going to wait for him coming back from Nam. Not her. She thinks that laughing was what did it more than his slaps.

One of the times Tom smacked her, he was raving about that fella from away who was big buddies with his dad. Hell, she never aimed to mess with that guy. Just a little fun. Get him all lathered up and then leave him standing there. Tom came home from an overnight with that guy and his own father out on East Jerusalem Lake, and it was fuck George this and fuck George that. She's pretty sure his name was George.

Anyhow, he told Poot to get some goddamned dinner on the table. She knew that was just so's he could give her an order. Mattie and Evan were off someplace. And it was only about three in the afternoon, for Christ's sake. When she told him, very polite too, not to bark at her, he took and backhanded her right down on the davenport. And her already pregnant, even if she didn't know it then. Or did she? She can't remember. It don't matter. All she was doing before Tom came home was watching a little TV. Never a thought of that George or anybody else.

When she got up, he slapped her down again. Open hand, but it hurt, no two ways about that. She put up with stuff like that one time before, just because he was drunk, and said I'm sorry later. She figured he wasn't in his right mind. Then he drank again a week or so later, same thing. That last time he wasn't even drinking, and he still laughed when she cried, which she couldn't help, goddammit. A girl shouldn't take that sort of disrespect. Not this one anyways. They shipped Tommy overseas, and he wouldn't be seeing her when he came home—if he did.

Sad in a way, because there were times before they landed in those godforsaken woods when things went pretty good, really. The mill where he worked in New Hampshire wasn't all that far from Concord, so they lived in an actual town. He came home every night tired, but still playful as a cat, and they ate together, or maybe went out to a movie or just drove along the Merrimack so he could look for geese and ducks or whatnot. That got her close to nature as she ever wanted, out the car window.

Then, between when he was drafted and when he went over, the two of them headed back where he grew up, and everything turned different quick. Tommy's folks didn't know about any of this. They're probably saying bad things about her to this day, except they're probably both dead now. Who cares?

She never even tried to find Donald and David, which must be grown men, of course, so they're probably as all right as they'd be if she stayed, maybe better. No sense to put her nose in. She wouldn't help a thing, and she never wanted to get in touch with nobody from that frozen goddamned part of the world again, period. The minute little Hughie came, it was like there'd never been no twins, like they turned back into the nothing they were before they came. Sure weren't nothing when she was pushing them out, though!

Little Hughie won't write, but he calls now and then. All the way from Germany, which is where she thinks he still is, for whatever oddball reason the government came up with. He's not allowed to say—for whatever oddball reason. Why's that? Who knows? But when he calls, he's sweet as sugar.

He was always a good boy. Oh, there was the usual cutup stuff in high school, skipping class or teasing some bookworm or whatever, but no cops or judges, no drugs or drinking. Not enough drinking at least to prove he was his father's kid. If he drank, he quit when it was time to. Not like Huge-ie or Tommy, for sure. More like Evan Butcher. Evan liked a taste, for sure. But that didn't really seem to matter. Whenever he drank hard, it didn't touch him. Poot thinks he was a pretty good old boy, actually. Mattie, now, she wouldn't care if Mattie fell off that pitiful one-lane bridge in Woodstown.

Little Hugh acted serious even from a baby. When he was still real small, she used to take him down to the Harborside aquarium and they watched fishes. He was the one liked it so much, but after a little, she got to too. He stood there by the biggest tank, never wanted to go, and Poot stayed with him, holding his hand, waiting for the big turtles to swim around, and specially one shark which he liked so awful well. Both of them did, that one with the spots. Sometimes she'd be there with Hughie so damn long she'd fall asleep on her feet, and when she woke up, why, he still wanted to keep watching. She had to drag him home.

Same with Legos. If he started in on some project out of that little book that came in the box, you didn't hear squat out of him for hours. Poot could do whatever she liked, even take a nap, and he never bothered her. Hugh Junior still keeps his eye on his business. He says his officers told him he was one hell of a soldier—born to it, always there when they needed.

Wherever it could be, there was where he was. Not here, anyhow, and fat Hugh neither, because he moved to Texas, she heard. Poot's headed to Anna Banana's and no one to say boo. She checks her bathroom mirror, front and side. She doesn't have to suck in any gut and never did, not even after two boys at once and then another one later on. Time's coming she won't look this good, but she ain't thinking about that right now.

XVIII

When George visited two summers back, Mattie told him, "All's he wants is to drink himself foolish." That's the same thing she said, over and over, a few years after Tommy came back from the war. When was that? George remembered the Watergate hearings were heating up. '74. She'd been talking about her boy, not her husband. George had been sober five years himself then, and he'd gotten over any bad feelings for Tommy. He actually felt compassion. Who knew what the guy must have gone through?

Sure enough, as soon as Tommy was back in the north country, living over in Codyville, it was one bender after another, and all the while he was bristling with ill-defined rage. On the few days when he showed up at his parents', he was pie-eyed even before noon. He kept getting kicked off one grunt job and the next. He kept having mad visions too, raving about a new order, about the coming of some God unknown to anyone but him. "Look to the mountain!" he'd suddenly shout. "Beware the Saducee!" Strange snatches of Scripture, imprecise, incoherent. Where had he picked them up? He could scarcely read.

"Comes in here drunk as a monkey or he's shaking like a dog trying to pass a peach pit," Evan remarked one July. Tommy had just sped away after another preacherly climax, gravel from under his tires rattling against the roadside wall of the shop. "Gets to raving about who the hell can say?"

"It's a disease, Evan. I really believe that," George said.

"Cusses on everything. Fishing's gone to hell. Ain't no deer in the woods. Nixon . . ."

"Well, Nixon . . ." George remembers trailing off with a wry smile.

Soon the church bell on Tower Hill struck noon. Evan cupped his ear, dramatically. "One o'clock Maritime," he breathed with a twinkle, or what he could muster of one. He'd already unhooked his pack basket from its nail. "Trouble you if I have a tap?"

"Not a bit," George told him. He meant it, a marvel. His over-whelming thirst had all but vanished since his last jackpot. If it ever returns, it's only as a passing fancy, because George can finish the movie in his sleep. It may start with him and Evan lazing on a Semnic beach, sipping something amber, and watching the sun fall. But it ends with that rat eating dog food.

He popped an orange Nehi as Evan uncapped his Old Crow. The soda hissed and ran down the side of the can. He can see each bead. A clear head, a working memory. A daily miracle has kept him going. Evan tipped his pint into a tin cup, smutty with wood smoke and old coffee. George watched him do it, fascinated, but not by the booze.

It's strange, George thinks, as so often, how the episodes in a person's life that lodge themselves in the mind are not necessarily impor-tant ones—fizz of a soft drink; louder hiss of a river fifty yards away; Evan's old hound bawling in his pen.

"Sorryface don't think it's a good idea, looks like," said Evan, smil-ing somewhat sadly, swirling the whiskey, head turned toward the dog's howl.

Sorryface III was a Walker-Beagle mix, with a voice like something out of those old horror movies George and his chums liked. He'd been one fine rabbit dog in his time: great nose, great bawl-chop voice, long legs for the deeper snow. Now his face was clown-white and his hips gone to pieces.

"I can't bring myself to shoot the old boy," Evan said, as if reading George's thoughts.

Evan raised a hand and smeared a fattening mosquito on his cheek. George wasn't shy about wetting his thumb on the soda can and wash-ing the blood off. He remembers such a detail, as if it were a lot less than two decades ago.

And Evan's words to him, his own words back at the older man, a mere sixty then, are exact in his mind. "Hadn't've been for rabbits and deer in the woods, fish in the lakes, and the first old Sorryface, my dad's dog," Evan breathed—"why, that dog-horned Depression would've drove us Butchers out."

"Glad it didn't, Evan."

"It drove a lot of them."

"I know, Evan."

"That hound . . . Why, Daddy said he got so poor he had to lean agin a bank to howl." They shared a laugh, though this wasn't the first time Evan had produced that one, and both of them knew it.

"Fact is," Evan went on, "that whole Depression mess pushed me right out of school to work when I was just a kid."

"You weren't all that fussy about staying in school anyhow, were you?" George joked.

Evan didn't answer. He seemed to have drifted off. Suddenly, he said, "Don't seem to care no more about them kids than if they weren't even his!" George could see a vein pop up on Evan's brow to think of Tommy's behavior.

"Let's pray he gets some help."

"Ran his wife right out of the country," Evan grumbled, "and his ma's raising their boys at her age! You'd think he'd come help her!"

"A lot never quit. It's not that simple," George answered, quickly adding, "but it can happen."

"You done it."

"Grace of God." The phrase came easily; it didn't embarrass him anymore.

"Never knew you to be so hellfire for God and that."

"Long story. Or maybe short. Hard to describe."

"Must not be the same God Tom keeps slattin' about. That one would make a preacher burn his book." Evan's expressions never got dull.

"No, I don't think so."

"Well, whatever did it, I'm glad you come around."

Evan stood, a bit wobbly, not from drink but from sitting for years in the stern of a canoe, or banging his legs around on river drives. He looked out the low door of his shop. A nighthawk dived to grab a bug ten yards away; they heard the boom of its wing.

Evan looked puzzled, as if the bird embodied all the confusion in his world. "What the hell's he doing sculling around this time of day?"

Tommy's twins would be harder for a grandfather to make sense of than an erratic bird. George remembers a sudden, superstitious, and unforgivable thought: maybe they'd been children of Tommy's God. That might explain their uncanniness. He shook his head to clear it of such superstitious nonsense, no less absurd than Tommy's.

At five years old, those boys scarcely spoke except to one another, their common language all grunts and mumbles, impenetrable to anyone but Mattie. "Heh!" one would say, the other answered in kind, and Mattie knew to fetch glasses of milk or cookies or find a missing shoe, a model car, whatever. The sound was always the same in George's ears, but she could distinguish its varying implications. Mattie was a little uncanny herself.

Don and Dave's amusements were all ones they invented. They'd simultaneously stand up from their toys and fling themselves onto the yellow couch. One would lean forward, then flop against its vinyl, while the other shot forward in his turn and in turn flopped back, little pistons. Or they'd be walking along the gravel road and stoop, as if on cue, to grab a stone apiece and throw it, always at the same apparently random target, a fence post, a dusting sparrow, a tree limb.

Stranger still, without instruction from anyone, the twins developed a precocious mastery over mechanical things. They showed no interest in their grandfather's knowledge of woods and waters, but they had many of a seasoned grease monkey's capabilities before they were teenagers.

The gift showed first in how quickly they took apart and reassembled the scores of model trucks, cars, airplanes, and bulldozers that came to line a shelf in Evan's shop and two in Mattie's kitchen. Then one winter morning, after their grandfather had spent more than half an hour trying to start his old McCullough chainsaw, David and Donald took over. They couldn't have been more than ten.

"I went in for dinner," Evan told George. "Left 'em right there in the dooryard, chirping like chipmunks."

While he was eating, they removed the carburetor, took it apart, and put it back on. Evan said he jumped for fright when he heard the engine catch outdoors.

"Heh. Dirty," the boys said as one when Evan rushed outside. And, together, "too rich." The strange part was that Evan had earlier fussed with the mixture screw himself, to no avail.

The twins went on to change belts on Ben Patcher's tractor, to fix the air volume control on their neighbor Wilma's water pump, and even took a screw and fashioned it into a brass key to replace one Mattie had lost for her mantle clock.

Time would come when they failed almost everything at school, despite the specialist help coming into use for children with learning problems even in their part of the country. The boys were barely passable readers, and unless they used block letters, their penmanship was identical—and runic. Only Mattie could read it.

They soon graduated from small engines to automobiles and trucks, David doing engines and undercarriages, Donald teaching himself to body work. They got so good so young that summer sportsmen from as far south as Boston were soon making the long trek to Woodstown at all times of year to have their high-end cars serviced by children.

The twins had traded repairs on Billy Miles's one-ton truck and Farmall Cub for use of his barn. Over time they filled it with a wheel balancer, an air compressor for their torque tools, and even a pit, which they dug and cemented, for procedures like brake and exhaust replacement. A lift would have been far too expensive.

How would such unusual boys have made their way otherwise in the world? Their mysterious command over machinery was indeed a gift in every sense of that word.

Or so people assumed in those days.

Evan had poured himself another inch of whiskey by the time the nighthawk dived again. Neither man spoke, but they looked at each other quizzically. Whenever George sees such a bird now, or hears the rattle of its stoop near his cabin, that visit to Evan's shop comes back. He couldn't block it if he wanted to.

XIX

Julie carefully nosed her van through town. She was headed home, and at this hour, the sun sat so low it was a job to pick her way among pedestrians and double-parked cars on Railroad Street. The glare off melting snow on the blacktop made things even harder. Thank God people ahead could see the stoplights. She only braked because they did.

The usual winos and dope fiends were taking up the little park's benches. Dead leaves and paper scraps scuttled across the slushed-over gravel, and raggedy sparrows bobbed around, hoping for crumbs, which these unfortunates would not be dropping. Julie wasn't old, but she remembered when you'd have looked pretty hard to find any derelicts in Glassburg. Progress? Poor things.

She saw the sign, Emory Unger Park. That was where most of the paint money went. To the town, of all things. When he was alive, George claimed, the only time old man Unger talked about the town was when he grumbled about school taxes or road maintenance or dumb cops. Then he died, and all of a sudden he's Glassburg's Santa.

The school gym was Unger Gym now; the public pool was Unger Pool; his big yellow house was the town hall, probably the swankiest one in the state, and the back fields and woods were leased to the Boy Scouts. Barely anything to her husband from the few bucks his parents left. Emory had likely used most of that to pay for that fancy college education. Not a cent from the uncle's own bundle, but maybe that was fair enough. George admitted he never tried to get close to the old boy. There just didn't seem any good way to do that.

Mary, that Irish maid he loved so much, died right after her boss, probably because once the Unger place was sold, or given away, more like it, where could she go? George said she must have been too healthy for the Mother of Consolation Home, and she didn't have a relative in

America anybody knew about. Emory didn't cut her a dollar in his will, either.

But there was a big surprise when Mary did pass on. Guess who had a pretty fair share of money? And every last cent of it, every scrap the sweet old woman had squirreled away out of her wages in all those years, with nothing to spend it on but the church plate, went straight to George.

Well, he was as close to a son as that lady ever had, Julie supposed. "God bless her!" she blurted, thankful to someone she never knew.

Mary didn't make George rich beyond anyone's craziest dreams, but he could pay for his last year of college with what she left him, and have some to spare too, though he told her he drank a lot of that away. Hard to picture.

A horn honked, and Julie jumped in her seat. The light was green. George claims he might be drunk today if Emory had left him a fortune. How would she know? She never saw him drunk. No one talked about it around here. He didn't talk much about those times himself, except he did say most of the people who knew him that way were probably underground.

Now her husband wasn't Christ the King when he was sober—who was?—but she'd talked to a lot of her girlfriends and figured she came out pretty darned well. She thought of Grace, say, who went with Julie from elementary through high school graduation.

"It feels like I'm walking underwater all day," Grace told her once. She'd gone on to Penn State back then, and now she was a paralegal. But for her that really meant a secretary, because her boss didn't hand her anything interesting or challenging. Grace hated Bob Mulder for his nose-in-the-air ways and for never once showing any interest at all in what she needed. Mildew, she called him. And Grace's husband Nick was good-hearted enough, but Lord, you never met anybody duller!

Julie liked her job, and there was no liquor to screw things up at home. No anything else, either. George didn't even flirt with women, let alone chase them. He was a steady worker, maybe too steady. Julie thought they could use a little more fun time together, but of course you aren't zipping off to the Bahamas or somewhere anyhow when you're raising children and running a business. She doesn't complain.

And after all, the kids were growing all the time. She was only forty-one, and even if George was in his fifties, they'd have more time right after his retirement, even if Julie had a hard time imagining her husband really retired. Not the type.

There were other blessings too. The girls got along better than most sisters, for one thing. There'd be some little snit now and then, sure, but mostly they enjoyed each other, different as they were. You noticed the difference as soon as they got big enough for a stroller. If Kate saw something strange or scary, she wanted to check it out. If they were in the Wild West or wherever and ran into a bear, you could almost hear her say, "Hey, let's go look!"

Mary kept more to herself. She liked to draw and read and write. She must have five diaries locked in a dresser drawer, which she started keeping as soon as she could make words, and that was even before first grade. Kate kept one too, but she preferred the outdoors, and she never met a dog she didn't love. She'd walk right up to some drug dealer's attack dog and kiss it smack on the lips one day if they didn't keep an eye out.

Kate couldn't get over losing Tabasco. She still thought the dog just ran away. Come her birthday, they'd have to buy another of some kind. Kate didn't care. It could be a Great Dane or a Chihuahua, as long as it barked and wagged its tail and slobbered. She told her mother and father, "I wish I owned twenty dogs—no, a hundred."

Julie sighed. Life was complicated enough without some puppy peeing all over the house again and chewing up cushions, but she and George had promised. They'd do something for Mary too if she told them what, but she never asked for much. It was almost worrisome, how guilty she seemed just asking for money to buy a party present for one of her friends. Where did that come from?

Well, George was like that too. He actually got the blues if he bought a pair of shoes, say. He'd wear the old ones till they were embarrassing, even though he could easily afford new. His business was a pretty sure thing forever, because kids had to go to school, and they rode to school in buses, and—unless George went back on the bottle, God forbid—he was the bus man. When the economy sank for a lot of their friends, their family's life stayed pretty much the same. George Bush? Bill Clinton? It didn't matter to their pocketbook.

"You're a pro. Look like a pro!" Julie smiled. She remembered she said the same thing about George's office a few years back. But she couldn't let him keep shuffling around in shoes so worn-out they hardly stayed on his feet.

Julie wondered if a pup would come between the girls. Probably not. The first few months they had Tabasco, Kate didn't want to be with anyone but the dog. No music, and she even skimped on her schoolwork, which wasn't like either one of the daughters. Half the other mothers she knew practically had to horsewhip their children to do homework. You had to drag Kate and Mary away from theirs! This changed during that little spell for Kate. It took her some time to get back to her routine, but she did, and she and Mary were fine again. Still, Tabasco was the first one hugged in the morning, and the last one said goodnight to.

Swinging east on Lewis Lane, Julie caught her breath. Shadows stretched on the farm fields, and they just looked so beautiful on the snow you'd think they were painted by some famous artist, with the sky dark blue enough it was almost purple. She still had the faces of her girls in mind, and she thought what good kids they were. George's drivers reported some stuff they had to put up with from a few brats on the buses. Not the brats' fault, probably. Some parents had the TV on all day and night. They used it to babysit. Why in the world have children if you don't want to be with them and watch them grow and learn things besides the latest jingle for Pepsi or Trix or Colgate?

Julie kept plenty busy bookkeeping and scheduling at the shop, and George always had a million things to take care of, but they never wanted to tell Kate or Mary to go do something on their own when they got home from work. Fact was that the kids were doing so much by themselves nowadays that she and George had to force themselves not to butt in.

Their girls lived in harmony. Actual harmony, sometimes: Kate played clarinet, and Mary played piano, and no one ever needed to talk them into practicing. They loved music, and they were good.

Julie needed to pull over. It was winter, all right, but she felt like she was getting into the same frame of mind she was in one afternoon seven or so months back. Right now, Lewis Stream was sparkling off to her right. The ice along the banks glittered like fire in the sun. On that July day, after the same kind of grocery trip as this one, she stopped in the exact same place. It was waist-high corn she saw in the fields then, and the sun on it was different, but just as pretty. She kept sitting there and breathing hard. She didn't know how long—long enough that she figured they'd eat the pork chops that night; they were half-thawed by the time she came to. Well, maybe they weren't, but she stayed parked there a long spell anyhow.

Later, when she popped her trunk open in their drive, she could hear Kate and Mary practicing some longhair piece. Julie didn't know a thing about classical music. George knew a little, and would know even more, he said, except the music teacher at his old school was a sadist. Even worse, he was George's fourth-grade homeroom teacher too. Her husband told her stories about things that man did, and they'd curl your hair.

George's truck was right there, so why didn't he come help with the bags as usual? Julie just stood by her car, looking up at the house and listening. No, she had no idea what they were playing. It could have been by Mozart, Beethoven, Roy Rogers, or Trigger. But Lord, it was beautiful. The afternoon started to cool off.

It wasn't only the sweet sounds of the music, though. It was how they just seemed to mix with everything around her. That sounded corny, speaking of corn, but this was one of those times when you think you know exactly what love is, or beauty, even if the best writer on earth couldn't put it all in words.

Their Mary's blonde hair falling in front of her, with her head bent over the keys, and Kate, all gristle and muscle, waving the clarinet back and forth the way she did if she was really involved—Julie could picture it all. When she was alive, Tabasco used to cock her ears under the clarinet and watch it move, swinging her head back and forth along with it, like one of those Indian snake charmers' snakes.

Swear to God, it seemed like the forsythia bushes all around the house started rustling and turning gold again, and everything just seemed to be vibrating. It felt a little scary, matter of fact. She watched a flock of white pigeons fly along Finland Ridge, pretty, as if God made them do it right then.

Was she crazy? She worried about that a minute, because right then the house just lifted off the ground, and she did too. She couldn't feel the stones under her feet or the bags in her arms. Her skin turned cold and hot at the same time.

When she finally went inside, the girls were back in the playroom again, quick as that. But George lay on the sofa with his feet stretched out straight as if he were dead. He had his eyes half closed. Was he okay? Oh, yes. In a moment, he rolled on his side and smiled, like when he woke up beside her mornings.

"I daydreamed the house just rose up like a balloon and hung there!" she told him.

"I bet it did," he said.

XX

George looks across the Mayes lot to where the water tower once stood. He painted his initials on it when he lived at Uncle Emory's. Although the man raised him in the eyes of the law, there were only a couple of times when he and George seemed the least bit close—or not close, exactly, but on the verge of something deeper than the old man's routine inquiry about his preparations for school. They never got much past that verge, unless George simply failed to recognize that they had.

What were his uncle's hopes and dreams? Did anything ever make him cry? George has lived long enough to think that almost everybody's life is probably more complicated than it looks. Shouldn't he have acknowledged living more than comfortably under Emory's roof? What accounted for the old man's deliberate solitude? Did he never long for companionship? George feels a touch of remorse.

He tries to reassure himself. Hell, he was just a kid back then! As ever, though, reminiscence can rule him. He closes his eyes against the sun, and suddenly he's in the farm Jeep, not haul-assing around the snow with his friends behind him on a sled but cruising the property with his uncle. He wasn't often invited on these tours, and he felt slightly uneasy, as in truth he always felt in the old man's company. He'd long for Mary's kitchen then, with its smell of bread and cream and something roasting, odors magical in and of themselves.

A single-shot .22 Remington lay on the back seat. Uncle Emory would now and again slip in a bullet and let fly at a groundhog—what Evan would call a woodchuck. Uncle wasn't much of a shot. George remembers his hitting only a single animal, which did a little bunny hop before flopping on its back, and Emory driving right on, not even bothering to inspect.

Mid-April, the country all budded out. The fields were their earliest green, almost neon, and the Jeep kept spooking cottontails from the lanes between pasture fences. They'd scurry into the brush but if you looked back, you saw them bustle out again to feed on new clover.

For whatever reason, Uncle put the brakes on after they'd flushed one of the rabbits, then backed the Jeep up maybe thirty yards. They'd already moved plenty of bunnies. What was special about this one? Of course, it hopped back out like all the others. Uncle dropped a new round into the gun, then, nodding at the rabbit, he wordlessly passed it to George.

"You want me to . . . ?" George stammered. The old man didn't respond. His look meant there was no choice. And so, steadying the barrel on the windshield, George squeezed the trigger slowly, as Nine had taught him to do.

He'd never known rabbits made any noise at all, so it shocked him when this one flung itself upward and screamed. The cry was like a terrified woman's or child's, and it came from a place far enough beyond his experience that it actually frightened George. Thank God it only lasted a moment.

The two of them got out. Uncle Emory picked the rabbit up, its back legs still kicking, and handed it to George, who was amazed by its lightness and softness. A fat tick showed like a blister on one ear; fleas wriggled in the scut. A runnel of blood seeped its shoulder, and Uncle swirled a bony finger through it, then dabbed a spot on both of George's cheeks. Taken aback, he made to wipe the blood away, but his uncle grabbed him by the wrist, stern as a schoolmaster.

"Keep it until it wears off," he commanded. "It's called blooding. Something you do the first time." This was not in fact the first time he'd shot a living thing, but George didn't protest. When his guardian wanted words, you knew it.

George, Nine, and Patrick had often gone to the dump on Emory's farm to plink rats. Pat had a battered Marlin with a clip, which they'd load with .22 scattershot. The crimped cartridges frequently jammed the gun, but when they worked, they gave the shooters better odds. The boys would wait for a rustle in the debris, then flip on a six-battery flashlight.

The shot made a pretty feeble load, and the rats often squealed their way to cover when they were wounded. None of the boys considered the agonies of the animals. A clean kill was preferable, of course, because it indicated good marksmanship, but the rats' pain was not part of the consideration. Rats were evil. Everybody knew that.

George winces when he remembers those outings after dark. These were just fat country rodents, after all, not doing any harm, with a function as scavengers, in fact. When he thinks of one different shoot, after more than forty years he still literally shudders, but for other reasons.

The O'Mearas lived in an ell off their cow barn. They had smaller kids sleeping on couches, mattresses, cots, and so on. One night, when Big Mickey and Esther were off at some Knights of Columbus event open to wives too, and the other O'Meara kids somehow sworn to silence, the three friends stood below a vine-covered barn wall. Nine, always the keenest observer, had noticed rats climbing in the foliage, especially in spring, likely on the lookout for birds' eggs.

The leaves moved when the rats did, which made for easier hunting than at the dump. Everything was relatively close here, while at the dump the boys couldn't always be sure a rat had come within range. That night, they picked up each kill with a rag and dropped it into a burlap sack, hoping not to leave any evidence for Nine's parents. They didn't know what the adults would say about their sniping, though his dad had given Nine the gun in the first place.

Nine's mother Esther was gentle almost to the point of inconspicuous. His dad, on the other hand, was intimidating, muscular and bull necked. George and Pat called him Big Mickey, though he only stood about five foot six. It was hard for them to understand his west-Irish brogue. He rarely spoke, but if he disapproved of something, you'd be aware of it. Those neck muscles would undulate as he clenched and unclenched his jaw, and you knew never again to do whatever it happened to be.

George once spilled a glass of milk at the O'Mearas' kitchen table. Esther tried to put him at ease—"It's nothin' 't all"—but her husband turned back-to in his chair. George could see the neck muscles pumping. After that, George was careful to say he wasn't thirsty whenever he ate with the O'Mearas. Mickey's censure seemed so unfair: didn't at least one of those dozen children spill now and then? Today he suspects the man's brooding had something to do with class resentment. A lot goes by a child.

That night, the boys, having shot up almost all their cartridges, were ready to quit when a rat suddenly rustled near the soffit, as close to a long shot as the hunt provided. Nine had the rifle; George held the light. Once the gun fired, the three of them laughed with savage innocence to see the rat clutching a vine, like an outlaw giving up his last breath in an oater movie.

"Go on ahead, boys! I'm done fer!" Pat drawled.

When the rat let go, Patrick reached for its tail, but it suddenly dashed for cover—straight up the leg of his jeans. The boy looked to be grinning as he stood there motionless, head scrunched into his shoulders. He wasn't grinning. Nine and George stood by, horrified and helpless.

At what seemed insufferable length, the poor creature fell onto Patrick's sneaker, smearing it with blood. He dropped his trousers. By moonlight, the boys saw claw marks all the way to his crotch. Now a rat was filthy as sin; everyone knew that too. Pat ran into the O'Mearas' boiler room, found a bottle of turpentine, and poured it all over his leg. They never hunted wall rats again.

Later, after his outing with Emory, Mary wouldn't bat an eye when George showed up in her kitchen with blood on both cheeks. "I killed a rabbit, and Uncle did this," he panted. By now, the stains had turned a somber brown.

"Oh yes," Mary said, "I mind they did that over home." But she didn't stop him from washing the blood off at the sink; Uncle Emory was in his den, waiting out his supper time; he wouldn't notice a thing.

"And why didn't you bring it here?" Mary asked. "Rabbit's fit for a meal." George suddenly understood that he'd never even considered what had become of his puny trophy. Emory must have tossed it into the brush.

Next day, when he told his uncle good morning, the old man surprised him: "The .22's in my coat closet. Bullets on the shelf. Just be careful."

"Yes, sir," George replied.

And so began the slaughter so many country kids used to practice.

Not many hunt around Glassburg anymore, partly because game cover seems to vanish by the month. If the hold-outs do go afield for pheasant or cottontail these days, they're considered monsters by some, and it doesn't matter if the critics are meat-eaters. George scoffs. Do they think their food comes straight from the feed lot wrapped in plastic?

Take the hunter out of Evan Butcher, he thinks, and what's left? He feels a gust of despair, despite himself. What's left of him anyhow, hunt or no hunt? Well, maybe something after all. George tries to brace himself by clinging to that idea. There's a catch in his throat, and not only because of what's happened lately. The world he remembers is irre-coverable, and he worries he'll never catch up with the new one. He goes back inside. This daydreaming will be the end of his business if he doesn't watch out.

Well, perhaps not. He's been scolding himself about that for a long, long time, and Mayes Transportation's still here.

Not that George has blithely been calling back the clichéd good old days. There was plenty of ugliness he'd like to forget. Why would he ever shoot a sparrow, say, like the one he picked off a mulberry tree by Uncle Emory's house after the old boy left for work one morning?

What was work for Emory Unger anyway? George had never really considered his uncle's business as a kid. It was only some mysterious realm into which the head of the household disappeared every day. It wasn't like Big Mickey's work, say; you couldn't identify a finished job—a harrowed wheat field, say. Did Emory's work truly engross him, the way running a bus operation has come to engross George? What kept a paint company moving along? Somebody must have peddled the product to the stores. Of course, he couldn't imagine his uncle carrying an actual can, but if he thought about it at all, he couldn't come up with a clearer notion of the old man's livelihood.

Just as Emory drove off, the sparrow fluttered into the little tree and George killed it almost before it had found its perch. "Old Betsy's in the groove today," he whispered, fondly appraising the .22. He'd read the phrase in some *Outdoor Life* or *Field and Stream* at Kirchner's bar-bershop in Glassburg. He liked the words the minute he saw them, and vowed to use them one day. They still have a satisfying ring in his ears. What a shame to waste them on a puny sparrow, but they just flew out of George's throat.

He lifted the tiny creature and rested it on a palm. If the cotton-tail had felt light, the sparrow seemed almost an antiweight. George jammed his little finger under the bird's breastbone and ripped upward, exposing guts and bones. He squeezed and squeezed, till the sparrow practically dematerialized. He flicked off the minuscule remnants as if he'd been picking his nose, though his actions hadn't been casual. He still doesn't know what he expected to discover, but something. Not that he did.

Groundhogs were the big game, though. When one scampered into its burrow, George would slowly count backward from a hundred, then whistle. Sometimes the 'hog would poke its head up. Whenever he managed to get one, George lugged it home and telephoned Patrick or Nine or both. They'd all meet at Elmore's.

Elmore, a small black man who worked the Morris farm, savored wild things. He couldn't understand why people turned down ground-hog. "Whistle-pig's cleaner'n a real pig," he insisted. "Just clover is all he eats." He convinced George to try a stew once, serving it with corn-bread and greens in his swept yard. It was delicious, but George didn't even know how to dress a groundhog off, let alone cook one, and he couldn't imagine asking even the ever-tolerant Mary to undertake the task. So his rare trophies went to the sharecropper.

When George turned fourteen, Uncle Emory added a 16-gauge Sauer to his arsenal. That's when the crow hunting started, the three boys taking turns with the scattergun, not that they often had a chance for multiple shots. George still shakes his head to recall how excited they got over those mornings, however futile they usually proved. The crows were smart as buck deer, and the boys were lucky to get a peek at more than one. If they built their blind properly, a single bird might fly onto a near enough branch, but once you killed that one, the morning was over. Still, George and Pat and Nine would tremble those dawns as the ghostly outlines of trees began to emerge along the fence lines.

Elmore would also eat a crow, as long as it still had a froggy voice. That meant a young bird, he claimed, and if you gutted him quickly, he'd be passable. "Ain't no treat, now," he said, "but he'll eat."

The three friends mocked Elmore for his bumpkin habits and tastes. They called him a hick, but in fact they admired the old man. He just knew amazing things the boys would never have discovered on their own. He'd come north after World War II to one of the whitest neighborhoods imaginable; but a wave of southland blacks soon followed, getting work when Weymouth Asbestos established itself in Norris. Most of them settled in a tiny rural village of their own construction, but Elmore remained a loner in the tiny house he built behind his boss's barn.

George wonders about a lot of those folks even today. What about their lungs? He even wonders about his own, not that he ever worked a minute in the asbestos plant, but exactly at four each afternoon, the factory blew out its stacks somehow. Often the boys watched the fluff settle like thistledown on the pastures, then picked it up to make beards and moustaches.

George never knew Elmore's age. He had no family, at least none up north, and he seemed ancient. When Uncle Emory died, and, shortly after, his boss Mr. Morris died too, what happened? Where did people go? Where did their possessions go? Where was the lore they stored? There was simply and suddenly no more Elmore.

By the time he got to college, George felt certain the man was still at his labor somewhere, hoeing in the hot sun, cutting with an old-fashioned scythe, hanging things from his smokehouse. Elmore kept a pig every year. By Thanksgiving you'd look in through the door of his dark little home—he never seemed to close that door, not even in January, and he never doused his wood fire—and you'd see big hams strung to the roofbeam, along with other less identifiable slabs. Bantam hens scratched around his dirt yard, dropping tiny eggs in the gardens and bushes, and sometimes Elmore had a turkey in a wire pen.

Quiet, sad, friendly, small, strong, savvy, Elmore had never worked except with land and animals. The black plant workers all called him "Country," and true enough, he stayed as rustic as he'd been born.

Why had he come north from Georgia in the first place? George didn't think about that. He was just there, as if there'd be no landscape on Morris's farm without him, his livestock, the giant tomatoes and squashes he raised, and his plot of cow-corn, which he shared with the land's supposed owner. He must have sold the rest somewhere, maybe to Morris himself, maybe even to Uncle Emory. So much escaped him as a child, George thinks again.

And then he thinks, no, it didn't escape him. He just never looked for much. The world was the world. It still is, and he needs to get to work, for the love of God! But when he's in one of his reveries, he can only surrender. He doesn't necessarily like that, but it's how things are.

Sundays, Elmore put on a double-breasted suit with ancient lapels that pointed forward like a bull's horns, and made for the one-story, cinderblock church just past the graveyard. George sometimes sneaked out there, where a sound swelled from the building, bigger, it seemed, than could be contained there: wailed choruses, sorrowful and beautiful both, mixed with the preacher's words, half sung and half shouted, along with a great deal of handclapping. George knew to be awed. He swore he saw the church actually quiver with the passion inside.

Apart from the Sunday meeting, Elmore stayed mostly to himself, and most people left him that way. Once, though, some older kids pulled a nasty trick. Their ringleader wasn't really a kid at all: Ketchup, everyone called him, though his hair wasn't truly red like Nine's. He obviously relished being the commander of a troop of high-school boys. He wore one of those shiny dragon jackets, like a lot of the scary older guys, because he'd soldiered in Korea. He wasn't any smarter or better for his experience. He lived to torment people, especially black ones.

Ketchup and his goons caught Elmore in his outhouse one Hallowe'en. They turned the little building over on its door, so the only way out was through the seat-hole. Good thing he was lean. The whole thing was shitty. How could you avoid the word?

Word got out about the prank, and everyone knew who'd played it, but nobody chose to do anything about it. So George worked up all his courage, perhaps as much as he's mustered before or since, and told Ketchup he was a bully.

"Is that right, kid?" Ketchup shot back. "Let me show you what that looks like." He bent George's arm behind his back so far there was an audible snap. His shoulder ached for a week. He'll never forget Ketchup's smug smile. With his two symmetrically chipped front teeth, he looked like some predatory fish or reptile.

It was Elmore—who else?—who helped George and his friends improve their crow hunts. "A crow don't like a hawk and owl," he drawled. The boys already knew that, but the papier-mâché decoys they used never made much difference.

Then one day things changed abruptly. Nine and George were complaining to Elmore about their bad luck while he whetted a scythe in his yard. After he finished, he disappeared into his shack and stayed long enough that the boys figured he was in there for good. They got ready to leave, but then the old man came out, blowing dust off a stuffed great horned owl.

"That'll work," he told them. Nine's and Pat's eyes shone, and George's must have too. Elmore smiled.

The man was magic! That owl looked so big the boys wondered where he found any space to store it in his small home. But the friends didn't know half of it. The sharecropper put the bird down and emptied one copious front pocket of his overalls onto an outdoor table. He produced a skeleton key, a brick-hard square of chew, three wooden matches, a small metal cross, and last, amazingly, a small ball of twine, a length of which he ran through an eyelet on the owl's wooden stand, then up to another on the arch, made from a wire coat hanger, that yoked the dummy's neck. When Elmore drew gently on the string, the decoy leaned forward, raising its wings. When he let go, the bird settled back. The boys blinked in wonder. "Carry it along with you," Elmore said. "Just bring it back one day."

They carried it, all right. They could run a line from a fence post to their blind, then they'd pull when the first crow came close enough to notice. They left that bird alone to squall at their owl till the flock swarmed, strafing and shrieking. The hunters could shoot half a dozen times before the crows left. They even had time enough, incredibly, to pass the shotgun around.

Strange, the fun that all seemed. George wouldn't cross the street to shoot a crow today, in fact would cross the other way not to bother one. Things were different then, not least because, after a hunt, their breakfasts tasted beyond delicious. The boys made a stone hearth, lit a fire to frazzle up their strips of bacon, and settled a can of beans next to the flame. They ate from tin plates with their fingers. Very heaven, no matter the blood linked to it.

As he idles in his office, George's right hand clenches. He once reached down to replace one of the fireplace stones that had rolled aside. He'd been distracted somehow, and forgot that of course the stone would be nearly as hot as the fire itself. When he gripped it, meaning to put it back into place, the pads of thumb and forefinger blistered instantly. Mary later wrapped them in gauze and some nameless gel she fetched from her room. George wishes he'd asked her what it was. The woman was magic too.

But getting hurt was a rarity, which seems a miracle: three rowdy, unsupervised boys with guns, shooting at whatever twitched. And George could so easily have died on his own. Every May, he'd ease open the door to his uncle's springhouse and fire at one of the big snapping turtles that always set up there through the warmer months. Once, his bullet zinged off a stone, ricocheted around the little building, and lodged in the sill on which he stood. But he kept at it even after that until at last he managed to plug one turtle in the neck.

"That ends that old pirate's career," he said aloud. He'd picked that up from a magazine too, something by Robert Ruark, he believes. But he'd saved the good words this time, maybe for as much as two years, to use on a trophy worthy of the rhetoric. The ridges on the snapper's long tail were sharp and ugly; its beak could have snapped a sapling; its shell was wide as a bathmat.

George hauled his ponderous trophy out and laid it on the lawn. He went in for lunch, and when he came back an hour later, its legs were still churning. A snapper clearly took a lot of killing. The whole thing gave him butterflies. He stood off a few feet and plugged the poor turtle's head again; then he lugged it deep into the woods and rolled it under a blowdown.

When Elmore heard about this episode a week or so later, he huffed. "That old boy'd give you the best soup you ever had," he lamented.

Once he got away to college, George didn't have anything to do with shooting until after graduation and his fateful trip to Woodstown, where the gun was simply a way of life. Evan had a good Llewelyn setter named Dale. He and George followed her after grouse and woodcock. Evan put George on deer stands as well. The two of them listened to Sorryface Jr. harry the snowshoe hare after first snow. They huddled together in duck blinds every fall. But his inheritance from Mary was dwindling. He was drinking much of it away. He needed a job.

George is a nonhunter these days, not that he wouldn't love to go on one of those outings again. Autumn's his busiest time, though, kids back in school, kinks being worked out of his bus routes, and his own girls are a presence he never imagined thirty years ago in Maine. His visits are achingly brief, and they're restricted to summers.

Evan would be too lame and too drunk to get into the woods or out on the lakes with him anyhow. The old adventures are gone, except from George's mind. And he has to be honest and recall that they weren't all wonderful—not by a damned sight, especially compared to what he has now.

It's a wonder he didn't kill himself in Woodstown, either, or worse, someone else. He doesn't think Evan knew it, but George often had a charge of liquor in him when he carried a weapon. He shot his share of game, but that was mostly because Evan would put him where he needed to be—on a likely deer stand, say, and even there he'd often drift in and out of boozy sleep. But about every other year he'd be awake enough to spot a whitetail wandering into a gap in the evergreen.

He particularly recalls one he shot in '63. The buck—over two hundred pounds, his rack as broad as a plow blade—fell on the near shore of Evers Lake. He came in nose to ground, following a tiny doe, who kept looking over her shoulder as if she were scared to death. Maybe she was. The buck had nine points, the odd tine drooped over its brow like a caribou's.

Evan looked oddly mournful as they dressed him. "You don't get a buck like that but once in your life," he murmured. George didn't comment, no matter he knew Evan had taken a lot more than one of at least equal grandeur in his time.

They hefted the carcass into Evan's freight canoe and paddled to a beach on Evers Lake to eat their lunch, jerky, and coffee and half a loaf of Mattie's anadama. The food was as good as the beans and bacon after those boyhood crow hunts. As they ate by their fire, snowflakes drifted down and settled on the deer's cape, but George felt as warm as if he were in bed. He and Evan took sips from a pint of Benedictine. Where in hell had *that* come from? Did Evan bring it, or George? It was just enough to get them toasty, not unsteady on the way out of the woods. One would drag the buck for a spell, then the other. By the time they lugged it to Evan's truck, they were cold sober and bed-ready tired.

George knows not to get too elegiac. Booze is patient. If you start romancing it, it's ready for you. He needs to recall his private celebration, for instance, after they'd hung the kill by his camp and Evan had gone home. Was it one or two fifths of vodka he drank up? The bottle has Evan on the brink of destruction now. It's already delivered more than one death to people they both know.

George walks out into the yard again, as if with a purpose this time, but that's only for show. Standing in bright sunlight, he suddenly thinks of one late September when he and Evan spent a night at the Semnic lean-to. Early next morning, despite a bit of a drizzle, Evan prodded him to produce some cream of tartar biscuits in their reflector oven. "See what we ate four meals a day on the drive," he said.

"I have, a hundred times," George answered. "Baked by you."

"You'd ought to know how."

Evan's biscuits practically lifted off the plate. Why not stick with them? But his mentor was adamant. He gave George a rudimentary set of verbal instructions, the went back under shelter to snooze—or pretend to. When George's biscuits were done, they were somehow hard as granite.

"Couldn't break 'em with a hammer," Evan chuckled, dropping them into a small gunny sack he pulled out of his basket.

Soon they saw a canoe emerge from the mist. It was Joe Mell, the one who'd made Evan's precious paddle. At well over six feet, Joe cut an imposing figure, and even at eighty he held his shoulders square as a young man would. His teeth still gleamed, and his hair was the color of iron filings.

Evan helped him pull his canoe up, meanwhile secretly slipping the stony biscuits under his stern seat. "What you doing out here this fine miserable day?" he asked Joe.

"Perch," Joe answered. Like most of the Passamaquoddy, he was sparing of words, and Evan followed suit. Joe showed a bucket with ten good fish in it; you caught bigger perch in the fall.

"Staying all night or going back?"

"Back."

"Seen any game?"

"Young cow. Horseshoe Cove."

So on.

Thirty minutes, and about the same number of words later, Joe rose and strode to his canoe, launching it before George or Evan could help. He back-paddled clear of the shoreline rocks, and then called out: "Evan! What you want me to do with breads?"

"Just get them the hell out of here!" Evan shouted, tickled.

The Indian smiled, swung his bow toward the carry, and sculled away. He left the biscuits where Evan had stashed them, at least until he was out of sight.

That was the last either of them saw of Joe Mell. Later that fall, he took to the woods for game to get his extended family through winter. No one ever found him.

Evan said, "That was Joe. Went somehow's made sense to him."

There's no order to these recollections. Rats, rabbits, crow and deer hunts, Uncle Emory, a dead turtle kicking for life, Patrick and Nine and Joe Mell and Elmore and Ketchup and biscuits and beans and burned fingers. And now Freeze-to-Death Island and a morning in '64. He and Evan had good luck with the black ducks that day. The birds just seemed to dive into their decoys. They limited out by eight, but they stayed on in their blind, just to see what else might show.

Suddenly Evan softly nudged him with an elbow, rolling his eyes northward. Two Canada geese were almost upon them, wings set. Why so quiet? Evan and George wondered afterward. In those times, on the rare occasions when anyone saw geese in that part of the world, they'd be honking with every wingbeat. This pair came in silent as death, back-stroking to land among the blocks, and even then they only gabbled once or twice.

Neither hunter raised his shotgun. It just didn't seem a thing to do. Instead, they quietly watched the geese coast around, calm as barnyard ducks.

"Could've hit them with a slingshot," Evan joked later.

"A badminton racket," George answered.

Five minutes or so passed before the men stood up together, as if on cue. The geese made racket enough flushing and squawking then, turning into specks over Porcupine Mountain and dropping behind it.

It seemed appropriate to celebrate, but celebrate what? Well, something. Not just a good shoot. They couldn't say what they felt, just that they felt it. So after Evan got a fire going, he began to clog on the island's granite apron, bellowing "Old Joe Clark" while George plucked and gutted ducks for lunch.

I don't want your old time religion or what you got to say
But pass me down that barley jug and I'll be on my way.

Kate and Mary sing that verse now and then, having heard it from their father. Whenever they do, George sees Evan high-stepping and tastes the ducks they ate with their fingers, sipping campfire coffee laced with bourbon. Another precious memory to guard against.

There are many good ones, though, having nothing to do with drink. In George's first sober summer, for instance, they took a canoe run from halfway down the Percy, all the way to the coast. Ben Patcher had agreed to meet them and haul them back from Doranville. At one point they slid into the mouth of a small stream and stepped out onto a gravel bar with a huge trunk lying on it. "We hossed on that one half a day," Evan mused. The log was almost four feet through, worth more than a penny or two.

"We even chained her to the bateau, and four rugged men just pulling till one of them oars broke in two, by the Jesus, and all that water in the river pulling right along with them." His eyes went wide at memory. "It was me and Joe chopped her," he whispered.

Back in his office, George thinks: So Joe Mell's the thread! He recalls how Evan said, "He kept you hopping at the other end of a crosscut saw, I can testify!" As he spoke, he looked, as if questioningly, deep into the second growth onshore.

George is someone remembering someone remembering. That's a motif in his life. It might well go on infinitely, unbroken, George telling stories about people telling stories about people telling stories. It would surely seem a curious process to others. His wife. His daughters. Yes, especially his daughters, sad to say.

It's sad, too, that some of those stories are lies. No, not sad. Vile.

XXI

If Mommy and Pop could see me, Melody thinks.

It's a long way from Pennsylvania to California, all right. Peta-luma, where the palm trees grow la la la. They wouldn't know what to make of it, God rest their souls. They were as sweet as you please. She feels a little twitch in her eye and tells herself, out loud, "Oh stop it!" But what can she do? She was always tender-hearted, that's all.

Not much to cry about, come to that. It's sad her parents have gone, but then they did all right and each one of them was taken quick, praise the Lord. She hopes she doesn't ever sit around in some home, like a lot of old folks do. Or wander up and down the streets in goofy outfits, either. The men that can't seem to hitch their trousers high enough to suit them; their wives with their hair dyed up to try and look seventeen; all of them grumpy about the government, high prices, children today and their bad manners, and on and on.

She specially prefers not to see some old gal in her Bermuda shorts, or whatever. Not that she has the figure she did herself when she mar-ried that lousy George Mayes. But Harold doesn't care. He isn't exactly what you'd call Charles Atlas himself. But he's a good man. Not a day goes by she doesn't feel thankful for him. What a relief after George! The creep. The drunk. At a party, the most you'll see Hal with is a wine cooler. Otherwise, it's one beer when they're watching TV, and he usu-ally doesn't even finish that.

George never drank one of anything. It'd be a wonder if he's still alive, and sad to say, she doesn't really care. This is the life for her. She never wanted to be anything but a mom, and Harold sold enough insurance, it's all she needed to be. Okay, they don't live like a king and queen; they also don't worry about the next meal, or car, or house or if one of them is shacked up in some motel. If George is kicking, he's probably doing just that or trying to. Same old George.

When they were small, Little Hal, Ricky, and Stella were always dressed as good as anyone in school. It seems like just yesterday when she bought the cutest jumper, all covered with baby lambs, for Stell, and suits like little men's for the boys. Those kids didn't have a thing to be ashamed of. What if she'd gotten pregnant with George? Thank God she didn't.

Out west she stayed home the whole time. Her best girlfriend Darlene is after her to come work for her at the travel agency. The nest has been empty a long time, Darl says. And she says they can train you in no time, and it doesn't matter Melody's fifty-something and hardly went anywhere in her life and would still probably be back in Glassburg if she didn't meet Hal. He was related to someone who threw a party someone talked her into going to. She didn't want to. Good thing she did, though. Hal was doing army training over in Indiantown Gap. His family came from some little town near Scranton. He didn't move out here till after he got through with the service.

They kept in touch all the while he was in Germany, which is where they sent him for some reason. She teased him in her letters: was he getting friendly with the froe-leins? She made like it was a joke. He claimed he was just living for the day he got back and could be with her, and now she certainly believes him. Clean as soap the whole time, she'd bet on it. He's different that way, not like most men, even ones that put on that innocent look.

Funny how she and Harold only dated three or four times before he left, and always in a group of people. But then they're this couple all of a sudden. So how'd that happen? Seemed like their friends were the ones who made it work out, almost like people's parents in foreign places where they set up a marriage for you. Anyways, she and Hal bought right into being steadies before they knew it, and her girlfriends even gave her naughty nighties and such for when he got home, even though the most they ever did before he went away was kiss, and not all that romantic about the matter at that. More like a peck or two, same as with your dad or something.

Yeah, funny how life turns out, and you just go along. When she thinks back, it's almost like she didn't have any choice when she married George either. Golly, she was so young! He just sucked her in, and

Mommy and Pop couldn't say boo about it, even if they did. "What are you getting yourself into?" She couldn't count how many times they said that back in '65 or '66. When was it? Yes, '66 was their wedding. And her just excited by the idea of marrying this guy from some hoity-toity college.

She should have figured George amounted to beans. A man with that education who was a bus driver with a bee in his bonnet about someday living in this backwoods part of Maine, which she never saw. Thank God for that too. He went there sometimes, drop of a hat, mostly to see his hero, he claimed, name of Evan. Bet he was a doozy. The man didn't even write to George, because he couldn't write very well at all, George told her. So why the big hero? You can't figure some things out.

Like no one can figure out George, unless he's a whole lot different now, and she doubts that. Melody doesn't think he understood himself, even. Get one drop of alcohol in him and it's off to the races, didn't care what he did. She had half a mind to tell the school board how he was when he drove. Maybe that'd change him. Just to think of her own three riding a bus when they were little with someone like George driving scares her to death.

"Wonder if he had girls up in the woods too?" Melody suddenly asks out loud. "Probably."

Hal Jr.—now he's going to be something. She's sure of it. Everyone calls him Skippy, even her and Harold. It was Skipper first, because kids in his grade thought he was the one who'd command a ship if they were on one. It was some play their class did for the school assembly, no parents invited. He got the captain's part because his friends voted him for it.

Harold the son, like Harold the father. They named him right. Her husband came from nothing. His dad worked in the can factory over near Wilkes-Barre, but Hal went to college down in Philadelphia. He had a license to sell insurance policies right after, and he went right to a job at the big company he worked at summers since his first year there at Drexel. Pretty soon he got the offer to come out here, and they took it. Better weather, and a very nice home. If Skippy makes the same kind of jump in life as his dad, well, sky's the limit, as they say. He's doing very good at his computer job, which she doesn't know a thing about. She doesn't think her husband does, either, but he doesn't let on.

Men!

Matter of fact, sometimes she wishes Skippy was a little less ambitious, less all work and no play. He doesn't seem to have much time for friends, not to mention the girls. He never had a steady, went stag to the school dances if he went at all, never danced at them, that sort of behavior. Maybe he's like his daddy in this way too. She believed Harold when he said he never had a fling overseas or anyplace else because he's not much for that, or not very often. Not like George, for sure. She whispers, "Just as well."

Drunk or sober, George was after her all the time at first, even when they were screaming at each other. He went after lots of other women too, darn him, and once, when she called him on that, guess what he said? "A stiff penis has no conscience." To his own wife! The mouth on him! He didn't care if she caught him or not. It was his life, he told her, and never mind he was supposed to be married. You couldn't make him change.

Maybe you could say about Harold, "a conscience has no stiff . . ." She bites her tongue, embarrassed, even though there's not a soul in the house beside her and their little poodle. Nikki doesn't miss much, Melody thinks, but she can't tattle.

"Come here, honey," she calls, and her poodle hops right up in her lap. Nothing but love, and small as she is, she'd tear up anyone who wanted to harm her, or else make them deaf just yapping. "That's a good girl!" she says, as if she were talking to Stellie a long time back, when she was just the cutest little thing, clomping around the house in Mommy's shoes and with her big beach bag like a regular grown-up, pretending they were at the beach. What was it she called the seashore? Oh yeah: wee-oh.

"Stop it," she tells herself again. Her tender heart again. But yes, time flies, all right!

No need to be gushy, though. If Harold isn't Romeo, she'll take the trade. Oh, it seemed okay when she and George were just dating, even if he was a regular wild Indian right from the get-go. Matter of fact, she kind of liked that about him till she figured out what it meant if you were his wife.

The best times were in summer when they went out to Riverside Ball Room, which was really just a big tent like the circus with a dance floor. George brought her corsages and got all dressed up, and she could wear her black dress with the little cut up just over her knee and there'd be some big band, and the players all guys that seemed her parents' age but never mind, and they danced old-fashioned steps till the wee hours. Fox Trot. Jitterbug. It was fun, she'll admit it. He even taught her to waltz.

There were plants in huge pots by every tent pole and waiters in tuxedos bringing you drinks, and these pretty chandeliers hung all around the tent. One o'clock came, and they wheeled out all kinds of little sandwiches and pastries. It was so romantic, and George didn't seem to have his roaming eyes those nights.

When they were out there, George didn't get as drunk, either, and she'll admit it too that she loved leaning on his shoulder in his little Volkswagen when they drove home. Sometimes it was full moon and the stars were out and all the countryside looked so beautiful. You could see deer in the fields, right in with the horses or cows, and the river sparkled like a necklace.

That ballroom was where she met George in the first place, when she went there with a bunch of her girls. She truly believed she was the lucky one that night, giving her phone to a fine-looking man, and smart. He even spoke French, he told her.

On other dates, she liked what happened when they went to his place too. Not that first night, of course, and not for lots and lots of other nights after. She didn't just give herself away like some do. Fact is, she never did spend a whole night at George's. Mommy and Pop wouldn't have been too thrilled to wake up and find her bed empty in the morning. Bad enough coming in late as she did sometimes. They gave her the business over that. Looks like they knew something she didn't after all. Why wouldn't she listen? She was a kid, that's why, and she really believed it was love. Melody doesn't miss any of it, not one bit.

You can have the romantic stuff. Yes, she'll take the trade-off on that one and she hopes their Stellie never goes through what she did. Let her wait for the right man, because she certainly did not, even if there was a good time or two. Stellie does seem to be waiting, all right. Her mother tries not to worry about that. Stellie's twenty-nine now.

Nikki starts yapping. Hal's home? Wow. She doesn't know how it got so late, just sitting there on the divan and imagining all kinds of silly stuff. But wait—the clock says it's only four. Well, her husband's his own man out here, by golly. He can come home when he likes. He'll be retired before you know it.

But she does wonder why he's early. They don't have any plans.

XXII

The hardest part was that he didn't have anyone to tell beside Nine and Pat, and he wasn't even sure they believed him. Well, probably most people wouldn't, unless they'd had the same experience. They'd think it couldn't be as bad as George claimed.

And what could his friends do anyhow? Or even Mary, his rock? Complaining would just upset her, maybe less for hearing about Mr. Calhoun's abuse than for having to reckon with her own powerlessness. Of course he wouldn't dream of talking about his terror to Uncle Emory.

If only his fourth-grade teacher would ignore him, go off and blow his darling trumpet for a living. How could anyone so goddamn mean sound so sweet on an instrument? To hear it, you'd almost forget who was playing.

Last night was another one of those when George couldn't sleep. There seemed reason enough for that. The incredible peace he felt when he arrived home just before supper was partly founded on hope. But in the night, hope gave way to anxiety, which became desperation. Does he think he can somehow change the world by force of desperate will? That's an old snare.

Everything's catching up with him, his head going wherever it wants. At four this morning, he came out to sit in the kitchen. The summer was getting old, and it would be a while before the creamy light of a mid-Atlantic August dawn showed up. There was some little creature making the bird feeder sway, trying to get at the thistle seed. Not a bird. Too dark.

Soon the flickers will be darting in the roadbeds, flashing their white tail-spots, getting ready to go. Yellow-hammers, Evan calls them. In an ordinary flicker time, George likes to hike if he's insomniac. Late summer dawns in the hardwood stands are still a splendor, even without children on his back.

A dream woke him up at four, one in which he was somehow both guilty of something and wronged. He can't recall a single detail, but it brought on a too familiar tautness in his face and gut, which remains these hours later. It's the kitchen radio's sappy Al Hirt trumpet number, "Here In My Heart," that brings back his unspeakable homeroom and music teacher.

The only good part of a day was when Calhoun broke out his own horn and played, as he sometimes did just before morning recess. When he sat on his desk and improvised, he seemed not just incredibly gifted, but human. Even his face looked different—dreamy. When he was running band practice, however, he acted the same as in his classroom. Pure hell, at least for George, the damnedest of the damned. No matter how hard he tried with his clarinet, he just didn't have a gift himself. But Calhoun interpreted his squawks and mistiming as mischief.

George strove for good behavior in every way he knew how that year, because he actually believed his life might depend on it; yet no matter how industrious and attentive he tried to be, Calhoun somehow had it in for him, no matter he'd lost his parents in a brutal way that very year.

There were as many shenanigans in George's head as there were in the next fourth grader's, but he wasn't trying anything like that crazy Benny Dinizio, always bent on trouble. Calhoun let Dinizio do almost anything he liked, though. When he made his blowgun, say, the teacher never sent him to the principal, let alone slapped him silly. He just confiscated Benny's weapon. One of them.

Benny would take the erasers off a bunch of pencils, push pins through the rubbers till the sharp ends poked out, and then blow an eraser at you through a pea shooter. It hurt like a bee sting, but once, when George took one in the neck and ran over to tear the little bastard's head off, Calhoun grabbed him by an ear and hauled him back to his desk. Then he swatted him across the back of his head for good measure.

"Dinizio," he said. "See me after class." He didn't even turn around to look at Benny. George did, and Benny just smiled that crooked smile he'd probably copied from some older boy. You could tell he wasn't afraid for his life. George saw odd shapes for minutes on end and his ears rang till late afternoon. What would be next?

He also summons the autumn morning when the boys were sent to the gym, two by two, for their football uniforms. There was a ninety-pound team at Glassburg. The kids would play actual games against other regional schools. They couldn't wait! George was paired with Artie Newsome, his best chum in the class. They fairly flew downstairs, across the courtyard and into the little gym, with its mixed reeks of sweat, the janitor's cologne and tobacco, and the rotted canvas of an overhead track.

George loved the place, even those weird odors. Athletics were fun, after all, even gym class, conducted by Mr. Denner, deafened by bomb blast in the war, nervous but still easygoing. George and his pals would hum during calisthenics, then watch the poor man fiddle with the hearing aid box in his shirt pocket, pacing front to back, uncertain he'd heard anything. What fool ever imagined that kids are naturally kind?

Calhoun was waiting at the top of the stairs when Artie and George returned. The boys had put on their leather shoulder pads, just to see how they felt. They meant to take them off, of course, before going back into the classroom. Only Artie got the chance. Calhoun grabbed George's pads and ripped them off, scraping his ears as he did. Why was it always ears? They stayed red right through recess, not that George was allowed out to play that day or the rest of that week.

Calhoun once assigned writing a story for homework, another degrading memory. Looking for comic effect, George conceived a roguish mouse named Mortie for his main character. He still remembers how he began:

> Attention, boys and girls. You there in the front row, duck down so Aunt Mabel can see. Uncle Mo too.
>
> Once upon a time in a huge old castle, and blah blah, never mind, there lived a very smart mouse named Mortie . . .

There were parts not only for Mortie, but also for a bunch of other mice, and for one big, not very bright villain, Roscoe Rat. George thought that had a ring to it.

Calhoun stood up, first thing next morning, and said, "I want you all to hear what someone thinks is a good joke on their teacher." Then he began to read in a silly whine, way up in his nose. When he got to "blah blah, never mind," he read it *blake blake*, even though George's handwriting was the best in the class according to Calhoun. That was the only half-compliment the bully ever paid him.

"But . . . ," George began.

"Shut up! Enough of your smart stuff!" Calhoun's face was tomato-red. It was so unfair. And that was only one of the countless mortifications he suffered.

George rises from his chair and paces to the counter for another splash of coffee. He can feel his pulse in his cheekbones, remembering how he worked past nine o'clock to make his tale amusing. He was sure he'd have gotten plenty of laughs from the other kids if their teacher hadn't ridiculed him.

The humiliation actually hurt George more than the beatings—he balls his fists more than fifty years later—and that wasn't the last time he'd be shamed, either. Not that the physical abuse wasn't awful. If anyone, anyone, ever laid a hand on Mary or Kate . . . George tenses in the half-dark.

Why is it such a struggle to let all this go? He should just toss that old cruelty into the trash. But no, the violence isn't what chiefly sticks in his craw this morning anyhow. That business with his mouse play was bad enough, but there'd be far worse come spring.

Some schoolmates were playing pick-up baseball one April afternoon. There weren't enough players to fill every position, so they'd close down the right side of the imaginary diamond for lefties, the other way for righties. Pieces of clothing or book bags were bases. Over the fence was out.

At some point, Monty Church tried to make it from second to third on a grounder. Artie threw from short in plenty of time for George to tag Monty, who couldn't run. He was a big, slow, friendly guy. Everybody liked him. But for some reason, that day he launched into a tantrum. You couldn't explain it. Monty Church didn't do that. "I beat the throw!" he yelled.

"You're out!" George shouted back.

"Am not!"

"Are too!"

"You're lying!"

"You are!"

And so on and on, just regular schoolyard blather.

Unaccountably, or so he thought, a number of others started siding against George. Outnumbered and frustrated, he shoved Monty, whose outsized feet got tangled in the third base sweater. He fell backward, bouncing hard on his backside. When he tried to sit up, his neck lolled like a baby's.

Artie's family lived right next to the ball field, and he took for home on the fly. Everybody knew something had gone wrong. Mrs. Newsome was a nurse, and when she got to the field, she warned Monty to lie still. "Don't anyone panic," she warned. Then she went back to call an ambulance.

George felt nothing but panic to look at poor Monty, whose face showed a rictus of fear, tears dripping till they puddled by his head where he lay.

No one muttered a word.

George feels a kink in own neck as he stands again. Two robins are hopping back and forth on his lawn now, and a pair of goldfinches squabble at the feeder. When Monty fell, George didn't yet have the escape into drink he'd use so hard later on. He just stood there and took it. He's known far worse emotional ordeals, but that one crushed him at ten.

The emergency squad carefully slid Monty onto a stretcher, and then the ambulance raced off, lights flaring, sirens screaming. George saw Monty's eyes as he was being loaded, nothing but white. He tried to believe it was just the angle, but he couldn't. This was curtains. He turned from watching the ambulance go. All his classmates had vanished. A single crow was hopping around near third base, but the marker jacket was gone too.

He walked the back fields from the bus to his uncle's as slowly as possible, imagining his future. He had none. You break your neck, you die; everybody knew that. George was a murderer, and murderers got the electric chair; everybody knew that too. Which was worse, that he'd killed a classmate or that he'd be executed? What difference did it make? His life was over.

When at last he trudged through the kitchen door, Mary smiled brightly. Ham and beans for supper, George's favorite. He usually loved to sop up the juice and grease with slices of Wonder Bread. But tonight, he just sat and watched the old woman bustle around, humming odd snatches of songs: Sonny, Come Home, A Galway Lad, so on. It almost drove him crazy. You couldn't blame her, of course. Good cheer was her nature.

At last, when he wouldn't speak, let alone eat, Mary fixed George with those eyes, so pale they were almost as white as Monty's. "What's the real trouble?" she asked.

The whole affair came out in a spate of words and tears that George couldn't check. Mary stopped him every few minutes, made him go back, clear up details. "There now, Georgie," she kept saying. As usual, he could smell her rosewater. "It'll be all right. Just watch if it won't." She was wrong, but he let her hold him. What else could he do?

He now knows how much courage it took for Mary, an unregarded, common servant, to telephone Monty's mother, the closest thing Glassburg had to a socialite. George's heart fills to remember her bravery.

Mrs. Church reported that Monty might miss the next day of school. A vertebra had been slightly dislocated, and he'd probably wear an Elizabethan collar for a short spell. His neck was a bit sore, but otherwise he was fine. He was doing his homework. Did George want to speak with him?

George shook his head violently.

The night still proved dreadful. Having seen those ashen eyes, he couldn't quite believe his friend was healthy. Some of George's school friends claimed Monty's mother Frances was a heavy drinker. What if she'd misunderstood the doctors? What if she found her son stone cold in his bed next morning? No one knew of a Mr. Church.

This wouldn't be the last time George fancied high drama as his fate. From early on, he's been inclined to embellish his own importance, to imagine himself colorfully wronged, and thus deeply tragic. Even sober, he can be inane in that way, can still cling to the performing arts.

He walked into Mr. Calhoun's classroom like a condemned man next morning but brightened to see Monty at his desk. He did have a funny collar around his neck, but he was very much alive!

George's peace was brief. Calhoun pointed at him, dawdling in the doorway. "Well, lookee here," he chirped. "It's our man-killer."

Whenever he thinks of this even these years later, George still feels like hunting Calhoun down in his retirement home or wherever the skunk lies up, reminding him of that moment. He'd like to dislocate *his* neck. That old siren, righteous indignation.

George knew the cliché about crawling into a hole, but he'd never known how dead-on it was. He wanted to hunker in one of his crow blinds, or to be a newt, a rat, a bug, a polliwog, a blue jay—anything but what he was, and where. He dealt badly with shame as a child. He still does.

Twelve years later, George ran into his old ogre. Calhoun had long since left the Glassburg school system, but even in his time there, no one ever saw him in town. It was as if he were always in the home room or the music room, his grottoes. It didn't take George long to recognize him at Simmy's Bar, prattling with the owner about the Eagles or Phillies or whatever. Man talk. George was struck by how small he looked in his late forties, just a pie-faced Joe in a cardigan, dated horn-rimmed glasses, his fedora with its limp red feather sitting on the bar in front of him. His hair was almost gone.

There's a wash of red light on the Mayeses' kitchen wall; the sun's just breaking through. George has all he could possibly hope for now. Yes, he ought to chuck this old business into the trash. He tries to breathe deeply and evenly, to let the soft sunshine filter through closed lids. But Calhoun's face lingers. This child-beating monster had been the biggest creature in the universe of a ten-year-old orphan. Now here he stood in a rinky-dink tavern, a doughy burgher, average size, doughy as a baby.

George was a grown man by 1965, of course, and he already had a little vodka in him, though he wasn't really drunk yet. A good thing too. He ambled over to the two other men. There was no one else in the room. Calhoun looked up, a smile still on his face from some remark about a team's misfortunes or some other trivial thing.

Hah hah hah.

Blah blah.

Blake blake.

"You remember me?" George asked, stony.

"No," said Calhoun, his smile melting.

"George Mayes?"

Calhoun looked like a small, cornered animal, and not a combative one.

"Can't say I do," he lied.

"Fourth grade, Glassburg Elementary?"

"Mayes, Mayes, Mayes . . . ," Calhoun said, as if musing.

"Don't give me a line of shit."

"What can I pour you, George?" Simmy broke in. He feared what might be brewing.

"No shit, okay?"

Calhoun forced another smile. "If I knew you'd get so big," he said, "I wouldn't've hit you so hard." He made to lay a palm on George's shoulder. George slapped the hand away and glowered. By now his old teacher had given up pretending he wasn't scared sideways.

What George did next was one of the damnably few things from those years that still seem well advised. One or two more drinks, and he wouldn't have managed it. He contemplated caving this vicious son of a bitch's head in. Instead, he just stood there looming over his old tormentor for a long, long moment. At length, Calhoun laid a fiver on the bar and scurried out the door.

All these decades later, his family asleep in upper rooms, sweet as angels, George wrestles with a brutal part of himself that lives on, that still wishes he'd taken the violent option. But he did the right thing. Besides, who could say what that miserable Calhoun's story was? Why did he single George out for abuse? That will have to stay a mystery. Yes, he needs to let it go.

XXIII

"I was tending beaver traps out to Tallow Stream. Camp there belonged to a man with the last name of Peep. Silly-sounding, sure. He was named Forest, but the whole town called him Lank, on account of being so long and tall. He was a good man, you know. Let me use that place, and me only seventeen years old. Think of it!"

George remembers Evan's tale almost word for word, no matter he heard it one time only. Evan wasn't old when he told it, so it's been years. George knows very clearly how it goes, because, for unaccountable reasons, it had a lasting hold on him from the start. It's among a handful of unnerving memories he'll never purge: humiliation at the hands of a savage teacher; the shocking deaths; Evan at Tallow Stream.

It's been an age since he gave up talking about the Tallow Stream affair himself, so that should be that. It's not. To his unending shame, cups he told the story over and over to crowds of nameless people, most of them drunk like him. He repeated it so often and with such different specifics that, in his cups, he half-believed it was his, not Evan's.

The tale's still full of anxieties and fascinations, like several other recollections that started well before dawn today. This one waited to assail him as he drove to work along the river. Perhaps it was the current that put him in mind of that stream, and of Evan beside it, old river-driver out on the water, riding the water, on the water's shore, his very language water.

George passed a blue heron standing absolutely still in the flow that rippled around its legs as though they were reeds or sticks. Evan called those birds shy-pokes. Suddenly a horn blared. George pulled the truck back into his own lane, heart thumping in his chest.

At the beginning of any story, Evan always follows a ritual, or he did in happier days. He crosses his legs, pushes his Effanem hat back, and leans forward. George has seen it a hundred times. He aped it a hundred more.

Evan's delivery is ritual too. He starts adagio, as if warming himself up. "Come along the end of February, it thawed a week." So he began on that day almost three decades back. "I like the smell of it, don't you? The woods all wet, and it gets right up in the air."

Then a long, long pin-drop pause in the little shop. "Heavy going on snowshoes, just slush," Evan went on. "Even snapped the bindings on one. So there I'm standing, fussing with it, you know. Trying to tie some sort of a knot to get me in."

Another pause. Evan lit his pipe. George once rehearsed and performed all these words and gestures, complete with the pipe.

"I hear a howl down in the swamp east of the brook. Someone's chasing rabbits, I suppose, though it's poor conditions for that too. Then a shot."

"Now they wasn't any knew it, but I had a woman staying to Lank's." George remembers how Evan stared out the window at this point. "If you seen how she looked, you wouldn't throw no bouquets, yet she was a fine person, I'll tell you. Mat and I wasn't married, nowheres near. Me with this older lady at seventeen years of age. Didn't I think I was something grand!"

Evan chuckled, a bit ruefully. It was almost as if he'd finished talking, but in time he went on: "She must've been thirty or such, but she didn't have no more teeth than her grandpa, which is gone to glory many years, I'd judge. He was a fine person too. Meddy is what they called him. Not too many got to a dentist in those times, especially ones in the tribe. Lord, though, she was put together nice . . ."

As he complimented the old lover, his face took on its distant look again. He'd probably never said a word about all this to Mattie. Why would he? She's had enough to deal with in her time. Even her husband knows that no matter his condition for half a decade. Poor damned Butchers, every one.

George couldn't shut Evan's voice off. "I'll admit I give her a little money when I sold them beaver blankets, but she weren't anything like some prostitute. I wanted someone to housekeep and visit and so I paid her, that's all. You get played out from running a big line like I done, even when you're young and rugged. I wasn't married, like I told you.

I knew Mattie, sure, but she was smart enough to stay in school after I got done. You didn't catch much sight of that one!

"So, Lena and I shacked up, as you'd say," Evan blurted. "And we done all right one March. No harm, was they?" Evan seemed to need reassurance, and George gave it in good enough conscience by shaking his head. George had never seen Evan blush before, and couldn't be sure that's what he was seeing now.

"Lena's the name some gave her. I did too, because I couldn't say her right name if it cost me my life. I just couldn't. She was good company, Mr. Man, and not just what you're thinking.

"And I'll tell you what. They ain't anyone, red or white or no matter, which could outbeat this Lena playing stud. I swore she was cheating me, but I'll tell you what too. It weren't so's a man could see if he looked hard as he could, which I certainly done." Evan shook his own head at that. "You couldn't've called her dishonest, and you couldn't say she wasn't a good woman. I don't know but I loved her a mite." The dreamy look again. "And another thing: you couldn't tell what in the hell you was listening to, but this Lena could sing like a heavenly angel. I craved to hear her, even if I couldn't tell you what any of them songs was about."

George fiddled with the truck's radio. Music blared, but he shut it off. He can't get the hang of this hip-hop. It doesn't seem he's ready for much in the twenty-first century just around the bend; he hasn't caught up with the twentieth. He longs as ever to hear the musicians from the Club Mayes of his old drunken fable, but you can't buy their records. George doesn't even own a CD player. And Lord knows you can't hear Mingus or Miles or the rest on the radio, at least not out here in Norris Township. He recalls Max Roach's drums in the Village. A miracle. Jesus. Nowadays the drums you hear are machines.

"Anyways, this man steps out of the woods quick as you'd change your mind. Poof!—there he is. And with him comes the goddamnedest rabbit dog as ever you saw. He don't look no more a hound than I do. Long-haired, and with a snout not much longer'n your finger, and those mixed-up eyes like a sled dog.

"Now this hunter, he's plenty scruffed up too. Long hair like a woman and a mouth full of snoose black as your boot. And he's a regular giant.

"'Get a run?' I ask him, just friendly.

"Course not," he says. "That's why I'm lugging him." Mean. Sarcastic. He holds up a hare.

"I just smile, but this fellow's making me uneasy.

"'Who's staying here?' he asks me.

"'Me,' I say.

"'You and who?'

"'Lady.'"

The story is clear as judgment in George's mind. He can't do anything but let it unfold.

"I don't calculate to say another thing if I can help it," Evan went on. "I'm thinking this ain't a gentleman, and I don't want to push him too far, for he's wide as a moose.

"'I'm Evan Butcher,' I tell him, and I stick out my hand.

"He only says, 'Let's go into camp.' Then by the Jesus, he lifts that rusty old pump gun and I'm looking at the angry end. I just stand there with my teeth in.

"'Let's go!' he says. Pushes the barrel right against me.

"Well, I about dirty my britches. But what're you going to do? I start down the path, stump-legged, one 'shoe on and one off, like the nursery rhyme. I was using the off one for sort of a cane to keep me up. And all this time I'm thinking this ain't going to be good for me or Lena either one.

"Don't ask how I get the gumption, but we haven't gone ten yards and I take that broke snowshoe by the stem end, and I slew around and catch him right acrost the face so hard the frame cracks.

"I don't waste a second. I draw that gun right out his grip and I fling it. It sinks right under the snow. I always carried a little .38, and pretty quick I got that pistol under his chin. He didn't go all the way down when I struck him, and he's that tall even on his knees, you see, I'm almost aiming up. I tell him: 'Lay down!'

"I was young in those days, all right, but if you asked me to do all that again, I couldn't in a hundred tries. No thinking in it, I just done what I done.

"He must've looked in the camp and seen Lena. But he don't know if maybe Lena's man, wherever he is, will show up with a gun. Which I did, praise be. He don't want no surprise while he's troubling her. But don't matter. He gets one.

"Now his dog just runs back up the trail soon's I spank that gorilla. I didn't even worry about the dog before. I might if I thought about it. But he ain't vicious a particle. Wants to hunt is all. I can hear him open up again in the swamp, chop-voiced like a little beagle.

"'Lena!' I yell, and here she comes on the clean jump. I ain't taking my eyes off this ape man stretched out on the snow, so I can only guess what she looks like. Is she scared? Don't believe so. She's tougher'n a boiled owl.

"'Evan . . .' she starts, like she's cross, but I cut her right off.

"'Go fetch that chain back of camp,' I tell her, a little snappish. I still have that one snowshoe on, but I don't dare try to kick it off.

"When she gets back, I give her the gun right quick. I have plenty of faith in her. They's something serious as a heart attack going on here, so she don't ask one question, just walks around behind him and puts the barrel right inside that awful hair.

"The chain must've been there ever since Lank logged that country, him and that bay horse he built the hovel for. Big yellow mare. June, he called her."

This sort of digression never troubled George; it always seemed part of a dramatic whole. In the old days, when he'd tell his version, he'd insert asides himself, sometimes Evan's, sometimes invented. George Mayes was a counterfeiting cur in his time.

"They don't seem no bad links in the chain—solid, every one.

"'Keep him covered,' I say to Lena. 'Blow his goddamn head off if he tries something.'

"Then we take for the hovel, and I loop the chain around this woodbug's ankles and tie it off—same's you would a birthday present, 'cept not in a bow. 'Happy birthday, mister,' I say. He don't have a small idea why I would say such a thing, of course. It's only I'm mad as a hornet. Son of a bitch out there botherin' people!

"I flop the one end of that chain over the roofbeam, and I heft on the other hard's I can. But this fool's so heavy he could have been Lank's horse, and I can't get him clear off the ground—only enough the foreparts to his arms is all that's touching. They're near big around as hams.

"Then I take my end of the chain and hook it on the hay crib, which is of good metal too, and bolted solid to the wall. Lank never done things partway. It's almost a comical thing, this monster hanging there feet up, snowshoes and all."

Evan knows how to play out a story's every part, humorous or dead-serious. Everything depends on that knack. When he spoke of the hunter's dead hare, he hung his neck just so and opened his eyes wide as plates; he plain became the animal. Same for that funny-looking dog, or the big hunter himself. Of course, Evan hasn't told many stories at all since the ruinous mid-'80s. The passion's gone, along with so much else. Maybe it'll wake up again.

"So, we almost got that big monkey strung up like a buck deer, and then . . . I don't know what you'll make of it. Lena and I get looking at each other like we should have us a time, and never mind that poor bugger upsided in the hovel. We didn't do nothing, but that's how we felt, whatever your judgment."

George didn't pass judgment. He felt he almost understood, but he didn't know why. That little part just seemed to make sense. He always got it into his own version, damn his soul.

"When we fetch help he's half froze, because Glenn Godshall, which Lena went for in my truck and which is our constable, isn't worth a copper penny for the job. He don't want an earthly thing to do with our prisoner, and the real police've got to come clear out from Marcus barracks. We wrapped a quilt around him alter along, but I never wasted no other pity on that guy. Come to find out he's raped a woman down Doranville way and even beat a man of seventy-five unconscious in his own store. No one knows where he came from."

As he finished, Evan looked out from his shop at what passed for a horizon. He put on a half-smile, and George wondered if it recalled Lena or the way they outfoxed that criminal. Maybe both.

"I could tell you where he's from now. Way out to some jail in who-knows-where, if he's still drawing breath. Habitual offender, they called him, and no Maine prison built to hold him. He was in and out of 'em all before his time. So I done the right thing. Have no doubt about it."

Have no doubt about it. Evan threw this in at the last. It must have meant something to him, must have had some formal ring. The story was his, after all, and with those closing words he somehow laid a special claim to it. Or so he must have reckoned.

XXIV

I made myself a lady's man, George muses. I made myself a brawler. I made myself a liar.

He knows everything's too thorny for labels. Lady's man. Brawler. Liar. They're only abstractions, though all of them, the lying one especially, are part of an old self-loathing he's afraid he'll carry to his grave. How many times did he tell Evan's story of the rabbit hunter? One would have been too many. His longstanding struggle with guilt over this violation attacked him again on the road a few hours back. Guilt? An abstraction too.

When he recounted Evan's narrative, he'd dress it up, which Evan didn't need to do, because it belonged to him. George doesn't want it anymore, but in the drunken days, the episode was his favorite in the barrooms. In his version, particulars changed, as if that excused his theft. George made the season late May, air swarming with black flies. He kept the setting, the forbidding, black-swamp country around Tallow Stream. He was out there for brook trout, not beaver. His lover was the storekeeper's daughter Brenda. And he was the hero. Of course.

George always took time to describe the red flesh of the fish, so newly caught they curled in the skillet. Brenda ate them like corn on the cob, head in one hand and tail in the other, fat from the bacon grease running down her arms.

"I can't say why that steamed me up," George would say when he added this detail. And the insane fact was, he did feel a subtle stirring, no matter that Brenda was pure fantasy: Billy Miles had no daughter; he never fathered anyone, never even married.

So, winter's big hunter became just a drifter with a rusty scattergun.

George sat among all the other winos and losers, whose faces weren't clear even then, in part because George looked just above the heads of his listeners, giving the false impression of face-to-face contact. It was also a way to deflect his self-reproach, which he was afraid eye contact, even with someone in a hopeless crowd, would undo him. He'd picked up his lecture style from a certain Professor Longstreth, a European historian.

Style! That's what he claimed for himself, a liar who might wet his bed on any given night. His stomach lurches when he recalls details from Simmy's, his favorite place: the pocked dartboard, the unchanging list of "cocktail specials" on a smutty mirror, the blinking Rheingold sign, its letters backward in the street-side window. He always stayed right up to closing time with the other wayward boozers, who trudged raggedly away in all directions when the door closed behind them.

George piled up his lies for far too many years, from his phony French thinkers at Yale to the hunter's story and beyond. The ones he fed poor Melody, before and during the early phases of their brief marriage, now feel embarrassing at best. No, he wasn't shacked up with that bottle-blonde from the five and dime, but gone to fetch a new inner tube in Norris. No, he wasn't conniving with some other woman when Melody lifted the upstairs phone, but a west coast parts rep. No, most commonly, he hadn't had a thing to drink. On and on. Duplicity became as much a habit as the alcohol that induced it. Lies felt as natural to George as honest speech to others.

In college, did he really try to prompt that Wellesley girl's sympathy by telling her that his mother had been murdered not in 1949 but the year before, just so she might let him sneak into that seamy, pale green room at the Taft Hotel, with its dim standing lamps, its yelping radiators, its silverfish among the bath tiles? What was the girl's name? Inge. Yes, that was it. She spoke German as well as English, something about an Austrian parent that George forgot as soon as he heard it.

He does retain impressions: a beautiful young woman. Willowy, he called her. Graceful too, sad-eyed for some reason. How could the poor kid buy his own sad story—or did she? Nothing came of his chicanery anyhow. Willowy, maybe, but tough too: "If you're staying here," she said, "you're sleeping on the floor."

George conceded, thinking she'd relent. She didn't. He lasted two hours on the bathroom tile, then crept to the peeling French doors and went down the fire escape, his back stiff as a plank. He heard Inge call his name from above him, which only made him hurry.

He never saw her again, but a few years later, he somehow learned she'd starved herself to death. Anorexia, it was called, something George had never heard of. He had noticed that evening that she ate nothing but bits of fruit and greens, how she kept gulping water, leaving aside the expensive entrée George had paid for in the classy restaurant. That both nettled him and confused him, but once the wine kicked in, he paid no attention.

But she starved? How could you rather die than eat? Pure insanity. But then wasn't there a time when George appeared to prefer death to abstinence? By now he has become wary of overestimating his importance in others' affairs, but he occasionally does wonder if he had some part, however tiny, in a delicate soul's dire pilgrimage to destruction.

And yet, against all reason, even so ghastly a fate as Inge's haunts him less than his appropriation of Evan's adventure with the big hunter. He was with the young woman for half a weekend, scarcely remembers her, but he's been with Evan for a lot longer. His thievery seems more unforgivable than so many of his other violations, though George knows it didn't really affect anyone else's life, never mind death. His reason rarely prevails, though, when his memory's hungry.

George feels chiefly troubled by having used Evan Butcher, even more surely than he once meant to use poor Inge and too many other people, young and old, friends and strangers, men and women. Things headed that way almost as soon as he left Mary's kitchen for the broader world and discovered what alcohol could do for him.

From the moment they met on Semnic Lake, Evan's behavior toward him has been anything but exploitative. He's always been generous with time, knowledge, loyalty, companionship, and until late years his heart and soul, not a common thing among men who drove logs, chopped mammoth trees, lived off wild creatures, ones disinclined as a rule to discuss fear or love. So George will never abandon Evan. That would be to abandon life.

One day he'll shed the weight of his piracy. He's been not only ungenerous, but also craven. He may have been physically brave enough in his time: he got big young, and he usually held his own against violence, though he largely avoided it. He was no giant rabbit hunter, but there were quite a few bar-hoppers who sized him up and thought better of starting trouble. If Evan hadn't spoken up on that Semnic beach, of course, he'd have taken a beating from his son, but George didn't run until Tom grabbed that axe. Leave the axe out, and he might have lost, but he'd have made sure Tommy remembered him.

He sneers at himself. Still the tough guy? Move on.

The fear that plagues him isn't physical. It's that he's been an emotional coward. What in the world, for the grimmest example, could have kept him away from Mary's hospital ward in those last days, when the imminence of her death was clear to everyone, including her? On his final visit, the week before her decline took a sharper, more obviously lethal turn, George detected a rattle in her breathing, caused by a lung ailment he never understood, for all the doctors' explanations. Surely it had nothing to do with the old asbestos plant? Mary rarely ventured outdoors, save for Catholic mass.

She was dying, all right, and yet it wasn't terror of death that halted him, but of inadequacy. If he couldn't save her, he'd be a failure. That old longing for heroism, the drive to be more than simply a fellow human, left him paralyzed on the sidewalk outside the hospital, his heart in pieces.

"Are you prepared for school?" He recalls his uncle's rote query. George's answer was always yes, even when school meant a whipping from that tyrant Calhoun. He could take that in the end, as it turned out, but he stood aside while the saint lay dying who'd nursed him through his younger life and, likely, assured his older.

Evan often broke that preposterous urge to heroism. He could admit to George that he frequently felt weak or threatened or awkward or above all, deeply confused, as over his son's ruinous drinking and the horrors to follow. He didn't try to be Hollywood manly.

"Grim," Evan somehow turned the word into two syllables. "How life takes ahold sometimes."

"I can only imagine, Evan."

"Be glad you can't," the old man corrected, truth prompting the comment, not malice. George would have noticed malice. Evan's own tears were as real as anything he knew, and so was the old man's need for a friend's compassion. Then one day Evan clammed up.

But that silence can't be permanent, George insists to himself. He needs to keep the candle burning. He mustn't say for good, mustn't say never or always. Hasn't he seen men and women crawl back from the lip of the grave? Something mysteriously lifted George himself out of the abyss, after all.

He never really knew another man in whom he could confide before he and Evan met. Not his roommate Farley, though he was about the only Yalie with whom George ever had the hint of a sober conversation. The roomie's yen for military glory would have shut George down even if Farley had truly wanted to soul-search with him, as he clearly did not. The frat boys whom he tried to dupe with his imaginary scholars and artists were irrelevant, of course.

He did have Mary when he was younger, but there were certain strictures even with her. When Calhoun roughed him up as a child, for instance, George kept that from her. It didn't cross his mind to confide in Uncle Emory, because he knew what his response to trauma would doubtless have been—the same as to sickness. To all appearances never ill until the very day a stroke undid him, Uncle seemed to consider even a head cold a moral failure.

"Buck up, boy," he'd say when George got hoarse or sniffly or even feverish. Had he whined about a little punishment, which is how Emory would surely have described Calhoun's assaults, he'd have been reproved, not consoled.

Liquor does stop a drunk in his tracks. But there wasn't much George could blame on an unhappy home life. At least he didn't think so, never considered the possibility until very recently. No, when time came, he would drink because he drank, nothing extraordinary about his case. He never considered his life unhappy. Unusual, maybe. Most kids lived with two parents, yes, but were any as good as Mary Conley? Even as a child, he knew to feel lucky.

All of which is not to say that George didn't have some sense of himself as an outsider. Observing more popular classmates, he half-believed that they'd learned their self-assurance in some secret alternative school. In eighth grade, when classmates started dating, no matter how short-lived each relation, he was befuddled: How did the boys get girls to dance with them, never mind kiss them? How did they introduce themselves to strangers, or look authority figures in the eye? On and on. Of course, he knew perfectly well that here was no underground school, but he did feel he'd missed out on helpful instruction, and no one was offering it to him now. Even in his alcohol-free adulthood, he can be stupefyingly awkward. A lot of drunks have similar misgivings, he's learned. No, nothing extraordinary about George.

The plain fact was, though, that once fate separated him from Nine and Patrick, George found he could more easily learn fluent French than cultivate new friends, let alone lovers. At college, for the first time ever genuinely on his own, George would discover liquor for real. It would be his ticket out of emotional encumbrance.

He remembers Yale convocation in the huge freshman dining hall called Commons. The famous art historian Vincent Scully was the speaker, and George had never imagined there could be such a voice or vocabulary. But he was stunned by more than rich diction: when Scully addressed what he called "a thousand future leaders," George realized he was meant to be included. He felt an odd charge. Frightening, sublime.

He may well have been the last student to remain in the hall. He sat unmoving until a man in green uniform, who'd come to clean up, politely suggested George needed to go home.

What would home be?

He did leave, but he loitered in the wide courtyard. The September night was unusually crisp and clear, stars glinting in their millions. He stood gawking upward, the charge still in his limbs. But suddenly, as though he heard the words out loud, a voice seemed to call out: He didn't mean you. What Professor Scully couldn't have known was that at least one member of his audience would be nobody's leader. There had been a mistake. The world would discover it soon enough.

George remembers huffing, as though his wind had been knocked out. His shoulders slumped; his chin dropped to his chest. But relief quickly followed his colossal disappointment, because if George would always be precluded from leadership, he had no reason to aspire to it. That awareness alarmed him, as a sailor may be surprised by sudden gale. If the triumphs of his classmates were beyond his grasp, what would he do with his life, even his student life?

George would shortly discover the answer. Whiskey, gin, beer, vodka, brandy—each was your man. Trouble with that term paper on Spenser? Drink. Want some sweet girl's phone number? Drink. Shy to get up and dance? You know what you need.

In spite of all, that last thought makes him chuckle. He remembers a night at the Sound Track, a black nightclub on Dixwell Avenue. The club's house band was The Untouchables, who played first-rate covers of famous R&B musicians: crooners like Chuck Willis, Clyde McPhatter in his down-tempo numbers, Bobby Bland, and others; flashy swingers like Bo Diddley or Little Walter; anything, fast or slow, by James Brown.

The Untouchables' singer was Little Barney Floyd, blade-thin, light-skinned, no taller than five foot three, but with a voice like a cement mixer. He was an even better dancer than blues-shouter, and he often ended a set by leaping up and landing in a split, his favorite James Brownism.

George was drunk enough to persuade himself that Little Barney's move was at least as much a matter of relaxation and confidence as of agility and flexibility. While the night's last tune was winding down, dancers whirling and dipping around him, George jumped and fell into a split, or what he intended as one. Both George's inseams had indeed split, ankle to crotch, along with every muscle in his right leg.

Earl, the band's laconic bassist, looked down at George with an ironic smile and muttered, "It was a good idea, though, man."

George hobbled back to his dorm. That escapade doesn't hurt now, but too many old ones do, even the ones some consider funny. There are more than a few he can't recall. Blackout. That's the apt word, all right.

The reckless young drunk grew into the emotional weakling. He has just banished it for a spell, but his theft of the Tallow Stream hunter, which he spilled like cheap beer in those dismal bars, comes back to mind. He suspects most of his listeners were blacked out too. No doubt many have long since drunk themselves into permanent quiet. They can't call George on anything, and his relief at that feels shameful.

XXV

Poot thinks, "It ain't like I never been here before."

She's bored, is all. Nothing wrong with the guy. He danced good at Anna Banana's. Good enough to wind up at her place. Hope he feels like a regular Lover Boy about it, whoop-de-doo.

Thump, thump. He's like a damned steam shovel or something. Poot watches his little Jesus cross swinging in front of her face. That's all he has on but his stupid black socks. Whoop-de-doo.

Maybe she'd ought to do something useful in her life, whatever that is. Like she was thinking, she's been here before. No surprises. No harm, but no fireworks.

For some reason she gets remembering the spotted shark she'd go look at with Hughie Junior in the aquarium at Harborside. She pretends she's standing there with him right now.

Romeo's grunting, but her and Junior are at their favorite place, right where the glass comes close to the water fountain.

Turtle.

Codfish, four of them.

Striped bass in a little school.

They learned how to tell each kind from other kinds.

Now here he comes, Mr. Shark, slow as third-class mail. Slow as this guy, matter of fact.

Spottie, they called that shark. Skin like a frog on him.

XXVI

Tommy Butcher drowned on his twin sons' fifteenth birthday, late April. He ran his truck off a rain-slickened mud road at Molly River Bridge and lay roof-down in the bog while water filled the cab. He'd flipped and sunk deep enough that he couldn't open a door or window.

Or maybe he lay unconscious there. Who knows? When George walked by the open casket later, he didn't see a mark on the man, meaning he may have been wide awake while he drowned. George hopes not.

George was at the birthday party. He, Mattie, Evan, and the twins went on with things. After all, they'd gotten used to Tommy's not showing up. Mattie had fashioned party hats, bought ice cream, made a cake, and covered the table with automotive tools, the only sensible presents for the boys by now. Everyone figured their father had gotten his usual snootful and ended up somewhere else, if he woke up before noon in the first place. He'd been behaving this way for almost a decade and a half, but things had gotten progressively worse by '85. Rage, crazy preaching, and booze.

Evan once showed George part of a letter their son had written his parents:

> a sord will flash in their citys; and eat up thier false profits and end thier evil plans! and
> They also take off their garments, and close their wifes and children.

Botched, garbled quotations, always from Old Testament prophets. But Tommy found nobody to listen to them or any other part of his wild preaching, which only deepened his fury. No one could turn him around, and no one believed any of his promises any more than his loony theology. He made pledge after pledge, especially whenever his father bailed his sorry carcass out of jail or brought him home him from a hospital. He broke them all.

"How many times did he tell us he got done with liquor?" Evan asked George, over and over.

George made the same sort of repeated promise at one time, but only to himself after Melody fled.

Tom would see God in the morning and hear Him right out loud. By the time he came by his family home to pass on the Word, though, it was rife with hatred and alcohol. He railed that sinful people ruled the world. Well, George wouldn't argue too hard about that, but Tommy Butcher made a damned poor example of the saved.

On that fatal morning, Tommy came toward Woodstown the back way, probably thinking he'd be safer from the cops. His driver's license had been taken over a year before, and if the county's police force had consisted of more than two overextended troopers, he'd have been picked up again long before and stuck in the can after the usual brawl. He found out what his idea of a safe route meant, the suffering fool.

How many times could George have died drunk himself, maybe taking innocent schoolchildren with him? He has no right to judgment. One morning, he woke up, staggered to the john, and saw a man in the mirror wearing a brown mask. He noticed that the toilet seat was shattered almost to dust. He must have fallen in the night and his blood was turned that dusky color these hours later. His drive home from whichever bar he'd chosen was an out-and-out blank. Now he didn't know his own face. But he didn't die.

And so, George has a nightly routine of gratitude, not least for still walking this earth. He can't remember how it got started. He's the only one to know about his little rite, though the last thing he frets over is how it would look to anyone else. The discomfort of kneeling would only distract him at his age. From what? Not religion. In fact, some churchgoing acquaintances say from what little they know of him that he's faking faith. Maybe. But the more George acts as if he has faith, the more its fruits show up.

No, he can't link any of this to doctrine. Doctrine's an enemy to George, especially any he might come up with himself. He long ago learned to resist his temptation to opine, however weak the resistance sometimes proves. He's simply confident there's something out there that keeps him going and keeps him stopping. It saved him from death for many years, after all.

His own skepticism of anything providential was loud and irrepressible in his so-called days of freedom, of what he considered independent thinking. But the best and fanciest of that thinking landed him on a filthy floor in 1967, crying for mercy—from anywhere—and watching a rat eat rancid dog food.

"The hell with your creeds and your skepticisms," George would announce to absent, faceless challengers of his beloved mumbo-jumbo, to anyone who'd call it a crutch, because George is happy for the crutch. It beats the hell out of puking. And it promises anything but ease and witlessness. It demands difficult behavior, and prohibits the easy kind, which once felt instinctive. To stay sober requires honesty, for one thing. There was a time he'd steal your belongings and then help you look for them. To behave differently remains a challenge, even all this while after that grotesque final binge.

And so, nightly, he stretches out next to Julie, waits for her breathing to steady, then ends his day in his makeshift way. First he recites a short passage he's memorized from the 28th Psalm:

To you, LORD, I call; you are my Rock, do not turn a deaf ear to me. For if you remain silent, I will be like those who go down to the pit.

George wouldn't claim that the psalmist's God has ever spoken to him, but he has explored the pit. Thoroughly.

Next, he calls to mind the faces of people who have particularly occupied his thoughts: the quick—Mary, Kate, Julie, Evan, Mattie—and the dead—Mary, poor Tommy, his own slaughtered parents, even Emory Unger. He doesn't need words. On a good night, he goes to a good, safe place, one as actual to him as Glassburg or Woodstown. *Selah*.

For a few years now he's added a prayer that Evan Butcher may come to know the grace George was granted.

Almost thirty years past, once his sobbing had exhausted him, he went into a sort of half-sleep, in which a faint bell tinkled. He's shared that recall with friends who've corked the jug. None defies him. The social drinkers, he's sure, would ask if George believed that sound was real. Well, he heard it. And he saw a light so small it might have shone through the louvers of a closet. Was that real? Well, he saw it.

No burning bush. No road to Emmaus. No ancient white man in flowing beard and robe. And perhaps not even a voice, but that George heard that too. It said, prosaically, "It'll be all right," and in that very instant, George knew it would. For his life to be all right represented a mighty leap upward. From where he found himself, nothing should have made it so much as conceivable. The world of living beings had looked impossibly distant an hour before, and then it suddenly opened to him.

He recalls physical sensations—his shoulders loosening, his fists unclenching—more vividly than any profounder things. For a minute or so, he actually believed he was being held above his encrusted floor. By something. Something that lived in that good place he seeks to enter every night before he drifts off.

Evan and Mattie Butcher were, of course, crushed by Tommy's death, Mattie less than her husband, or apparently so. George wonders if women don't own some inner strength that men can't know. Not that they're immune to panic or despair, of course, but when things bear down, women bear up.

Of course, such a notion may be nonsense, or more likely something sentimental, based on the particular women who have blessed him. In his nightly ritual, Mattie and Mary Conley and Julie and even his daughters, still children, walk in vaguely visible procession, as if behind a film of gauze. The little group circles a stockade of some sort, its fences far taller than they are. But they can scale it at will. You could save the world with the picture he conjures.

It's always about saving the world.

After Tommy's funeral, he and Evan retreated to the shop. The freshets were musical on the hillsides, the aspen leaves the size of a quarter, their green as bright as coin too. The woodpeckers' sounds were different from winter ones. One of them banged on some neighbor's metal roof, a mating behavior, as Evan once told George.

It was the sort of information that used to intrigue him, but it seemed almost idle then, the atmosphere in the shop so changed, small wonder. If Tommy had pranged his pickup a few weeks earlier, when the ice still covered that pool, he'd have skidded on his roof and ended unharmed in the alders at its far side, but he flipped in the season of skunks and skunk cabbage, of woodcock whistling up from the ball field in courting flight, of loons regathering in the lakes—of everything starting over.

But not for Evan: "I feel like the oldest man God made," he murmured that day. He poured a dose of whiskey worthy of George in the bad old times. Well, he has a right, George thought, though the thought was idle too, and he felt a twinge of anxiety for his friend. There's always an excuse if you're hunting for one.

Mattie looked dead-tired, but she kept herself busy. She ran the Bingo games at the church vestry and on odd days the register at Billy's store. "I ain't going to die on the vine," she told George, though her eyes bore witness to the strain she faced, and the lines in her face, for all her valor, looked deep enough to hold the rain.

So George's proposal seemed logical: he'd take the boys to Glassburg and have them work for him. He always needed good help. Their grandparents would mend as they could, would start living like an older couple again. As for the twins, who knew what they thought of George's plan?

Mattie put up a fight over the whole idea. "They ain't even your kin!" she complained.

But her objections weren't truly deep, or George would have felt it. No one ever claimed Mattie Butcher was a soft touch.

Don and Dave sat in the backseat in near silence for thirteen hours. By the time he passed through Bangor, George had quit trying to converse. The journey passed as quietly as the ones he'd so often made alone.

Much farther south, as settlement became thicker and thicker, he'd check his mirror. The kids' faces wore the same expression, or nonexpression, each time he looked. When he pointed out the Manhattan skyline, and next the infernal New Jersey oil fields, each said heh.

Once in a while, a twin would make a slightly different sound, little more than a breath, nodding at certain cars they passed on the turnpike. Jaguar, Mercedes, Lincoln, Porsche, Cadillac. But they'd worked on them all by now in Billy's barn, so the noises were casual, not urgent.

Back in Glassburg, Don and Dave got the spare room. At mealtimes, Mary and Kate, in total quiet themselves, studied the speechless pair almost as if they were exotic pets. Julie quit trying to draw them out after their second supper together.

After ten days, the Tommy and Poot's twins joined the Mayes Transportation crew. He'd found them a place with housekeeping privileges near his shop, not without wondering what their housekeeping would amount to.

XXVII

Donnie give Dave socket wrench. Nine-sixteenths. Donnie bodywork but know what brother need.

Dave wiggle other hand god damn give me give me give. God damn nut too tight. Donnie put WD-40 in hand. Spish spish spish . . .

Heh.

Heh.

Dave smoking. Sit on floor what-the-hell dirty anyhow. He sound like drunk Dad cough and cough.

Heh. Dave and WD40. Look. Head gasket all holes. Jesus.

T-bird. '56. So clean but gasket. Have to order. Okay but cough cough. Put stinkin' cig out Dave.

Heh.

Lunchtime. Sun in window make you blind. Gammy Mat. Soup. Baloney.

Heh.

Heh. Hurry up Davie. Tall lady drop off gray man soon. Jag ain't ready gray man angry. Long trip for him. Probably done fishing. Lady just sit with book and then book. Swat flies and burn up. Sit on wharf all day dumb ass in sun. Pink as bubblegum.

Just bring your money tall lady gray man.

Don't yell Gammy Mat. Coming coming Jesus.

XXVIII

Rob stares at the papers on his desk. Their words and numbers swim. His gut churns. He always had heartburn before, but it got a lot worse when he set up on his own in a brand-new part of the country.

"Is it worth it?" he whispers.

Well, yes, sure. He always meant to be his own boss. But worries! Great Scot, that mess on the New Ohio Insurance blotter doesn't just make Rob uneasy. He's frustrated too. He likes solving mechanical problems, hands-on, but sometimes there's just so much else in the way! Not good for his health, no. His stomach is like when he was a kid.

He walks to the door and looks at the job list he posts every day for himself and the men. It blurs too. He checks his watch, and that's enough to make him lose his train of thought again. It's hard to ride these spells out. Rob never predicted the tangle he's involved in. Or tangles, plural. He's got no gift for—prognostication. Never did. As far ahead as he ever looked was, he wanted to do better for himself, to find someone who'd help him, to raise a family, run a business. He just wanted to sign up for the famous American Dream, not doing any harm along the way.

He can't decide how much of a part he played in the harm that came to the Butcher boys anyhow. They'd probably have ended how they did even if they never left the woods. There's bad luck all over their family—a father drowned in a drunken rollover, and next the poor guy's sons wiped out.

Rob fights hard against the idea of guilt, but he can't be dishonest. He's at least a little responsible, no doubt. He can't wave his wand and—what's the word?—exculpate himself. He's not built that way. He'll keep going, of course. Giving up isn't in his character. But he's got some baggage, and he can't dump it on the side of the road. Who on earth could say, Oh, just a couple of suicides? Not him.

Rob flips open his dinner pail and peels back the sandwich paper. Cerise always packs him a good lunch. Baloney and American cheese, the twins' favorite. Bad reminder. He wraps it up again, queasy. He likes it a lot, baloney—bologna; but right now he doesn't care if he ever sees it again. It's no good for your system anyhow. He read that somewhere.

"When they came to Mayes, who treated them like humans?" Rob asks the air. The sandwich has gotten his conscience rolling again, as if his wife had deliberately packed something to bring the whole sad story back. "What am I, crazy?" he thinks. Cerise would never do that. "Bite your tongue," he tells himself. He likes that expression, which he never used until recently. Cerise is too good for him by half, whatever it took for her to be with him.

But yes, who supported those kids back in '83? *He* did! George too, of course, but after all he knew those kids when they were little babies. That is, if anyone could know them.

Rob looks at the closed lunchbox again. It seems to weigh on his desktop. How many noons did he take the boys' trades? How many slices of good sandwich meat did he swap them for their garbage? Olive loaf or luncheon loaf, whatever that is. Dry bread. Bile rises in his throat at the thought of all that, but really of any food just now.

That food trading wasn't half of it. In the Butchers' first or second week, he told off Herbie and John Henry, George's other men: "You think those kids chose to be what they are?" The two looked sorry enough, but Rob went on: "When you bastards come up with work as good as theirs, you can make fun of them then." He remembers that a little painfully. He didn't have to rub it in.

Herbie and John Henry used to mimic the kids saying *heh* at one another. Once Rob watched them giggle like a couple of schoolchildren, moving their bodies in sync, the way the twins did. It looked like a strange little dance. If Herbie handed John a tool, or the other way around, they'd slap it in the other guy's hand, same as the Butchers did it. All that came to a stop after Rob's tongue-lashing.

Rob feels a pressure on his forehead, a tingling in his fingers and toes, and breath that's shallower than it ought to be. His bowels mumble. He can scarcely recall the looks of a driver who started the real disaster. Earl something? Yes, that was it. Earl never knew it, but he had a lot to do with Rob quitting George. And it wasn't fair. Earl got away from there pretty much untouched. George caught him drunk at lunchtime, called him into the office, spoke with him for a long, long while. Suddenly, Earl got very loud. You could hear him through the closed office door. Then he came busting out, slamming that door hard enough to make cracks. You could still see them when Rob left later that year.

That was that for Earl. But earlier in the day, probably loaded already, he'd crimped a fender on 13, newest bus in the fleet. He must have taken a turn too wide and popped a culvert marker or something, just ahead of the door. It was a shame, with the bus so new and all, but it wasn't a big deal. There hadn't been any riders and the damage was light enough. At first, Rob told Earl not to worry. Unless you were pretty damned negligent, George Mayes had a long fuse, but not long enough to keep Earl on the crew. It was the smell on Earl's breath that turned things around.

Donnie wasn't long rolling out the dent and filling in the ripped sheet metal. That kid was a wonder. They both were. The Bondo was just setting up when Herbie decided to take time off from good behavior for a moment, and he was going to regret it. He must have figured nobody was watching when he scratched the word *fuck* into the Bondo with a screwdriver. The paint would have covered it, and nobody would be any wiser.

The boys couldn't read very well, but the writing wasn't the point. Somebody was messing with their work. Their work, because one's work was the other's too, if he lent a hand or not. David happened to look up from some engine job and he came running. He punched the side of Herbie's neck, and rolled him right down the lube bay, end over end. It looked like some sort of cartoon.

Now Herbie probably outweighed David by fifty pounds, but as soon as he got up, Dave flew through the air like a linebacker and crossbodied him down into the grease again. The kid was quick as a cat. He didn't have a dirty spot on his clothes himself after everything settled. They never got dirty working, those boys, and even a knockdown fight didn't put a smudge on Dave. He was on his feet before you could blink.

Then the real gory part started. David kicked Herbie's head till he slumped him sideways, then he straightened him back up with the other foot. It went on and on while Rob stood in his tracks, like someone had cast a spell. Then he started to scream like a baby. That beating was like nothing he ever saw before or since. But yelling was all he could do, and the sounds didn't even feel like they were coming out of his mouth. He couldn't recognize his own voice.

John Henry was outside. Who knows what he was up to? He was no worker, that's for sure. He should have been fired way back, except that George had taken a liking to him. They'd been going to those meetings together. That was probably it.

Rob never knew John Henry had an ounce of energy. He used to stop every few minutes and wipe sweat any time of year, even if he was only changing oil or whatever. But here he came running in and grabbed the iron bar they used for tipping up the fuel tank cover. The bar was long and heavy. It was—unwieldy.

Rob can't help himself. Even while he's recalling that awful brawl, the raspberries on Herbie's cheeks, the red stream from his nose, the blank expression of the kid who was maybe thrashing him to death, Rob pictures his beloved words. He can't help it. He's crazy, that way. Compulsive. That's the term, all right.

Now and then a word even seems like it rises up over his head as soon as he thinks of it, like those thought balloons in comics. He sees it spelled out: *E-x-c-u-l-p-a-t-e. P-r-o-g-n-o-s-t-i-c-a-t-e*. But is it *i* before *e* in *unwieldy*, or is that one of those weird exceptions like—well, like *weird*? He pushes back the parts order on his desk, reaches into his lowest drawer, and fishes out his O.E.D.

Okay, he's compulsive. *Unwieldy* comes off the page now and goes up in the balloon with the others. That's satisfying. Rob makes a small humming noise, the way you do after you've taken a bite of something tasty. The word is there for good now.

When Rob's daydreaming quits, he goes back to that day in the shop. It's a good thing the bar was unwieldy, too. Who knows what John Henry would have done to David's skull if he'd managed to raise it and bring it down? But suddenly Don came out of nowhere and chopped John's legs with his cross-body block, just like his twin.

Rob would bet those kids never played a sport in their lives. Where did they learn these things? Not that it mattered, really. The kicking started in for John Henry too. It was like the boys had been practicing for years. The goings-on were something out of a dream: two blond kids, skinny as duckpins, no expressions on their faces, kicking bigger guys' heads the way a boxer smacks a speed bag.

Rob said to himself, Do something or you'll be sorry the rest of your life. And so he did, exactly when George did. George grabbed Dave's shoulder. Rob grabbed Don's. Crazy, the way those boys acted together, with no signals. George and Rob did too. Was something contagious? The fight, if you could call it that, was over right then.

But oh, that bus shop saw its share of bloodshed and then some in its time.

Rob puts his lunchbox away in a closet, just to be doing something. He still can't get over how strange that day was. He knew, the minute the beating stopped, that he'd be leaving Mayes Transportation as soon as he could. George and he understood for years that that was the plan, and George kept encouraging it right along. But they both likely imagined the change would be a few years down the pike. On the other hand, neither one of them predicted those awful beatings. There wasn't any prognosticator in them. That day just left a curse on the shop for Rob. He needed to go.

So here he is. Three cheers or whatever. He belches, winces.

XXIX

Yesterday morning, Evan laid his chin right down on the windowsill. He remembers it well. There was a damned spider acting up right in front of his eyes. Horrible bug, when you think on it. He had a housefly snaggled in his web, and he kept shinnying down to play it out. He went ahead riling it and the poor thing fought back a little bit weaker every go.

Evan thought about saving that fly, but it was a long way past saving. Hell with it. Too late to swat the spider too. Why'd you do that anyhow? One of God's creatures. Oh yes: ain't we all God's creatures? Sure enough.

He tried to look past this spider-and-fly fuss to the river. He's been hearing it run all his life, and now his life seemed like a blur. You was a young fit man just yesterday. Now look. That river never changed. But all he could make himself do was hear it. He couldn't quit watching this Christly spider, smaller than your fingernail, sliding down that strand like a fireman's pole and tickling a fat old fly till it got done.

And soon it was. The spider wrapped up that poor little bug same's you would a present.

Fact of the business, he'd as lief the damned river just shut the hell up. Now where in tarnation did that come from? How would he take to despising water he heard all his life, or take and get weepy over a pesky fly, come to think? He'd slap the damned thing and not think a thing of it on a regular day. Was that what he was, weepy? His mind weren't where it ought to be, and he knew it, and even to known why.

There's a way out, George always claimed. Out and up. But what did he know? Oh, he lost his mom and dad awful, no argument there. But hell, he was a kid at the time, and a kid don't know so damned much.

Or maybe he does. No, don't get to picturing things, he told himself. Don't even bring up Donald and David. Leave it all be.

Evan meant to get in his right mind, but he didn't even know what that meant anymore. Who did? Sometimes, half the people in Wood-stown sounded like Psalm-singing preachers, the way they'd try and perk you up. Look on the bright side, they said, you got to see things clear! But if Evan didn't see things clear, how in howling hell did he see them? You take and put your bright things to one end of this bench. I'll put the rest over here. Now you watch which end flips up.

Mr. Spider got his mummy all closed in, shot the poison in it, and was just waiting on his own good time. Probably coming back down to eat it up for lunch or supper or whatever meal it would be for a spider. It'd been a long time since Evan really wanted a meal himself. He'd eat to save his life, that was all. But you wondered some days why you would save it.

He guessed he might like George's idea of a way out, but he weren't even sure of that yesterday morning. It seemed okay to drink what you like and let the hours roll right along just like that damn river. You feel like a stunned ox in the morning, sure, but you can liquor that away and if you're in any luck it's the next morning before you know.

That was about all the luck Evan Butcher expected now. He'd be the last Maine Butcher on this wide earth. He was the dead end, and a good thing too. Cut the damned line right off here. Butchers just seemed like magnets for troubles.

Then again, Evan knew a fellow ought to be more than a stumble bum that can't get nothing done, shouldn't he? But right off he thought, what's left to get done now—or any time in your life? One day you hewed thirty-two railroad ties, and no one else ever got near to that till they started making the ties with machines, for the love of the Lord. Could you take pride from running a machine? Evan didn't know too much about it.

He was the best of the best making sleepers and riding logs down-river. Where'd that land him? Couldn't keep his goddamned son from turning tits-up at Molly River till he was only another drowned man like some Evan remembered too well. Couldn't keep his grandsons alive, neither, even if he and Mattie done what folks like them was never meant to do, the best they could. No one should've been raising grand-children from babies when they was so old.

Evan fumbled under his bench and pulled out his pack basket. It gave him the nerves doing that, because you don't know of a morning just how much you left last night. He grabbed the neck of the jug without a look at it right then. When he did look, there was a good quarter left, praise be. Praise what?

It was like finding a five-dollar bill in your jacket or something. You want to celebrate, because you wasn't expecting that. He lifted the bottle and started to open his throat. Come on, Rosie, he thought, and he well knew it would keep coming till he couldn't swallow no more. But he didn't take a yank right then; he put the bottle right back under the bench for the time being.

His eyes was all tears again, but not over some spider, and not over whiskey. He really couldn't tell what for. He turned over on his stomach and stretched on the cot. Seemed like the sobs could go on till he died. That's how steady. They felt terrible and they felt just right. Evan couldn't have told you about that either.

And if you asked him how long he kept laying and bawling, he couldn't answer that one any better. All he knows is that right at the end, he let a great big breath out of him, hard. He liked the hot feel of it in his throat and up in his nose. But it wasn't a whiskey burn.

He pulled the bottle back from underneath. They's just them few inches, he thought, but then he thought no, by the Jesus, I won't. Not now. What'd George tell poor Tommy that time? You want to start stopping, then stop starting. 'Course Tommy damn near started a fight on that one.

Evan went over to the door. It felt like he was walking the way he used to, almost, steady up and straight. He held the jug just a second and worried some. What if he changed his mind? Well, he just wasn't going to think about the business right then.

"Someone'll help me out," Evan whispered, but he didn't believe he was thinking of a ride to the junction for a fill-up. He never liked beer that well anyhow. It did for other times when he couldn't get a better, or he could put the vanilla to him, which he kept for emergency. He got thinking everything would work out, yes, but maybe not because he was getting cocked. Another way.

Looking out at his dooryard, he thought about Bert Morton, and who knew why? Bert ran the bateau on that first drive Evan made. He was a very nice man, one-eyed. And Evan stood right on the bank by Mopang, nineteen years old and the greenest man in the gang, and he watched Bert and that big boat catch big water side-to. His bateau flipped like Tommy's truck. He saw it, though, not like Tommy's truck at all, which you could only picture, even if you never wanted to.

Two of the boys was thrown free, which they fished out, colder'n ice but living and breathing, maybe even now. Hard to say. People scattered all over these days. The other four was crushed like bugs, and what you pulled out wasn't fit to show anybody that cared for them. This wasn't a good story to tell their wives and mothers—now was it?—never mind their little ones.

The upset was handy enough to the launch that a bunch of the boys carried the dead ones back up to the dam. Then it was out to the marble orchard. But everyone else was on the river again soon's they were in the ground, because now the drive got two days behind.

And then there was poor old Brad Llewelyn, which they salted down like a beef and stuck in that bedroll for thirty long days and more, too far downstream to lug him the other way like that bateau bunch. These things came on Evan drunk or sober. Clearer, sober.

How long did he stand there holding his whiskey bottle? So much kept coming to mind. Take Baptiste, which played the fiddle so well. Tiny little mite. He put that fiddle down right beside him while he worked one end of a saw, and if you got a break, or played yourself off your feet for a bit, you'd lay up a while. Not the Frenchman. Maybe he'd sit, but now he'd be sawing on a violin while you took your rest. And play and clog at night in the camp. Wasn't that young, neither. More energy than a good hound.

Slow airs was what you called the ones Evan liked best. You ain't ready for a reel when your back feels like it was just in a vise and you been yarning on that saw all day out straight. One of them slow airs was what you wanted in these circumstances.

Baptiste had something carved on the back of the fiddle. It was in French, but he told Evan what it meant:

> In life I was silent,
> In death I sing.

That was what the maple it was made of could be thinking, if a tree could think. You sure hoped a tree didn't think if you cut a million board feet off the stump in your life, but the magic saying was nice anyways.

Evan never believed in magic, unless it was some kind of black magic. You could almost buy that, Mister Man—Devil's magic. Maybe Evan done something or his own parents done an awful thing that pleased that old Devil, and he's been taking away ones you cared about since they got born. Or however that works.

The crew heard about Baptiste maybe two, three years later. He went back up home somewhere, they said, but he kept working same as out here. Someone told the boys he was playing music when this widow-maker limb falls on his head. Then it's goodnight, Frenchie. Just sitting and playing his instrument.

> In life I played the fiddle,
> In death I'm silent.

How was that for a saying?

Then a damn strange thing happened. Evan saw he was pouring his whiskey out. He told himself for the five hundredth time he just drank his last drink. Why was anything different this time? Hard saying, not knowing, but it just seemed he cried a lot of poison out of him, and when he watched the whiskey soak in the ground, he could feel that weight, same as if you was carrying a canoe and just set it down—that weight was gone.

He left the shop and smiled at Mattie. She stood there like a stone, seemed like, and watched him walk right by her through the kitchen to pick up their phone.

He called George, but he wasn't home. Julie said she didn't know where he could be. "Well, tell him I got done with the bottle," he said. And then he said goodbye, right away quick, before he heard an answer, so's to go back to Mattie.

XXX

fter the Glassburg cops sent it to her, Mattie mailed the note on to George. It was scrawled on the back of an invoice for a state inspection and tune-up. David had filled the copy in, parts and labor, so crudely only Mattie could truly have read what he wrote. One word, in block letters, was clear enough: PAYD.

George has kept the scrap. It's smeared and crumpled, as if someone had folded and unfolded it over and over. Who? What difference would that make? It's dated July 12, 1987, just a few days after Don took his own life and just before David was dragged back to the asylum. Mattie included a note in her neat hand: "I never did show this to Evan God forbid."

George feels honored by her choosing to show it to him. The rough letters could still make him weep if he looked at them.

I GOT NO BRUTHER

No point in life, Davie had clearly decided. His grandmother had been right in her prediction.

XXXI

George's anxieties last night represented a wild yawing from his recent optimism. Now hope returns in an equally wild rush. So on, so forth. What's next?

The night thoughts are nothing new, of course. He remembers going to his office on a certain late afternoon five years back. He probably passed Julie on the road without knowing it, lost in thought. She'd be fetching the girls from day camp. Summer hours, his crew gone home. He looked at the job list by his door: yesterday's, July 6. That meant, come twelve o'clock the night before, the world had proceeded to July 7.

This exact date half a decade back had marked one Butcher twin's death. Twelve months later, the other killed himself too. No wonder George had been a wreck in bed in this most recent night and early morning. For one thing, there were still a couple of weeks before he traveled up to visit Evan, or what was left of him, and he feared he'd never see the old man again. The cold fact was, he could be gone by then.

When he calls Woodstown after supper tonight, he'll ask, "Can I speak with Evan?"

Mattie may answer as usual, after all, "Not unless you know how to wake him up, you can't. I quit trying an hour ago." Or words to that effect.

George will tell her: "Don't lose hope, Mattie."

"Good-bye, George."

It's as though he actually hears the click.

He's never been one to keep track of significant dates. "You just don't notice things sometimes," Julie will tell him if he forgets Katie or Mary's birthday, say, or their wedding anniversary. He hates embarrassment more than he can explain. His response, too often, is petty anger.

"Women!" he barked once. "Don't they have anything better to pay attention to?"

He apologized soon after. Where would the girls be if a certain woman didn't tend to details? Where would he be himself?

But that morning in '89, the one of the dry drunk, remains distinctive. Back then, he wanted to forget the whole indescribable mess involving the Butcher twins, but he kept getting caught up in it, and he's still not done. It turns out the brain may falter, but the soul—in fact, even the body—remembers what's important, even actual anniversaries. He couldn't do a thing about that then, and not now, either.

He remembers closing the door, though he was all alone, and cranking the air conditioner. Out the window, two high school seniors were cutting the grass in his back lot. Good kids. He still knows them. They could be corpses, like the twins, for different reasons and like so many drunks George has known. But they aren't. It's a great thing, people that age getting into recovery; you wouldn't have dreamed it in the '60s. He hoped they wouldn't come knocking. If they'd seen him like that, shaking like a leaf, God knows what they'd have thought. They didn't, thank fortune.

The moment he stood out of bed that morning, it felt like one of his old white-knuckle hangovers, a side of his face numb, his vision doubled, a painful throb behind his eyes. George imagined chasing it all away with a yank of booze as he used to do. Incredible. No, abstinence is what's incredible. His Satanic addiction is willing to wait however long is necessary.

Say it, Satan coaxes: *Just one.* In fact, on that awful night, George did dream, precisely, of a devil. That's as vivid as his waking memories. Satan—in whom he didn't exactly believe, and in whom he did not exactly not. That will forever be mere semantics.

The Satan of his dream was scarcely imposing. He somewhat resembled the manager of then new McDonald's in Norris. Short-sleeved shirt. Soft paunch, though otherwise not chubby at all. Pallid skin. All false heartiness: he wants you to keep coming back. Over 90 million served or whatever. In the dream, he wore a chef's hat and the comic apron some men put on for outdoor barbecue. George read its block-letter inscription: KISS THE COOK. Ha ha ha. Inane.

And yet George did kiss him, right on the slack mouth, and got head-spinning drunk in the instant. He smelled vodka in his sleep.

He should have been more than happy to wake up. He doesn't have many drunk dreams anymore, but it's always been good to discover they were only dreams. They've been among the things to keep him clean. Coming out of them rekindles that wondrous just-out-of-jail sensation. Thrilling relief.

So why didn't the feeling come on him in the predawn hours of July 7, '89? Who can say? Satan is insidious. Rob would like that one. *Insidia*. Latin for trap. Another scrap from George's hodgepodge classical schooling.

"There's always a trap set for you in the woods," Evan Butcher once told him. "On the water too." He said that as he was showing George how to keep the bowed trunk of a hung-up tree from knocking your lights out when you cut through it.

Here he is, back at it. Remembering himself remembering. "Which is not a great sin." He says out loud.

The traps aren't only in the wild. Evan knows that now. Or so George hopes, who barely knew it well enough himself during this spell he remembers, and he'd been sober over twenty years by then.

When he came downstairs that morning, it was cool outdoors. Crows cackled nearby, and he heard the cheery sound of bustled cookware and children's chatter in the kitchen. George was sound of limb, his business was sound too, but none of it mattered. His mind was on a tear. He clattered his own breakfast dishes, railed at the girls and at Julie about a toaster setting, for God's sake, and snapped at the poor dog, shooing her from under the table.

When Julie reminded him it was time to get to work, George shouted, "I own the business! I'll get there when I damned well please!" Even as he bellowed, he recognized the absurdity. He was a busman. Not exactly the Oval Office, Yalie-boy.

Mary and Kate skittered out of the room like mice, and George stormed back upstairs. Soon he heard the van's engine catch. The kids had day camp, and Julie would be at the office on time. She knew what needed doing at least. No bus rides to coordinate, but bills to pay, papers to file with the state. The rest of July and August would hurry by. Let the boss help himself to tantrums.

Julie wouldn't be bullied, still won't. That frustrates George now and then—and also endears his wife to him. He once joked that she married him because she wanted a father she could disobey. Father? George was the child.

When he came down again, he saw a note on the coffee maker: *Planning to stay crazy all day?* Julie had inscribed a Valentine's heart below the question. Evan, as he raved, George knew how he was acting, knew he just wanted to indulge his insanity a little while, to take a psychological holiday, to wallow in self-pity and resentment.

Still, he tore up the note, yelling, "So why in hell do I have to be a good boy all the time?" No one to hear but Tabasco, who must have reckoned herself the target again. She leapt from her bed and wetted the tile by the fridge.

"God damn you!" George screamed. He lifted the poor dog by the scruff and threw her out the kitchen door. She went on peeing, leaving a wavy, damp line as he carried her, which just seemed too much to cope with. He wouldn't clean up that mess. He'd never wanted her to begin with, or any dog. He hoped her piss would stink to high heaven by the time the girls got back. What a prince.

At some point he flopped on the porch hammock, entirely wrung out. He must have fallen into a weird sleep, because he had another dream. No devil in it. No, Allen Ginsberg.

Before he got sober, George had gone up to New Haven to see Ginsberg. Who knows why? Mere impulse, hardly unusual for him in those days. It was the middle '60s, when the poet's shenanigans were appalling every stuffed shirt in the Ivy League and elsewhere.

America, go fuck yourself with your atom bomb!

What Ginsberg presented wasn't a reading, or none of the kind George had ever imagined. He can't recollect specifics. He was drunk as ever, which was apparently okay. He remembers at least that Ginsberg kept saying everybody ought to be drunk or drugged or whatever could get a person crazy. Did he quote Baudelaire? *Il faut etre toujours hivre.* Probably not.

The whole event was Bacchanalian.

Bacchanalian. Another one Rob Beam would like. George huffs.

He was young again in the dream, dancing in that motley crowd. But suddenly Ginsberg's beard fell off, his hair shortened and fell to one side, and he was Hitler. Holy God, what could that have been about?

Hitler was stabbing the twins with a knife like Evan's, the one with 1915 scratched on the sheath. A lot of blood. Mattie was shrieking at the dictator that it wasn't the kids' fault they were so much the same. Their suicides were George's fault, and everything would have been different if they hadn't been taken out of Woodstown where they could be watched over by their grandparents and neighbors and people who knew about them knew about them knew about them.

Knew about them . . . Mattie kept repeating the phrase, and as if in response all the blood evaporated and the twins stood up. But they fell again. The blood spewed again. Two pools of it ran together and became one—so big it could drown a person.

Mattie started melting, and quickly. The last George saw of her in the shocking vision was her head, which lay on the floor like John the Baptist's on the famous platter. Hitler-Ginsberg had disappeared, and that bodiless head kept mouthing one word over and over now.

What word? George only knows that it had a drawn-out *O* in it. He could see the shape of Mattie's lips; they kept *O*-ing and *O*-ing until her face was snuffed, and in the blackness only the *O* remained, briefly floating knee-high, then dispersing like a smoke ring. George remembers coming to from whatever his state was. Even the hammock's weave was soaked in sweat and perhaps something else.

George had read a totally different sort of poem as a Yale freshman, and one of its lines never left him. *After great Pain a formal Feeling comes.* Apart from the Ginsberg show, all of it a blur now, that would be one of the few times he paid any attention to poetry. If every line of verse struck him like that one by Emily Dickinson, he'd read nothing else nowadays.

He doesn't remember the rest of what Dickinson said. It's that solitary line that gives a name and shape to something George has felt more than once in sober moments. He can relive how it came upon him as he emerged from that afternoon's odd and powerful slumber. It was like what he experienced once just after a pneumonia fever broke. The twins were alive then. It was before the deaths. BTD.

He felt weak as a baby from his illness, but everything looked so—composed. Through the window he gazed at the cherry tree he'd planted when they first bought the property, and it appeared to be exactly right in its placement and structure. And the flagstone walk from house to driveway seemed to have dropped into its position for George's sake alone. The very pea stones in that drive showed a bluish color that echoed the blue of the asters in a bedside vase.

The formal feeling was the one that first overtook him when he heard that voice back in '67, the one that turned his life around: *It'll be all right.*

He picked up the phone to call Julie at the shop that afternoon, but realized she'd be picking up the girls from camp. He sped home. Less than an hour later, a miracle, those very girls were hugging him. And Julie understood when he explained. Or she came as close as anyone could who'd never been a grave-bound sot.

"You meant to do a good thing, George," she told him. "Remember that."

She was right as usual. He'd wanted to give Tommy's orphaned kids some challenging work, but mostly to give their aged grandparents some rest. Mattie and Evan had raised Don and Dave right up to their own seventieth years. Then it got to be after the deaths. ATD—after which Evan kept drinking like the lost soul he was.

Rob Beam had a lot more to do with the twin disasters than George. That's a perversely bitter thought, because George still doesn't like being an incidental figure in any drama, or, more accurately, because deep in his soul, he clings to the preposterous notion that by sheer will and keener attention he might have altered the course of events. But it was Rob Beam, a man Evan and Mattie would never meet, who did more to bring death and horror into the Butchers' world than anyone, unless the whole wretched business was somehow fated.

After his unnerving dream-vision that July afternoon, once again George savored the assurance that his own world was still intact. The best woman he knew was at home, Mary and Kate safe and well, having splashed in the camp pool or woven raffia or shot harmless arrows at straw bales all day. They'd been picked up on time, and whatever they've been doing since they've done in a trim, all-but-paid-for house. Wasn't this payoff enough to a man who spent his late twenties telling lies in sleazy bars and risking the lives of kids whose adulthoods he could so easily have canceled?

And yet George still can't help thinking he should have seen some omen in the boys' double beating of his older mechanics over a mere scratch, should have seen how the next tiny spark might turn into conflagration if they stayed in Glassburg, should have hustled those mysterious twins back north where they came from. But he couldn't imagine reburdening Evan and Mattie.

Who the hell does he think he is, in any case? No one could have foreseen the tragedies. Surely, he has learned by now that life makes up its own stories, and it's only after the fact that George or anyone else can see them whole, if they ever do. The very details have blurred in his mind. Whose work had Herbie messed with? That was the one named Don, no? Wasn't he the first to do himself in? Wasn't he the one with the mole below his ear?

They might as well both have worn that mark, both gone forever. And Herbie's been sober since. He wants to be Herbert now. John had already been sober a while by the time of that mauling, and he's stayed that way, thank God. He's been as good a worker since, as he was a lousy one before. Earl, the one whose ding in the fender had started the whole brushfire, the only one to escape the brutal attacks, was still ripping and running. The last George heard he'd landed in jail. Again. Beating up his girlfriend. Again. Drunk. Again. Two out of three in recuperation: not bad, above average. But it's surely a mixed bag, this realm of hungry, addicted ghosts.

Of course, he can't help thinking over and over about Evan, whose vows have been worthless for some years by now, as his son's had been before him and George's even before that. After his annual pilgrimage this year, the cold weather will soon enough drop on Woodstown. There may be no one to get Evan home from among the headstones. Few in the village want to deal with him at all anymore. Cowards. Turncoats.

The twins could have killed those two men that day, but George never lifted a finger to get them out of Glassburg and back home until it was obviously too late. His head had stayed in the sand. So had Rob's, more deeply than George's, given what happened later. George didn't see change coming, at least not so soon. It would always have been too soon, though.

Rob gave his notice before anyone expected. At first George blamed his bolting on the tension at Mayes Transportation, which had naturally lingered after what the twins did. Anyone would want to get away from that.

He'd considered firing Dave and Don, but to his private embarrassment, he was scared to do it. He rationalized that he couldn't just send them back north, after all, not with Evan's drinking the way it had become, and Mattie's heart, for all her toughness, so close to broken for good. Dead son, drunk old man.

He couldn't very well fire the other mechanics, either, for the sin of having had themselves kicked senseless by two skinny demons with the wallop of TNT. He actually prayed nights that one pair or the other would just walk out. God forgive him, he hoped it would be Herbie and John Henry.

But all this was before Rob showed his colors. George recalls how the two of them choked up when they met at work that final morning. No hard feelings—there couldn't be any, really—on either side. It was only that they'd worked together for quite a span. They'd watched one another grow up in a way. Rob turned into a man. George turned into one too at last. Partly, anyhow.

Having as clean and steady an employee on his payroll as Rob epitomized George's life since the last of the sixties. No more mouthwash cocktails. No more doing his job plastered. '68 was when Rob first came to Mayes Transportation, as if to model the kind of existence George had forfeited at his age, having persuaded himself from his first year in college that he could function as well as the next person, even better. Didn't he hand in all his papers on time? Didn't he ace most of his exams? Vodka was the best friend he had. The only one, really.

Rob Beam worked hard to improve himself, not just to get paid. From day one, he had instincts that came to George only well after he'd settled, if that's what this is, for running a school bus service. He knows he shouldn't harbor righteous indignation against the boy, because that's a time bomb for him. As his friend Al always said, "It's like drinking poison and hoping someone else will die."

But he soon discovered that Rob had meant right along to steal the twins. Their ferocity apparently didn't matter to him after all. He was smart enough—and sneaky enough—to know he wouldn't find better engine and body men than the Butcher boys unless he wanted to pay wages he couldn't afford while starting out on his own.

Rob's shop got established quickly enough, and Don and Dave were crucial to its success, as he knew they'd be, the crook. He didn't care whom he cheated in the bargain. The twins had just thrown their tools into the back of Rob's pickup.

"I thought they gave you notice," Rob lied when George confronted him. So he's a weasel, your all-American boy, George thought. He couldn't have felt more shocked if a spacecraft had touched down in the yard.

"Did you? Those kids don't have any idea about things like that, and you damn well know they don't, Beam!" George had checked his own urge to physical violence. There'd been more than enough of that in his recent life. He wasn't a match in his late forties for a strong kid like Rob anyhow, and Lord help him if the boys interceded on their new boss's side. So George ended up sounding merely peevish.

He didn't blame the twins. He'd been right about them: beyond their hands-on work, just about all of the world was foreign to them. They likely went with Rob because they figured they were meant to. Don and Dave couldn't keep a checkbook; they paid for everything, even their rent, in cash, the same way George paid their wages. All they'd ever done was tightly circumscribed. All, including that feral vengefulness, owed itself to their extraordinary gifts. They could easily be killers if they got into another fight. That had made everyone, George included, step lightly around them.

The niceties of contractual obligation, spoken or written? Hell, you might as well have discussed Emily Dickinson with those kids. Or Ginsberg. Or the Second World War and Hitler himself. Zero. You might have spoken of macroeconomics or baseball, the same. They knew almost nothing. They were only uncanny.

But Rob knew. It was perfectly clear to him how George had helped his career, offering constant approval as he developed the experience and contacts that would free him to be his own man in time. But not so soon, and not at such cost to Mayes Transportation. Traitor.

A hell of a thank you gift, dirty as soot, taking himself and two others from the crew fewer than eight weeks before the schools opened. It wouldn't be easy, either, to assure the kids' grandparents that everything was all right, because it wasn't. Rob will always be unforgivable, wherever he is with his underhanded woman and his goddamned *Oxford English Dictionary* and his so-called solid character. George longs for him to request a letter of recommendation, though he knows it's a vain wish. Rob will be working for Rob from now on, as he always has, in a sense.

After he left, at least Rob posed no threat to George. All he serviced were cars and light trucks, and the two men Don and Dave had half-killed came right to the front. Maybe Herbie and John Henry didn't have the talents of the three who'd abandoned him, but at least they were stand-up guys.

On the other hand, George suddenly reflected one evening, it wouldn't be beyond a tricky bastard like Rob Beam to underbid him at some point for the school contracts. He banished the thought as soon as he had it.

George's imagination is too keen if anything, but there are things he just can't imagine. Norris is only twice as big as Glassburg, which, for all its late sprawl, is pretty little, and the twins were surely still inseparable. So how did one of them fall in love? Where did that one meet a girl to begin with? Was it at the Rexall where Rose worked? How could the boy get around to proposing? Did he say *heh*, and she said *heh* back? And how did he break his plans to the other twin? *Heh*?

But all of a sudden Donnie was in fact married, and the girl seemed more than perfectly normal from everything George heard. Her name's Cerise, but everyone calls her Cherry. Don married Cherry, and overnight the other boy found himself in a locked psyche ward. Who'd intervened and gotten him there? Rob? How?

One with a wife, the other in the hospital, and George making a flying visit up north to lay all this on poor Mattie and Evan, though

Evan was a little bit drunk the whole day. Not as bad as he'd become, but he likely assumed all this confusion and sorrow gave him permission to head in that direction. As he drove home in the dark, George wasn't entirely sure that everything had truly sunk in for the old man as it clearly had for Mattie, who said, "Now David will get married too." George looked puzzled, so she added, "That—or he'll be dead before you know it."

George clucked his tongue: "Don't talk like that, Mattie. Neither one of us has a crystal ball, do we?"

"One of us does," she said.

George's soul chilled at that. He didn't ask for elaboration because there were things he plain didn't want to hear. He hopped into his truck and started south. The whole business can still give him those damp-cold jitters, so much having seemed to follow an ugly, foreordained path to bloodshed.

In fact, the Norris cops later told him there was little blood. Don had taken a spoke from a motorcycle wheel and thrusted it up through that mole below his ear. He may have lain there a while. Who knew? And how had he decided the world was too much to bear? Why hadn't the fatal crash of their father set the boys off? Because Tommy was a separate being from them, George guesses, while the twins were one.

He's been trying to puzzle everything out through half a decade, but he knows he'll never penetrate the mystery of those Butcher kids, up there now in a graveyard among such different folk—woodsmen, pie-bakers, river drivers, tie-makers, wives and grandmothers, venison harvesters, tree scalers, surveyors, men deft with paddle and fishpole, women deft on their feet, do si do, chassez, people deft with their fists. Who will watch Evan Butcher wheel his beat red pickup in among those stones, knife-thin and new alike, to drink himself insensible?

Wherever Rob Beam roams now, having abandoned his Norris shop in its turn, he's the chief villain. So, a curse unto his progeny too, George thinks, although of course, if Rob and Cherry do have children, the kids won't deserve a curse. But neither did Don and David and the rest of the Butchers and even his own family, who must still now and then suffer George's ludicrous rage that everything can't be undone, and his bouts of profoundest dejection.

Mary Conley should be alive too, and his slaughtered mother and father, and even Uncle Emory. But these days it's chiefly that old Wood-stown drunk in his truck, with his little crumpled hat and his god-damned jug who's on George's mind. Evan needs to be magic again.

When Cherry ran off with Rob, David came out of the Kuehntown Sanitarium. The banker who held the note on the Beam garage repos-sessed it and put the place on the market. George also brought the Butcher twins back to work for him, at least pro tem. Herbie and John Henry were uneasy about that, but their jobs instantly got easier.

Pro goddamn tem.

Donnie wouldn't work. He missed Cherry. He cried all day, right in the shop, until George had him admitted to the same Kuehntown clinic where his bosom twin had been. He stayed a month, got a prescription for his nerves, came home, quit taking the prescription, rammed that spoke through his neck and died on the garage floor after hours.

That was July 7, 1986. George drove the body north and watched the kid buried. A moose wandered through the cemetery at the far end just after Mattie's much younger cousins, the Pruitt sisters, finished singing *Lead, Kindly Light.* Some wanted to see the big cow as a sign, but what sort of sign might she be?

Back at Evan's shop, the old boy did get dead-to-the-world drunk even before they could start a proper conversation. He watched his friend grab his whiskey bottle by the neck and tip it straight up, sucking till he couldn't swallow any more, just as he used to do himself with his vodka fifths. So George drove home right after dark, through thunder-storms that tracked him all night long. He hoped the rain might keep his old friend from his typical graveyard visit.

Why was everything in shreds? George egotistically found it unfair to him. He was sober, after all. But the thought put him in mind of an old saying of Mary's, when in so many words he told her the universe had turned against him: "All the world is out of step but Georgie."

Dave didn't attend his brother's burial. He went straight back to Kuehntown, where he stayed off and on for just short of five months. At last, he was discharged with a prescription for his nerves. He came home and went back to work at George's shop. But in due course, he quit taking his medicine. Then he found an identical spoke to ram through his own neck and died on the same spot as Donald. The only thing he'd lacked was that mark under the ear, and so, astoundingly, he drew one with a black felt pen and drove the metal in just there. July 7th, 1987. A year to the day from when his twin had done it.

Mattie sounded relieved when she heard the news: "It was going to happen."

She and George propped Evan upright at graveside until the last clod fell. George did so on his own while Mattie, tearless, laid some Black-Eyed Susans on the fresh dirt, same as the ones she'd picked for Donald from among the ragweed and hardhack in their back lot, where the grass grew long, right up to the edge of the woods, no one fit anymore to scythe it.

Once again, a moose skirted the far margin of the cemetery. As George loitered by the Butchers' before heading south, Evan's snores coming rough from the shop, Mattie remarked that it was the same moose as last summer's. "She got into some wire or whatever," she said. "I see the mark on her hind quarter, like an *X* with a short arm to one side."

XXXII

George went back to Woodstown a month after the second twin's funeral. July had always been the month for his short stays at camp, but the burial had soiled it. He'd needed some time, for one thing, before he could put up with Evan again, if he could at all. The old man's behavior from well before the first suicide broke George's heart, but it enraged him too. At the same time, he worried that none of his north-country history would stay intact if he ever voiced his anger outright to Evan. He needed to cling to something.

Evan may have been thinking likewise these days in such odd moments as he was lucid. He had little enough to cling to anymore. Only faithful Mattie, and he was paying her next to no attention, a further prod to George's deep irritation with him.

George hadn't told the Butchers he was coming to town, and when he arrived, he decided to lie low for a spell.

What was the point of being up north, then? In a village of eighty souls he'd have to hunker in his tiny cabin to avoid notice, and even then would likely fail. So he decided to make himself scarce, at least for a day, waiting to see Evan Butcher when he felt up to it. He'd no more popped his padlock, though, than he knew he couldn't face him at all. His conscience pricked him, but he told himself he needed to think. Or not think. Maybe if he spent some time in a place that once meant so much to him, he'd find a little equilibrium, even a little courage to combat the old emotional cowardice.

Before dawn, he lashed his canoe to the rack on his truck and headed to Semnic Lake with what few clothes he'd brought, along with an old spinning rod and a boxful of rusty lures, some tinned vegetables, a rasher of bacon and a sleeping bag. The worst of the mosquitoes gone by, he'd sleep in the lean-to, as he'd done in better days. He'd sneaked into town at night, and now he sneaked out. Coward, all right.

Maybe he'd stay at Semnic the full week. No one would show up, least of all Evan. The fishermen's bass and trout had gone into the deep holes. So what did he mean to do? His conscience kept pinching. He called himself a weakling more than a few times.

He meant to relive, as much as possible, that stay near forty years back, after he breathed the word *north*, put the aluminum canoe on top of his Volkswagen, and followed his nose, though there'd be no Evan this time. But how on earth did he dream of recapitulating that summer when his friend was not in the picture? Lord, was he as directionless as decades ago? So much for progress. Still following the same old nose.

He'd be the only soul to fish, though he probably wouldn't be able to troll deep enough, not with the crude outfit he'd packed. But fish were scarcely his real aim anyhow. What, then? Memories? He inwardly knew that retreat to a place where so many of them had been spawned wouldn't improve much of anything.

The dead coals from the '56 burn were now turned to a sooty powder and the brush was beaten down. The carry was a regular hiking path these days, same as anywhere else. Yet the portage trail proved harder than ever. By God, he was fifty!

Stopped for breath at height of land, George reckoned the years since he'd been out this way. He'd arrived with Evan over fifteen years back, when he came close to a brawl with his son, well before Tommy landed on his roof below Molly River Bridge. That was before George dreamed of hiring Tommy's sons too, before every dreadful thing that followed. His grandkids' model car days already lay behind them then, but they were still kids. Or were they? How quickly life forced them to grow up, and how quickly they died, one at seventeen, the other a year older. Hurricanes blew through their brief stays on earth.

George set his canoe down on the Semnic shore and paddled to the lean-to site. He rolled it over by habit, for all the fine weather, storing the paddle underneath. It was a good paddle, made by Evan himself, maybe not in a league with the one by Joe Mell, but straight and flexy as an amateur could want, and a treasure.

George saw right away that one of the lean-to roof's support poles had snapped off. There were tarpaper strips flapping from the roof in a rising wind, rough siding was woodpecker-dotted, mushrooms grew among the floor planks where rain and snow had seeped in. To George, the little structure had an implausible look of physical pain.

A slab of wood didn't feel, and the world at large didn't care whether some cobbled-together old shelter was there or not. Nor, sadly, did it care that three man-children from one family were gone, or that a surviving grandparent had turned to ruination. The wind blew regardless, small waves slapped at the shoreline, ravens gawped and stuttered, bass gulped minnows. Come the cold, turtles would sink into the mud and slow their heartbeats almost to zero, little golden-crowned kinglets busy themselves to eat three times their body weight just to make it through a night, moth larvae go stiff in their frail cocoons, bees stay hive-bound.

George was unconsoled to know that things would start all over again afterward. If he'd been a songwriter, he'd have written how the skies cried, never mind they didn't. No, the sun bore down, magisterially, and those skies were bluer than blue, and he could lift his eyes and see clear to Mt. Katahdin, a rare sight from that spit of land.

Once that mountain view would have made a whole trip worthwhile, but all the beauty he beheld now somehow irked George. He slammed his pack down on some floorboards still intact. They'd hold his own bulk through one night too. A small animal rustled in the pine spills drifted along the back wall.

He collapsed on the shoddy floorboards and slept three hours, as he had all those years back on the thorny trip with Evan and Tommy. But he slept sober, not drunk.

When he came to, the sun stood high. George started a fire, just to keep busy. He'd skipped breakfast so he could sneak out of Woodstown without detection by men and women who hadn't worked for wages in years but who still got up by five. Old habits die hard. Headlamps off, he'd left town before a hint of dawn. The only light that shone was the flood at Billy's store. He'd swung his truck onto the ballfield to stay beyond its arc.

But he wasn't hungry. Still angry, rather. Now he flung his axe into the hovel. The animal rustled again. George would wait on the fire; the bacon would keep inside his pack; or maybe the vole or mouse or whatever it was would have it, and welcome.

He might yank a bass or perch with a Daredevil or Mepps. He could weight his line with a staple from the wounded lean-to's tarpaper roof. But he really wanted to fish less than he wanted to eat, and the wind was rising by the minute anyhow.

So at least there was no canoe on the water, no matter the carry path was worn by foot traffic, and its brush vanished. What else had changed in a decade? Maybe his and Evan's sacred spot had become just another place for fishing, or more likely partying. He spotted a patch of tin foil and an empty beer bottle in the brush behind his camp. Ashamed, he left them there. His stake in this little patch of territory seemed to have shrunk to almost nothing now, however he resisted that notion. He decided to walk the lakeshore, just so he wouldn't sit there brooding.

Evan always called the first cove George came to "Miller's Mistake," but even he couldn't say where the name came from. Its standing rocks were throwing up spume, which caught the sunlight, leaving rainbows to shimmer and vanish. His bitterness was starting to fade. He heard the scream of an eagle behind him, the wind bringing it his way. George could see the bird above Prune Island. He envied its effortless ride on the blow.

Then he heard other noises from upwind. Curious, he walked back past the lean-to, into the gale. At the first cove north, small and nameless, he saw half a dozen aluminum cans rolling up and back in the rote. What sort of person could chuck trash into these woods, let alone into the cleanest water on earth?

Then someone shot. There was no doubt about it. George froze. Another shot followed, and a weird whanging sound, then a burst of collective laughter. He moved on, but more cautiously. There were people out here after all. Armed people, shooting, laughing, drinking beer. Where had they come from? One of the haul roads must reach the lakeshore somewhere even out here now. Another thought to depress him.

Ahead, the point ran down a bluff into the water. He'd have to cut through the woods unless he wanted to wade around the headland. He moved from tree to tree as if he were stalking game, though most of the hemlocks and pines were second growth, nothing like the trees that had stood there decades before George's time.

He suddenly recalled an article in a very old *Bangor Daily*, something Evan had kept for whatever reason. He paused to reconstruct it; there had rarely been an urgency that could block George's recourse to remembrance.

The article spoke of a certain Willem Ellsley, who'd been busy one morning to fell a great pine. No one would imagine a tree of that scale today, but that one—according to the newspaper—was fabulous even then. Ellsley been sawing for half an hour, the story said, when he heard something. Circling the trunk, to his surprise he found a man sawing on the other side. The article was dated January 11, 1897. Couldn't Willem hear the other lumberjacks? Could you believe such a yarn?

Well, maybe the day had been howling like today's. George wanted to believe. How he wanted to believe. What a world of wonders it must have been! A hard life for the likes of Ellsley. Hell, it had been hard enough for the likes of Evan, of Brad Llewellyn and Bert Morton and Louis Maclean and all the other men whom George always thought of as the old-timers.

Back then, men and women and children died miserably in childbirth and of infection and lockjaw and drowning and malnutrition and common or garden influenza and dead limbs dropping silently, as on poor Baptiste the fiddler.

And what a world of wonders it must have been.

From the brow of the hill, George looked into the wetland on the far side of the ridge. Some half-dozen people stood on the sand, all looking inland too. Where were their boats?

He caught motion out the corner of an eye, and on the beach, a man raised his barrel to fire across the swamp. He heard another whang, then the laughter again. He followed the rifleman's aim and found, suspended from a cable, a metal deer. One of the men, his pants rolled above the knee, was mucking his way toward it through the tussocks and beaver channels.

When he reached the sham buck, the stranger grabbed a cord and turned in his tracks, headed for the same ridge that George stood on, but farther inland, east. He towed the metal cutout behind him. George could just hear the squeal of steel pulley wheels on the cable.

While the fetcher waded and stumbled, George crept downhill, closer to the shooters by two hundred feet or so. Coming from downwind, his movement would be inaudible, and the brush was still thick enough to hide him. The men's yammer grew clearer, though he could only make out scattered words. *Jimmy. Trigger. Beer. Walt. Son of a bitch. Engine.* He couldn't piece the fragments together.

At water's edge, he slipped behind a boulder. The man who dragged the target was climbing up into the trees. There must have been a post there, like the one George noticed now, some seventy-five feet out in the bog. That was how it worked. The deer slid down along the cable and over the wetland. They shot.

Soon George heard full phrases: *Let 'er rip! Send him! Giddy-up!* Knowing what was what here made the words come clearer. The effigy coasted along the wire, slowing as it got closer to bog-level. The shot that followed brought on boos and catcalls. The rifleman had missed.

What in the whole scene was dismaying enough to make George queasy? He couldn't have said exactly. And yet, though he was still a bit weary from the carry a few hours before, he made a snap decision. His cabin was locked; all he'd brought to it lay in his pack; he could hang his canoe in the shed at home. When the wind calmed at evening, he'd load up and head south. He wasn't spending one more hour in this despoiled place.

Another year might be better. Maybe he'd get back to Semnic and find it the way he'd hoped before dawn that morning. More probably, he'd have to find someplace else he needed. Semnic wasn't that anymore. There were strangers here.

"Tourists," George snarled out loud. But what was he, if not a tourist himself? A tourist, apparently, no matter where he went now.

For the other tourists, it was adequate fun to be out with their six-packs and rifles and phony animals to slaughter. For them the beautiful day was simply a beautiful day. They had nothing to attach it to, while George had too much. And it turned out he couldn't deal with it all in such a summer. Another time, perhaps.

XXXIII

At ten p.m. in Sidon, a dot-on-the-map town in northern New Hampshire, a vaguely familiar, delirious fatigue came on George, the kind pneumonia had once brought on. He knew he wasn't fit to be at the wheel. The early departure to Semnic, along with the carries in and out, had caught up with him.

He found a nondescript motel whose sign was all but ludicrous, *Heaven At Last.* When he rang the bell at the office, the proprietor showed up, bleary but extravagantly polite. No doubt he needed to cultivate what little custom he could in this lightly traveled spot, even if the client who'd risen out of the night was some disheveled camper with a canoe on his truck. There wasn't another car on the lot.

The owner turned out to be Cambodian, a fact he offered without George's asking. How on earth had he landed here, among the moose and black bear? George was too tired to ask, even though his host clearly wanted to tell a tale now that he was up. George felt guilty to disappoint him, but his legs were buckling and his eyelids heavy as anchors. He stumbled to his room and fell onto the bed, shoes and all, too exhausted even to douse the lamp.

He came to at about three. His torpor had passed. He sat bolt upright, hearing the slow cry of a loon somewhere not far off. What lake lay in this part of the world? Evan said that doleful song meant the bird was calling the wind. George has always loved the expression. It means the birds want a blow to head into; otherwise, they struggle to get airborne.

The idiom was simply descriptive to the local folk who used it, but George could make all manner of connections to it. He'd often heard the wind-call after a cold rain in autumn, back when he had time to make more than one visit to Woodstown. He pictured yellow leaves falling along the landing road in a mizzle, the whole sky low, the red squirrels more active than ever, and flickers flushing along the ditches, their tail-spots brilliant against the slate of November. In a severe drought year, he once saw an army of eels migrating overland in evening dew around dry spots in the river.

To picture Woodstown in these conditions, though it was still mid-August, bred an inevitable melancholy. Of course it had at least partly to do with time's velocity, which wasn't an abstraction anymore, as it was to his younger self, when, if he felt it all, he could drink it away like everything else. Or he could wallow in it, persuaded that his melancholia showed him to be uncommonly sensitive. Oh yes. That's surely how Melody remembers him.

George's tears came on like raindrops themselves, the broadleaves sifting down through them, Evan melting away in mind, until only his crusher hat was left, and then it too vanished, as in some cartoon of loss. The migrant birds in the grizzled sky pivoted and in a flash were gone south. Was he awake or asleep?

For what may have been the first time in his adult life, since he can't remember his feelings at ten, in that motel his mother and father rose from the dank basement at Mayes Hardware. George has a couple of photographs, but they're of his parents' wedding, or portraits taken at other more or less formal occasions. The two don't look like anyone, really, or rather look like everyone: bride, groom, graduate, soldier, bridesmaid, team member.

But certain moments that returned to him in Sidon were far more specific. Was he six? Seven? He knows he'd been playing for hours in his sandbox, having run a tiny pinwheel's shaft into the sand. He repeated a little chant: *Windmill, windmill. Come see my shiny windmill.* He'd nearly hypnotized himself as the tiny blades turned, and suddenly it was getting dusky. Time to go inside.

As a father now, it stabs his heart to recall what happened next. Charlie McLeod, a neighbor almost twice George's age, walked into the yard, snatched up his toy, broke its shaft, and plucked its blades off like petals.

"Little sissy!" he spat. Then he rode away on his English bike.

George felt he'd just seen some strange big animal, whose first effect was to arouse an odd wonder. What did such a creature eat? What sort of bed did it make? George knew Charlie only by name and appearance, a big guy who had nothing to do with the likes of him. In a twinkling, his astonishment turned to grief. He wailed in the sandbox loud enough that his father came out.

His dad took him by the hand and walked him to the back step of their little house, fireflies pulsing among the sour cherry trees his parents were so proud of. His mother made sensational pies from their fruit. George specifically remembers that much of home life at least.

"What is it, Big Sonny?" He'd forgotten his father's pet name until just then in the motel. George recalls feeling anything but big. Hiccupping and sobbing, he was explaining to his father when another neighbor passed by the yard. It was Bobby Loenig, something of a friend, maybe two years older. George wanted to die, or at very least not to be there blubbering like a baby.

"Why is Georgie crying?" Bobby asked.

"He's not," his father answered.

"He looks like he is."

"He's just breathing hard," George's father insisted. "Shouldn't you be home, Bobby?"

It may be the first time as an adult that George remembers how he ached with gratitude to his dad. He aches again now.

Mother had been listening through a window. She came out and said that she'd speak to Mrs. McLeod, and that nastiness like this wouldn't ever happen again. She opened the kitchen closet and brought their son another pinwheel, newer, shinier. Plastic was still something of a novelty in those days. "Always good to have something extra," she said. George felt nothing would hurt him now. And he felt, and feels, that same all but overwhelming gratitude.

At the motel, he marveled at how few such memories he owned. At nine, he suddenly had no parents. Dave Butcher's note after his brother's death flew to mind. George shuddered to think of his own kids: what would it be for them if their parents disappeared, let alone if they were butchered by a stranger?

He'd lived a long time with Mary Conley's love, and later with the avuncular generosity of Evan Butcher. He was living now with the often-unmerited loyalty of Julie, the sweetness of Mary and Kate. But he'd never truly known till that night how the loss of his mother and father had wounded him. Maybe it had cut him so deeply that at his age he couldn't properly evaluate the wound and so looked away from it, because how could that blow not have hurt him, and why should the pain now flood him like revelation? George tends to focus on one thing at a time. Work. Love. Fatherhood. Stories. Evan. He doesn't put things together until he's slapped in the face.

What was that uncharacteristic, American-sounding idiom Mary used? "You're slow on the uptake, pal."

He sees, and scarcely for the first time, that his drinking career accounted for much of that slowness. His addiction was so consuming that his needs remained obscure for just shy of twenty years. His habit's demands were what mattered. George had kept searching for an indefinable something, until the object of pursuit became drink only. At length, he reached a point where he'd either die or discover the available world. That world would always contain its share of pain, but at least the pain would belong to him, no longer to the bottle.

How little he'd learned as a boy and a young man! His weeping went on almost till dawn. It remembered the emotional storm he endured years back when he recognized, at last, the diabolical grip that liquor had on him. And similarly, when it ceased, everything looked orderly. The formal feeling. Out the window, a string of grackles sat just so on a phone wire. The proprietor was mopping the concrete slab in front of his office door, and the suds refracted the blue above. Man and mop and walkway were also meant to be just so.

By eight, he was ready to head south again. He felt as if he'd run a race, but he could drive through the fatigue. Before he checked out, though, he'd ask for the Cambodian's story. He still had a lifetime to sort the world out, and he couldn't know when he might hear something to help him.

A gust of the old melancholy did blow in briefly. How to help Evan? Yet the settled feeling overcame it. George hoped he might in fact be helpful, if not to Evan, then—he winced at his own fulsomeness—to others.

"How'd you come to be here?" he asked the motel owner, who smiled shyly and leaned on his mop handle. It appeared he had as much time as George could allow him, which suddenly felt like plenty.

Heaven at last? He would see what the jovial fellow meant by such a silly claim.

XXXIV

None of this would of happened if that darned George just listened to his wife. They both probably think Rob's dumb, which he's a long way from, thanks. He leaves his brand-new shop back there in Norris, which is making good money in just a short time—people know what quality is, and you get what you pay for. Then he leaves that shop on the fly and he's saved enough that he's got the new one up and running in no time, and the bank gives him a good deal too. You can't give the twins credit for any of that. Sad story about those two. She won't say it's not.

Julie never wanted her husband to hire them in the first place. She just said, "No twins." They didn't realize Rob could hear, but there was something about a little hole Rob drilled and a tube or part of a tailpipe or something. People might think that was sneaky, but like he always says, if you don't look out for yourself, who's going to? He just did what he had to do, no matter where he was. Not that he'd trick Cerise.

Julie knew hiring those boys was bad luck. Rob heard her say, "Mark my words," but George just told her she was superstitious. There wasn't any curse on the Butcher family. Or maybe she didn't say a curse, but something like it. Guess who turned out right?

Well, in one way it's good Julie couldn't put her foot down. Cerise doesn't like to think like this, but yes, you look after yourself. If one of the twins hadn't brought her into the picture, then she and Rob wouldn't be together. That's just the way the world works. She won't say it's always hunky-dory.

She doesn't let people call her Cherry anymore. Too much stupid stuff about that when she was in high school. And Cerise isn't hard-hearted, no siree. Maybe she's not the sharpest tack in the pack, or she wouldn't have married Donnie. Okay, you got her there. But she didn't mean any harm. Now she lives with a normal man, what she did does look crazy. She still can't believe it herself.

Crazy, you said it. She always had her pick of guys. Girls in high school hated her for that, which she loved. You had to love something those days. But it wasn't love with Donnie, no matter how you slice it. She just wanted something—well, different. Let all the little hussies go all trembly over some big ape in shoulder pads. Let them go to cheer-leader camp and make like they'll be coming back to boy heaven. Not Cerise. Something different, that was all.

It's awful to say, but it was kind of a challenge, too, getting one of those twins away from the other, because you never met two people that stuck together like that. In a way it wouldn't matter back then which one took the bait. Each of them was different than anyone else you could find, all right. This makes her sound cold-hearted, which isn't true.

They used to come in the Rexall together every morning, ten o'clock on the dot. If it wasn't too busy, she saved two stools, and she had the raspberry Danishes and the coffees, mostly milk and sugar, on the counter right when the big hand touched twelve.

They'd do that sort of a smile at the exact same time, and say that *heh*, ditto. Then they swung the same leg up over the stools like you were seeing double. Cerise didn't tell them apart by the mole. That was other people's trick, and hers too at first. But pretty quick she noticed Donald-the-mole always sat on the last stool toward the street, and his brother on one in. She didn't have to peek under their ears anymore. If they couldn't sit in their places, they'd just have her wrap up their order and they'd go.

Then one afternoon just before she got off, here comes the Mole all by himself. He gets a bag of chips, but he sits there a while and looks at her with that nutty smile, which you wouldn't even call a smile unless you watched them a while. They were real interesting somehow. She studied them face to face, and sometimes in the mirror. They didn't know about that. She's a crafty one in her own way too, she's proud to say, which makes up for being a bonehead sometimes. One time anyways.

Look at what she's got now. She's not saying she couldn't've han-dled things better, but she and Rob are renting a sweet little house, and they'll have a chance to buy it if everything works out, which it might do. Paying off the mortgage on the shop comes first, she supposes. Rob got permission to put on a redwood deck in the back of the house. They can eat or just sit there when he's home, even if you can't keep him still for long. He built the deck himself in about a half a minute. Rob can do anything.

He redid the floor in the kitchen. He got permission for that too, which you'd give same as the landlord, because whether the Beams can work it out to buy the place or not it'll be better than what they moved into. Floor all done over in squares that look like real tiles. Nice-looking, and easy to clean.

So, Donnie starts showing up most days for a few weeks. Then one afternoon he walks her to the bus stop and does that for maybe ten days. Next thing, he gets on the bus and just sits with her all the way to where she lives. He must've turned around somewhere along and rode back to the shop.

Cerise never thought of asking her husband what Donnie kept telling him around two o'clock. But then she wasn't with Rob then, either. Anyway, that boy was strange, and Rob told her later he just let the twins be that way like George did. No harm, he said.

Maybe a month goes by and one day Donnie gets off the bus and walks her to her door. But he walks away right off quick.

Maybe another month and he comes up the stairs.

What was in her head? He didn't have a single idea how to behave. Cherry—Cerise had to show him everything, and crazy, okay crazy, but she liked that she could do that, because it really was different, like nothing else in the world. *Heh heh heh*, so she almost laughed out loud. But you know? It was almost like an animal. She never wished to be with an animal. She doesn't mean that. God no.

So, then they're married. May's well be a loony. She was the one popped the question. Probably Donald and David didn't know what marriage even was, exactly. They weren't going to propose like someone normal. Their father was dead, and no one had any idea where the mother was. She isn't sure if Donald even thought about things like that anyhow, if he ever thought about anything. You probably wouldn't call it regular thinking if he did.

Okay, she should talk. She did the dumbest thing a girl could possibly do. She can't quite say how it happened. She didn't take any time to figure out what things would be like, and pretty soon you just get tired of nothing to say, not so you're understood anyhow. *Heh*. What in hell's that? He said a few other things too, but not many. Mostly it was that. And she was forever fighting David away from their door, which made Donnie sad, you could tell, and the whole thing was just a regular circus.

Rob was a gentleman all during that stuff, no googly eyes or whatever when he came in for his own snacks or she stopped by the garage. Still, a girl knows things, and she must have let on she liked him too. And by and by, things happened. Matter of fact, she'll admit it—she started the whole business.

So, they just had to get out of there if they were ever going to be together. Rob told her what those squirts did to men twice their size. He said he could run a shop anywhere, and that's what he's doing, only in Ohio. He could do it on the moon. She's sorry stuff went the way it did, but she's proud of her husband. She don't even have to work. Cookie in the oven too.

She didn't want anyone getting hurt, Lord knows. She never had some evil plot. She only did what her heart told her. Her old girlfriend Bessie was the only one back home that knew where she was. Once she told Cerise the scary news about Davie, it was straight to that Cincinnati JP for her and Rob. Bessie wouldn't say boo to anyone about where they were. She was the best friend you could ever have. Cerise misses her awful.

So being married to Don was nuts, like she says. Same as being with Rob makes sense, and she hopes they'll be married fifty years. He's going places. She did the right thing the second time around, for sure.

And those boys were bound to do something oddball even if she and Rob stayed. Look what Dave did when she married his brother. Headed for the funny farm in Kuehntown, probably in a straitjacket. Rob never wants to talk about it, and she can't blame him. He likes to keep his mind on . . . well, on going places.

And what if she and Don stay married? Then it's Davie who commits suicide because he can't stand not having his brother to himself. And then Donnie has to kill himself too because the brother did. That's the way they operated, amazing to say. She stays and they just reverse the order: Davie first, then Don. Would that be better? No matter what she did, they weren't going to act regular. Crazy isn't half what those poor boys were.

XXXV

Graveyard to graveyard, George thinks. It's not magic, no, but a wonder.

He feels his fatigue in every vein and fiber, but it's a pleasant feeling. Pleasant? Too tepid. He can't find the right adjectives, and what difference does vocabulary make anyhow? Leave that to Rob Beam. God bless him and his stolen bride. Bless all creatures great and small. Something like that. He floats on the glories of the given.

He and Julie sit on the porch, not speaking. She's reading the paper, probably the advice column George teases her about. He imagines her scanning counsel on how to deal with an intrusive mother-in-law. There's a sister, maybe, who refuses to come to another letter writer's second wedding. Still another writer, Troubled, reports that Uncle Steve gets drunk at every family reunion, and now he wants to take Troubled's daughter to a dude ranch. Uncle Steve is the daughter's godfather too, and Troubled is—well, troubled.

George, for the first time in his recent recall, is not troubled. Or only slightly. Every so often a chill does momentarily descend when he thinks that maybe he shouldn't have sneaked away from Evan and Mattie, who don't even know he spent one night at his camp and part of the next day at the Semnic lean-to. Evan's still capable of drinking himself into perdition, no matter the message he left with Julie.

And yet the old boy may not go back after all. With each day that passes, George is living evidence himself that marvels can happen. People can come out of some very deep holes, so why not Evan? If he does, it won't be by way of George's will. It never has been. A relief, really.

Inside, the girls giggle over something, their voices low in the kitchen, but for flashes of vibrant laughter. Their father is just another man, George knows, resting in a recliner at day's end, stroking the head of a dog, who squints with contentment. If he interrupts the petting,

Tabasco butts him like a kid goat. Her desires are simple, like his own just now. "Good girl," he whispers. Tabasco II.

Who'd have thought such a moment would be almost everything George ever hoped for? The sublime's all around him; it's inherent in a normal day, if that's how he can truly describe this one. What was he looking for all those drunken years, and even lately?

If he backslides now and then, as he will, he'll have this peace to refer to. In that Sidon motel, he let something out of himself. It was further purged by hearing of the Cambodian's resolution and resiliency, not only in his escape but also in what felt to him like success enough in his new life. In fact, it felt like a miracle—like heaven at last.

The drive home after, and all that has followed, seemed even more cathartic. There are doves in the Mayeses' driveway now, pecking gravel, cooing to one another. Such song makes an apt coda to the hysterics of brighter birds in spring and earlier summer. It meshes perfectly with George's quiet quickening.

The world will return to its full complexity; but he means to savor the state of mind he's in. Exhaustion has narcotized him, though he doesn't feel threatened by slumber. He can lie back and replay a whole life if he wants to. He smiles at that idea: "It's my hobby, I guess."

"Did you say something?" Julie asks.

"Just muttering," George replies. She goes back to her paper. What could he possibly tell her anyway? That a lifetime's emotions have compacted themselves into the last couple of days? How long has it been since he burned his letter to Tommy? He begins to reckon, but no measurement or logic is pertinent. How rarely the purely rational has ever really guided George's experience.

It was after the family's supper by the time he got back from his visits to the graves at Fields of Peace and Our Mother of Consolation. Day camp was over, and the girls could sleep in tomorrow, out-of-school latitude. No buses running yet, either. Mary might stay in bed till noon if no one disturbed her, but Kate's not like that. And even at only eight years old, she's capable of amusing herself. Precocious that way. Other ways too. She'll likely go downstairs, make herself a bowl of cereal, and go find Tabasco. She can spend hours simply hugging her pet.

Could it have been only the day before yesterday afternoon that George packed up his things and drove south into the darkness, far ahead of plans? He took the long way to blacktop, the Molly River road. Stopped at the bridge where poor Tommy came to grief, he snapped on his dome light, then snapped it off. The moon was big enough to write by. He can't say where the writing impulse came from, but it felt strong.

He used a sheet from a pad of lined paper that one of the daughters probably left in the truck one day when he ran her to school after she'd missed her bus. George smiles again. A Mayes bus, that would be. The notepad had sat in his glove box at least since the end of the school year, then.

George stood on the bridge and read his terse letter to Tommy out loud:

> Forgive me for lusting after your wife. Forgive me for provoking that fistfight. I pray you can rest, because you had more trouble than anyone ever deserved, and may the same peace come to your children.

Not eloquent, of course, but that didn't matter a bit. George touched a match to the paper and set it on the gravel. He waited till nothing was left but ashes, which he scooped after they cooled and scattered onto the bog below the bridge. A bittern thumped. Postdriver. Bats deftly cut the fat moon. It was so still you could hear things scurry through the woods.

Afterward, George drove on till he reached that Sidon motel. He had made a start on something.

It was noon by the time he reached the New York border yesterday. He still had four hours to go, and Julie didn't expect him till week's end. He could just keep on to the graveyard where his parents lay and no one would worry about him. But he decided to call Julie anyhow and tell her his plans for the afternoon. He swung into an Atlantic station and dropped a pair of quarters into the pay phone.

"What on earth are you thinking?" Julie asked. "Just come home, George."

"Trust me," George said, "I know what I'm doing."

"It sounds crazy." She was clearly worried.

"Maybe it is. But it's the right thing. Trust me."

"If you say so," she answered, hesitantly.

The mid-July weather at Fields of Peace wasn't particularly hot, but the haze over the county, part man-made, part natural, betrayed the awful summer mugginess. George missed Woodstown for the clear air alone. But he'd missed home up there. True home.

At Fields of Peace, trees served as grave markers. Small brass plaques on their trunks were all that indicated who was buried where. Had his parents left some document, asking for flowering crabs to be planted above their plot? Why had they requested Fields of Peace anyhow, and not the Lutheran cemetery in Norris, where atheist Uncle Emory lay, along with half a score of other dead Mayeses and Ungers?

Who had arranged the parents' funerals and burials anyhow? Emory? Some lawyer? A preacher? What preacher? All George remembered was the graveside ceremony itself, and only bits of it at that. He recalls how hard the wind blew, ruffling the minister's papers so that he spoke in intermittent phrases. A flock of rackety geese passed over the field where the few mourners gathered. The minister's eyeglasses caught the sun.

George must have wept. He was nine years old, just a year younger than Kate. But standing before his murdered parents' plaques, under trees long past bloom, he didn't remember tears. Indeed, he remembered so little it stunned him, as if life had begun at Uncle Emory's, or more accurately in Mary Conley's kitchen. It began with an Irishwoman's love, before the merciless thrashings he got from a music and homeroom teacher, a sociopath and a player of sweet melodies on a trumpet, who like anyone must have had his own story. George strained to forgive him, though he's doubtless as dead now as anyone in the ground at that sylvan cemetery.

His thoughts went on and on as the sun lowered, to Elmore and Pat and Nine and crows and his obscure uncle dabbing rabbit's blood on his face and George scrawling his initials on a long-razed water tower and Iggy Mook and Boardie Bennett and Julie and two children and Rob Beam and the Butcher twins.

And, forever and ever, Evan.

But George had never till now properly taken these two into account:

Nicholas Mayes, 1919–1948
Jenny Unger Mayes 1921–1948

There was no further inscription. Fields of Peace rules.

His father had been twenty-nine, his mother twenty-seven. Lord in heaven. George knelt to read his second letter. Sweat ran into his eyes and dripped onto the letter, blurring a few words. But George knew what they were. He asked for forgiveness that he'd never adequately considered the man and woman under that sod.

I was a little boy, but I should have tried to find out more about you after you'd gone. I just didn't know whom to ask, I suppose. I will be uncertain about everything, forever. Please forgive me.

His short prayer afterward was no more than that Nicholas and Jenny might rest in peace. As he had with Tommy's, he set the leaf of paper on fire and watched it disintegrate on the grass. He rubbed its ashes into the turf, beneath those arching trees.

Walking back to his truck, he surprised himself by how light he felt, how cool. The weather hadn't changed. Something else had.

He parked in front of Our Mother of Consolation and circled the building on foot to find the cemetery just before sunset. The stone seemed scandalously ineloquent.

Mary Conley d. 1960.
Salve Regina.

Not even a date of birth, but then who would have known? Generic inscription, but who could have been consulted for a better? Perhaps the stone served as proper testament at that: Mary had been a solitary soul, great beyond calculation—and anonymous as field dirt.

George went into the sanctuary and knelt in a pew. Someone, perhaps the sexton, entered quietly as he reflected, did some business in the apse—George could hear a soft metallic knocking—and left. Pigeons gurgled in the steeple, sole ornament atop the plain poor people's church. Traffic chuffed by on the road. George heard music, very faint. There wasn't any, but he heard it nonetheless. Something by Brahms, he thought.

Mary Conley had spent a half-hour in this chilly sanctuary every morning for decades, so something in it was part of what made her the woman George remembers. She was the light that never went out, even as he knelt retching on the floor of a Glasstown duplex twenty-seven years earlier.

His letter owned up to his insufficient gratitude, which, George claimed, there were no words to express. Like both the others, it was brief:

> I should have been holding your hand when you died. There's too much I should have done. I beg your forgiveness, and I cling to your memory with more love and respect than I have words for.

He lit a candle, Roman Catholic fashion, then touched that paper to flame like the others. He dropped it onto a tray under the candles just before it burned his fingers. After the last scrap curled and vanished, George went back to his truck, somehow certain that in fact he was forgiven, at least in this case. Mary always forgave him.

There remained only the one letter. He knew it didn't matter that the words would be as wanting as they were in the other three. Mattie would be the one to read them aloud. Among other things, George begged forgiveness—perhaps in larger part than his violation warranted—for stealing Evan's tale of the rabbit hunter. He suspected the apology would strike Mattie as strange, as indeed it was, and it might well strike her husband the same. Maybe they'd both even find it foolish. George didn't understand why it meant so much to him, either, but he had the rest of his life to think about that. He was disburdened.

He'd written out Evan's letter on the dashboard of his truck, even before he left the Cambodian's motel. He kept a few envelopes and stamps in the Chevy's glovebox, the ones in his office always disappearing so quickly. The letter was already addressed, no need of anything but Woodstown, Maine, and the postal code. George was determined to mail it, even if Evan instantly forgot what it said, if he read or heard it at all. George simply needed to send it for his own peace of mind, if for no one else's.

He passed Mayes Transportation, deserted on a weekend, on his way home. There was a mailbox on a corner just a few hundred yards up the road, and George pulled over. As he reached to drop that final note in, though, he abruptly changed his mind. Or something changed it for him. He didn't believe in magic anymore, but yes, he did believe in wonder. Something told him there'd come a better time to send his note, if it needed sending at all.

He came wobbly-kneed into their house. Julie smiled and put her arms around him. Mary and Kate tumbled down the staircase and hung themselves on one leg: Daddy! Daddy! Tabasco put her forepaws on the other, squealing her happy yawns. The moment, like this whole day, was perfect. All of it will pass and the world go on, as George knows too well. But it's all his for right now too.

He hears his wife chuckle quietly and ruffle the Glassburg Eagle. He wonders what's funny, but he's too lazy to ask. The universe will sort things out, likely not as George Mayes thinks it should, but as it must. There has never been a guarantee of anything. And yet there's always something to hold onto. The important things are small ones.

He replays this morning's phone call to Mattie from the motel office, after the proprietor had recounted his own story. George needed news from Woodstown, no matter his recent evasions.

How had he predicted that news wouldn't be dreadful, as it has been in late years?

"He ain't drank since day before yesterday," Mattie said.

One day and some hours are not much, George thought. And yet a day is what Evan has, same as he does, same as anyone. "That's good, Mattie," he answered. He knew better than to gush.

"Told me, 'This ain't me.' Those was his words."

"Well, he's right about that."

"There was something different, seemed like. Don't know what it'd be. But different. He's outdoors mending the back lot fence. 'Bout time!"

"I believe something is different. Don't ask me why," George went on.

"Told me he wanted to go berryin' last evening."

"That sounds good."

"'Twas."

"You went."

"I guess by God we did," said Mattie, rather jauntily. For her own reasons, she added, "We'll both be eighty soon, George."

"I know."

He wanted to speak to Evan, but quelled the impulse, for fear he'd launch into a spiel about recovery, about calling him day or night if he got thirsty, about how life could be peaceful after all. No matter his years without alcohol, after all, he has truly seen that peace himself in these latest days of his life alone.

There'd be abundant time, he trusted, for amplification. That part can wait.

"Hope you found a bunch of berries, Mattie," he said.

"I judge we did, Mr. Man. Like I told Wilma a few minutes ago, they was just hangin' blue out by Molly River."

ACKNOWLEDGMENT

Chapter II of this story originally appeared in my collection *A North Country Life: Tales of Woodsmen, Waters, and Wildlife* (Skyhorse Publishing, NY, 2013).